THE BEAST

THE BEAST

A DARKDEEP NOVEL

ALLY CONDIE
BRENDAN REICHS

BLOOMSBURY
CHILDREN'S BOOKS
NEW YORK LONDON OXFORD NEW DELHI SYDNEY

BLOOMSBURY CHILDREN'S BOOKS
Bloomsbury Publishing Inc., part of Bloomsbury Publishing Plc
1385 Broadway, New York, NY 10018

BLOOMSBURY, BLOOMSBURY CHILDREN'S BOOKS, and the Diana logo
are trademarks of Bloomsbury Publishing Plc

First published in the United States of America in September 2019
by Bloomsbury Children's Books

Bloomsbury books may be purchased for business or promotional use.
For information on bulk purchases please contact Macmillan Corporate and
Premium Sales Department at specialmarkets@macmillan.com

Library of Congress Cataloging-in-Publication Data
Names: Condie, Allyson Braithwaite, author. | Reichs, Brendan, author.
Title: The Beast / by Ally Condie and Brendan Reichs.
Description: New York : Bloomsbury Children's Books, 2019. | Series: [Darkdeep ; 2]
Summary: Middle-schoolers Nico, Opal, Tyler, and Emma face a more dangerous threat and
must uncover the whirlpool's origins, as well as those of that freaky
"Thing in a Jar," while fending off paranormal investigators.
Identifiers: LCCN 2019004264 (print) | LCCN 2019006487 (e-book)
ISBN 978-1-5476-0203-2 (hardcover) | ISBN 978-1-5476-0204-9 (e-book)
Subjects: | CYAC: Supernatural—Fiction. | Monsters—Fiction. | Houseboats—Fiction. |
Friendship—Fiction. | Northwest, Pacific—Fiction. | Horror stories.
Classification: LCC PZ7.C7586 Bc 2019 (print) | LCC PZ7.C7586 (e-book) |
DDC [Fic]—dc23
LC record available at https://lccn.loc.gov/2019004264

Book design by Jeanette Levy
Typeset by Westchester Publishing Services
Printed and bound in the U.S.A. by Berryville Graphics Inc., Berryville, Virginia
2 4 6 8 10 9 7 5 3 1

All papers used by Bloomsbury Publishing Plc are natural, recyclable products
made from wood grown in well-managed forests. The manufacturing
processes conform to the environmental regulations of the country of origin.

To find out more about our authors and books visit
www.bloomsbury.com and sign up for our newsletters.

For Cindy,
who took a chance on a
wild idea, and even
bought us a whiteboard

THE BEAST

PART ONE

FREAKSHOW

1

NICO

Nico Holland was about to get eaten.

Chewed up. Or maybe just chomped. There were a lot of unpleasant possibilities, but one thing was clear: the furious creature facing him was definitely going to bite.

Nico dove left as razor-sharp jaws snapped right where his head had been. Yelping in terror, he rolled to his feet and swung his Torchbearer dagger wildly, but the figment leaped back. It moved faster than fast, and Nico had made the mistake of jumping out of the bushes in front of the charging creature.

Dumb dumb dumb.

But he'd had to cut off its escape. They couldn't let whatever this snarling, red Creamsicle–colored lizard-thing was get away. The figment had appeared out of nowhere, casually strolling up to drink from the pitch-black pond. As they'd watched—slack-jawed and bug-eyed—through the house-boat's bay window, the creation had scampered for the hidden tunnel leading off their secret island.

Nico and his friends had raced from their floating club-house, chasing the monster down into the passageway, which burrowed beneath Still Cove and then climbed up the other side, to the clifftops surrounding the fog-choked bay. There Nico had watched in horror as the figment's flaming tail disappeared into a dense stretch of woods north of town. Thankfully, the afternoon weather was absolutely terrible—a steady, cloying rain punctuated by icy gusts that snuck under your shirt—so no one else from Timbers was likely to be outside. They could still contain this disaster.

"Nico, back up!" Opal Walsh shouted, her long black braid slung to one side. She was behind the creature, angling into the clearing from where it couldn't see. To her right, Tyler Watson and Emma Fairington were huddled in the brush, keeping perfectly still. Nico spotted Logan Nantes creeping around on the figment's opposite side. Soon they'd have it surrounded.

Great. Then what?

The creature glanced over its shoulder and spotted Opal. Its tail flame blazed like a welding torch. The temperature in the clearing shot up. Steam began rising off the grass.

"Oh, it's a Charmeleon all right," Tyler said, pawing at the collar of his hoodie. "Maybe we let this one go, huh, guys?"

The figment swung to face him, blinking luminous blue eyes. Ruby scales gleamed as the creature bared its fangs.

"Okay, bye!" Tyler's head disappeared in a whirl of snapping leaves. Emma's bouncy blond curls vanished beside him. "You three have this covered, right?" she called from somewhere in the shrubs.

"We can't just let it go," Nico grumbled, running a hand through his rain-slicked brown hair. "We don't even know where this dinosaur came from."

"Charmeleon," Tyler corrected, still cowering out of sight.

The figment turned back to Nico and flexed its claws. The blue eyes narrowed.

Nico retreated another step, then called out in a shaky voice. "Did anyone go into the Darkdeep again?"

"No," Opal said immediately.

"Of course not!" Logan snapped. Emma and Tyler both called out denials from their hiding places within the bushes.

"Then how is this guy here?" Nico muttered, as the hairs lifted on the nape of his neck.

Figments came from the Darkdeep—a black, swirling pool hidden in the basement of the abandoned houseboat they'd discovered. When someone entered its inky water, they were spit out into the pond on which the houseboat floated. And whatever they'd imagined while inside the Darkdeep would suddenly appear on the island with them, like a dream come to life. At least for a little while. It had been fun at first, but

Nico and his friends quickly learned how dangerous these creatures could be. They'd inherited the risky job of controlling them.

But if no one entered the well, how'd this monster appear out of nowhere?

"What *is* a Charmeleon, exactly?" Opal asked, as the creature stamped and hissed in the center of the clearing. It seemed to be considering how to rip Nico's head off.

"Come *on*. I tried for years to get you guys to play Pokémon." Tyler's face reappeared behind a pine tree a dozen yards farther back, his dark skin slick with sweat. "Now I'm the only one who knows anything useful!"

"It's a nasty fire creature, maybe level thirty," Logan said, not moving a muscle. "Not a fully evolved Charizard or anything, so we're lucky there. But watch out for those claws. It's got a long reach, and this species is always looking for a fight. Plus, that's a healthy tail flame."

Tyler stared at Logan. "How did we never hang out?!"

Logan shrugged uncomfortably. Son of the richest man in town, he'd only recently stopped being a jerk to Nico and his friends, initially to impress Opal. Nico had avoided him for years—their fathers did *not* get along—but the battle with the Darkdeep had brought the five of them together. They were all Torchbearers now.

"Can we focus, please?" Opal gripped her dagger with both hands. "Same as last time?"

Nico shook his head. "This bad boy's way bigger than a rogue gingerbread man. We need a new strategy."

The Charmeleon shifted, glaring around the circle, muscles tensed as if ready to attack. This was the third figment they'd had to chase down since sealing off the Darkdeep weeks ago, and by far the most deadly. Nico racked his brain for a way to get close enough to use his dagger without losing a hand in the process. Cornered figments were testy at the best of times. This one looked ready to chew nails.

"I . . . I have an idea," Nico stammered, wiping the back of his hand across his brow. "Logan, can you get it to look at you?"

"Yes. But, um . . . I don't want to."

An instant later, Nico's half-formed plan went up in smoke. Tail-flame flaring, the Charmeleon launched itself over Nico's head, raking for his eyes as he dropped to the dirt. The creature landed behind him and prepared to bolt into the woods.

But Emma stepped from the trees directly in front of it. The figment froze, growling as she held out her hand. The Charmeleon tilted its head, then sniffed. Its tail fire died down abruptly, like a burner switched to low. The creature hopped forward and snuffled Emma's fingers.

"Emma, what the heck?" Tyler hissed, darting from the bushes. Nico's heart skipped a beat as the figment snatched whatever was in Emma's hand and held it up with a squeal of delight.

It was a package of M&M's.

"Candy," Logan breathed. "That's how they evolve."

"Don't let him eat it!" Tyler shouted, waving his hands. He stormed into the clearing despite his fear. "We don't want any part of what comes next!"

But Opal had slid up behind the creature, which was now glaring at Tyler. She tapped her Torchbearer dagger against its red scales. "Sorry, friend. But this isn't your place."

The Charmeleon made a disappointed noise, then disappeared from sight. The M&M's dropped to the grass.

"Nice job, girls." Nico was slowly picking himself up off the ground. He wiped dust from his sweatshirt and blew out a long breath. "That worked great. Maybe clue in your buddy Nico next time though, okay?"

Tyler narrowed his gaze at Emma. "How did you know to give it candy? You'd never play Pokémon cards with me."

Emma rolled her eyes. "You have a *very* selective memory, doofus. You made me go through your collection like every day after school, no matter how much I whined. I just never liked it."

"Well, you're welcome," Tyler said smugly, buffing his nails on his sweater. "I saved your life, no big deal. But maybe listen to me more in the future."

Emma snorted.

Opal pocketed her dagger and crossed her arms, staring

at the crushed grass. Nico caught her eye and nodded in thanks, and Opal nodded back, but worry lines marked her forehead. Getting that close to a fully present figment—one able to manipulate the world around it—was always dicey, even if they were getting pretty good at stopping them.

Nico knew they didn't need to actually stab a figment to dispel it, or maybe even use the daggers at all. The weapons only served as a focus. When facing their nightmares, they'd learned to accept their fears as real, and then push back against them. That was enough to banish an imaginary creature scanned from their minds. That's what Torchbearers had been doing since forever—monitoring the Darkdeep and catching whatever came out of it. It was their responsibility now, and they embraced it. *But from whose mind did this guy spring?*

Opal must've been thinking the same thing.

"That's three stray figments now," she said. "Too many to be leftovers from the radish festival disaster. Which means these are *new* imaginings. Which means someone is creating them. But who? And how?"

Nico blew out a breath. A few weeks back, their hometown of Timbers had decided to honor the area's most popular crop by throwing a big festival celebrating radishes. But the night before the festival, the Darkdeep overloaded and a gang of figments invaded the sleeping town and trashed everything.

Nico and the others had barely been able to lure the creatures away in time. The town remained in an uproar about it, with crazy theories flying everywhere.

Nico scratched his cheek. "I checked on the Darkdeep two days ago. It was totally quiet and not moving at all. I'm sure the creature who'd been manipulating it from the inside is gone, Opal. We severed the link."

Opal turned a critical eye on the rest of the group. "There haven't been any *private* experiments, right?"

Everyone shook their heads. Nico and Tyler both stole a glance at Emma.

She didn't miss their attention. "How rude!"

Nico held up a placating hand. "No one is accusing you of anything, but—"

"I haven't touched that pool since it tried to kill me," Emma said indignantly. "Believe me, the sparkle wore off after that."

Emma had initially been enamored with making figments, likely because of her obsession with movies and special effects. She'd gone into the Darkdeep more often than anyone. But Nico believed her now—Emma might crave excitement, but she wasn't crazy. To defeat the Darkdeep, they'd been forced to face the things they feared most. No one escaped unscathed. Nico had a hard time believing anyone could dive back into that frigid pool after seeing what it could do.

"Maybe someone else discovered the Darkdeep?" Logan suggested, his expression souring at the thought. "I found the island on my own, so it's possible a stranger came across the houseboat without us knowing."

"You *found* it by spying on Opal," Nico snapped.

"Does it matter how?" Logan fired back. He was taller than Nico, with glossy black hair and dark eyes.

Nico winced, then rubbed a hand over his face. Sometimes he and Logan still had a hard time getting along. They were wired so differently. Nico loved being outside, and communing quietly with nature, while Logan liked to tear around on his ATVs and play action sports. Plus, their fathers' feud always simmered just below the surface. Nico's dad worked for the National Park Service—his report on endangered spotted owls had made business tougher for Logan's dad, who owned the timber mill employing half the people in town. In retaliation, Sylvain Nantes tried to get Warren Holland transferred away from Timbers, and the matter wasn't settled yet. Logan and Nico had managed to work out their differences, but the bad blood sometimes threatened to resurface.

Nico sighed. "You're right. My bad. I just don't understand how figments keep escaping the Darkdeep while it sits there, totally inactive. I thought we were done with this problem."

"The fact that the Torchbearers were a thing at all makes me wonder if the problem might *not* go away," Tyler said quietly. "Maybe random figments popping out of the Dark-deep now and then is just how it is."

Everyone fell silent. They were the new Torchbearers, had even signed their names in the crumbling record book. But for all their commitment, it didn't mean they understood the job. They were guessing at pretty much everything.

"Figments have to come from somewhere," Opal insisted stubbornly, pulling her rain jacket tighter. "They don't just appear out of thin air."

"Let's check the Darkdeep again," Emma said. "The well chamber might have clues about how this one came to be."

Tyler shivered. "I hate going down there. I feel like it's watching me."

Opal shifted, eyes uneasy. She scooped up her backpack off the muddy ground and hoisted it onto her shoulders, hooking her thumbs tightly under the straps.

Nico understood her agitation. The Darkdeep's shadowy lair gave him the creeps, too. "We've been lucky so far," he said. "Nothing's gotten past us."

"That we know about," Logan countered darkly. "We aren't watching the island around the clock. An airplane full of glowing chicken monsters could materialize while we we're in school one day, and we'd have no clue."

"We'd know," Tyler said doggedly, then shrugged at Logan's flared eyebrow. "If we hadn't spotted the Charmel-eon lapping up pond water, it would've gotten loose in the hills. Eventually, someone would've seen the thing, or its tail flame would've burned down the forest. The fact that Timbers is still in one piece means we haven't missed any yet."

"*Yet*," Logan muttered under his breath.

"We need better answers," Opal insisted. "We need to locate the source of these monsters."

Nico exhaled deeply. There was no way around it.

"Let's go see the Darkdeep. Let's make sure it's really asleep."

2

OPAL

Opal stared at the inky black pool.

"It's not swirling."

Her words echoed in the houseboat's gloomy lower chamber, where she and the others were cautiously examining the Darkdeep. When motionless, its surface looked both smooth and hard at once, like silken glass.

"It's freaky seeing it like this," Logan said, shoving his hands into his pockets.

They'd come straight from the woods to the houseboat, heading downstairs immediately to check on their charge. Emma and Nico stood shoulder-to-shoulder with Opal, as if remembering the battle they'd fought here not long ago.

Tyler waited at the foot of the spiral staircase. "Okay," he called out. "We've seen enough. Come back up now."

Opal didn't blame him for being scared. Admittedly, Tyler

was afraid of most things, but the Darkdeep chilled her blood, too.

No one moved.

"Guys?" Tyler urged. "No point in hanging around."

Emma knelt before the pool and peered into the still liquid.

"Emma," Nico warned, "there's no reason to get that close."

"It's like obsidian," Emma said. "Almost . . . solid. But it's not. I think water is still moving somewhere below. Not in an unnatural way, though. Just in a weird-hole-in-the-pond sorta way."

Tyler chopped both hands down to his sides. "Do. Not. Touch. It."

"I won't!" Emma sounded annoyed. "I'm not even tempted, honest."

Opal glanced at her friend, surprised. Because despite everything, *she* was.

Didn't the others feel it? An urge to reach out and skim the surface, just to see what it was like. Wasn't their skin tingling with some kind of inexplicable electricity? *It can't just be me.*

Opal linked her hands behind her back. Touching the well could only lead to trouble.

"Well, this is good news, I guess," Nico said slowly, scratching the back of his head. "I mean, we still don't know where that Charmeleon came from, but the Darkdeep seems under control."

"Upstairs," Tyler insisted, tapping his foot on the bottom step. "We can discuss this *upstairs*."

Nico nodded. The group clomped back up the rusty metal staircase.

"Maybe the Darkdeep is coughing out *old* figments," Tyler suggested, as they filed through a trick wall panel into the houseboat's main showroom. Logan had repaired the figment-smashed entrance the week before, using boards from his dad's scrap yard.

The chamber was full of oddities in display cases, trunks of ancient books, bizarre artifacts and random weapons, even a huge unidentifiable animal skeleton hanging from the rafters.

Outside, thunder crashed as the rain picked up. Opal was glad they were snugly indoors, even if it was the strangest place in the entire world. As eerie as the houseboat might seem to others, it was their secret clubhouse. Their safe place.

Tyler spread his arms. "Like, maybe we created some extras back when the Darkdeep went wild, but they didn't all escape right away. Logan and I were both into Pokémon cards. Maybe it just took a while for this Charmeleon to get ejected from the vortex."

"Maybe this last one emerged as a *Charmander*," Logan said, stroking his chin excitedly. "And it had to evolve from that

16

earlier form. The creature could've been hiding on the island while it powered up."

"Exactly." Tyler held out a fist. "You still have your cards?"

Logan made a face. "*No.* Dude, we're in seventh grade. That stuff's for little kids." But when he thought the others weren't looking, Logan bumped Tyler's fist.

Nico shot a smirk at Opal. "Is this what everyone else was doing while we rode bikes?"

She grinned. "Don't you mean motorcycles? TIE Fighters? Talking dolphins from the Bermuda Triangle?"

Nico grimaced. "Okay, okay. We were nerds, too."

They passed the pedestal with its large glass jar. Inside, a spindly-armed green blob drifted in luminescent fluid like a tiny alien corpse. They had no idea what the creature was, but Emma had started calling it Thing, and the name stuck.

Opal paused, struck by something she couldn't quite define. Had Thing changed since she'd last seen it?

No. It looks the same. She sighed. More tricks inside her head.

A few weeks ago Opal had gone temporarily insane and thought Thing had spoken directly into her mind. The words still gave her chills.

Come, Opal.

Come and see what I have for you.

Opal scowled at the memory. She'd imagined the whole thing, of course. Lifeless green blobs didn't communicate telepathically. Opal had always been like this—making up stories in her head, like when she and Nico would race around town as kids. She still did it now, writing down weird ideas in private notebooks she kept in a secret desk drawer. That's all it had been—a scene from one of her fantasies that crept in while she was tired. *That's all*.

"You guys could trick-or-treat as Charmandles," Emma said, her eyes lighting up. "I think I'm dressing as Rey, but I haven't ruled out Captain Marvel."

"Charmanders," Tyler corrected, then he gave her a level look. "Emma, we're in seventh grade now. You know we're not going trick-or-treating, right?"

Emma's eyes rounded. "We're not?"

"No way," Logan said. "There are like five cool parties we could go to, plus Halloween's on a Saturday this year, so we can stay out extra late."

Emma turned to Nico, who shrugged guiltily. "It does feel like we're a little old for it."

"Let me make sure I'm hearing this right," Emma said, pressing a fist to her forehead. "We're not going to collect one-hundred-percent free candy this weekend. This is something we're *voluntarily choosing* not to do?"

"Correct," Logan and Tyler said together.

Emma spun to face Opal, eyes frantic.

"I'll go with you for a little while," Opal offered. "If you want."

Emma covered her face, then trudged over to a chest in the far corner and lifted its lid. "Who wants a snack?" she grumbled, removing a box of Hostess CupCakes. "Gotta have *some* sugar this week. Since we're too cool for Halloween now."

"Oh, don't be like that," Tyler said. "We'll still have a great time."

Emma stomped her foot. "Free. Candy."

"We'll talk about this later," Nico said. "Right now, let's see if we can find anything about random or time-lapsing figments in the Torchbearer records." He intercepted a plastic-wrapped pastry hurtling toward his head. "Um, thanks, Emma."

"No one touches a page before wet-wiping their hands," Tyler scolded. "Remember the rules."

Tyler was fascinated by the old books on the houseboat and spent most of his free moments poring through them, searching for anything about the Darkdeep, or his other obsession—the Beast, a legendary sea monster rumored to live in the treacherous waters of Still Cove.

"My hands are clean, see?" Nico shoved a whole cupcake into his mouth.

Tyler folded his arms. "Barbarian."

Opal was brushing wet dirt from her backpack when she paused. A weird feeling nudged her. A gentle tug at her . . . attention? Imagination? Thoughts? Her gaze shot to Thing, bobbing in its liquid enclosure. But the little green creature looked as lifeless as always.

The odd vibe came again, nibbling at the edges of her consciousness. She tried not to shiver, but it was like an itch she couldn't scratch. An impression was dancing around her brain, yet stayed frustratingly out of reach.

Growing alarmed, Opal squeezed her eyelids shut. Counted ten breaths. The sensation faded. When she reopened her eyes, she was looking at the far wall, where a battered metal lunch box sat on a cobwebbed shelf next to a pile of dusty sketchbooks.

Opal frowned. Then she surprised herself by getting up and walking over to it. Why was this random object jumping out at her now?

The lunch box was the curve-topped kind she imagined grizzled old fishermen using—solid and durable, made of metal. She'd never paid any attention to it before. There were literally hundreds of amazing-looking things stored on the houseboat. This wasn't one of them.

"I found something interesting," Tyler announced to the room. "There's a line in this book about chain reactions!"

Opal nodded encouragement, but found herself turning back to the shelf. Shrugging, she took the box down and opened its lid to discover a red-and-white checkerboard napkin. Her heart sank. *Just a boring old lunch box after all*. With maybe an ancient, moldy sandwich still wrapped inside. She wrinkled her nose, ready to snap the lid shut, but something stopped her.

She picked up the worn napkin. Felt a weight at its center.

Opal glanced over her shoulder at the others, then began to unfold the weathered cloth. Layer after layer loosened in her hands, until a tarnished bronze medal fell into her palm. It was the kind you pinned to a uniform—heavy, attached to a blue-and-white ribbon with a red stripe down its center, and topped by a solid metal bar. The front was a simple raised shape that reminded Opal of an airplane propeller.

As Opal examined the medal, the strange feeling returned, but stronger than before. She was suddenly sure the decoration was important. That it was . . . *something*.

"Never mind," Tyler grunted, closing the volume with a thud that caused Opal to jump. "This doesn't help. But FYI: us all going into the Darkdeep together wasn't very smart."

Opal dropped the medal into her pocket. As she put the lunch box back on the shelf her fingers brushed the sketchbooks stacked beside it. They were a motley collection, with different sizes and bindings. One was bound in crinkled leather and seemed like the oldest of the bunch.

Opal was a sucker for a cool notebook. She unzipped her backpack and stuck the leather one inside, where it joined the just-in-case gear she now carried everywhere—first-aid kit, flashlight, water bottle, granola bars, a Zippo lighter they'd found in the Torchbearers' tunnel chamber, and a change of clothes. She wouldn't be caught unprepared again.

Shrugging the bag onto her shoulders, Opal heard a commotion behind her and turned.

"Oh *wow*." Nico had pulled the neck of his shirt over his nose. "*Logan*. Seriously, dude. Go outside next time."

"No way!" Logan wheezed a muffled laugh, shoving Nico good-naturedly as he covered his face. "Everyone knows whoever smelt it, dealt it. Don't try to pin this one on me!"

"*Ughhhh*," Emma moaned, her face buried in her elbow. "I can taste it in my mouth. Boys are so freaking gross."

Gasping, Tyler fanned the air furiously. "Make it go away. Somebody make it go away!"

The odor reached Opal and she gagged. "*Ohmygosh*."

The room smelled like the worst fart in history, combined with cow manure, and something else—something oily and earthy that instantly coated Opal's skin and settled into her pores.

"Outside!" Nico yelped. "The door! Go!"

Everyone ran through the showroom's velvet entry curtain into the foyer. Opal threw open the houseboat's front door and they spilled out onto the porch, piling up like a car crash as the stench surrounded them. The driving rain had stopped momentarily, as if an accomplice to the nasal mayhem.

"It's worse out here!" Emma yelled. "*Back back back!*"

Opal froze, staring at the pond. The water was the same limitless black as usual, except for a wide circle around the houseboat that had turned a gross reddish brown. *Burnt sienna*, she thought automatically. One of her crayons from when she was younger.

The red-brown circle hissed as fat bubbles boiled up through its surface, turning the rings a putrid neon yellow, like a volcanic spring. For long seconds the water frothed, then the roiling stopped. The reek was so awful, Opal could barely keep her lunch down.

Rotten eggs. Was that a sulfur odor? Opal thought so, but wasn't sure.

Whatever it was, the foul smell lingered even as the colors dissipated. Nico appeared at her elbow, eyes watering, still burying his nose under the neck of his shirt. He waved at the now-calm pond. "What was *that*?"

Opal shook her head, anxiety crawling over her skin.

The Darkdeep might be quiet, but there was something very wrong with the pond.

And that feeling she'd had earlier. The tingle in the back of her skull.

She'd felt it once before, when she'd thought a floating green blob had smiled and winked at her. Opal's instincts screamed the same warning now as then.

The sensation didn't feel like it came from *her*.

And it didn't feel human.

3

NICO

The snarling Beast soared skyward like an eagle.

Nico watched the balloon float past with a frown.

"Oh, forget it, he's a goner," Tyler said, as the sinuous black shape rode the wind, growing smaller and smaller down Main Street before passing over the waterfront and into the stiff ocean breeze. The shimmering Mylar caught a rare sunbeam on the chilly, overcast day before sailing out of sight.

"That's littering," Opal muttered, shaking her head in annoyance. "Even if it won't land for miles."

Nico agreed. They were sitting on a bench outside of Fish & Game, the sporting goods store Emma's parents owned, hunched over hot apple ciders Mrs. Fairington had whipped up in the break room. School had just let out for the long weekend—Timbers kids had both Thursday and Friday off for fall break, leading up to the glorious Saturday Halloween.

Nico was pumped. It was his favorite holiday, even more

so than Christmas. He loved how downtown businesses went all out with their decorations—fake cobwebs, jack-o'-lanterns, black cats, witches, and skeletons. Store owners wore costumes and gave out free candy at the registers. If it were up to him, the fun would last all year.

Except for this Beast hoopla. I could do without that.

Opal was frowning at the crowded town square. "I don't mind all this . . . stuff going on, but these vendors need to be more careful."

Nico silently agreed. *This place has gone nuts. Again.*

Around them, Timbers bustled with activity, the kind of polite but quick-footed energy found in Pacific Northwest towns on blustery October afternoons. And it seemed like everywhere Nico looked, he saw Beast paraphernalia. After the disaster on the eve of the radish festival—an event locals had begun calling "Beast Night"—the town had suddenly caught creature fever.

Beast mugs. Beast pins. Beasts carved out of wood or molded from plastic, in different shapes and colors. Not everyone agreed on what the mysterious sea monster looked like—there were Loch Ness versions, weird ET smiley ones, and some that seemed straight out of the *Alien* franchise—but Timbers shopkeepers were united on one point: there was money to be made, especially this close to Halloween.

"Whoever blamed the Beast for destroying town square was a genius," Emma said, blowing on her steaming drink.

"Look at all these people." She pointed to a line of tourists walking off the ferry, giddy to visit the scene of a real-life monster attack. At least, that's what the charters were selling.

"It's a disgrace," Nico said bitterly. "Why are so many people buying into this story?"

Emma slugged him in the shoulder. "Because it's *fun*, you goof. And Mayor Hayt denying the rumor every chance she gets only makes people believe it more." Emma leaned close and lowered her voice. "Besides, it's not like the rumors are that far off. Monsters *did* destroy the radish festival—just not the Beast. But now everyone gets to have some excitement."

"More than that." Tyler nodded at a sign for *The Beast's Slathered Sundaes* on the front door of the ice cream shop across the street. "People around here are cashing in. My dad's got his hands full with all the boats in the harbor, and my mom's hitting up tourists for donations to the Lighthouse Preservation Society." He sighed happily. "The festival was supposed to give Timbers a shot in the arm. Well, it *did*, kinda. These Beast rumors are pure gold."

"It's been really good for the store," Emma said. "My parents are selling binoculars and rain gear like crazy, not to mention bear repellent. That stuff is going by the case."

Tyler's head whipped to Emma. "Bear repellent? Because of a sea monster?"

Emma laughed. "You can't prove that it *won't* work, right?"

A knocking behind them caused everyone to twist around. One door down, Logan was standing in the window-display area of Buck's Home Goods, smiling wide as he pressed a T-shirt to the glass.

Nico suppressed a groan, pulling his jacket close against the biting gusts. "Jeez. Even Logan?"

Logan stepped outside, grinning like a loon. "What do you think?" He lifted his prize up for the group to see: a black tank top with a goofy cartoon sea monster smiling in the center. Block letters above it read: *TIMBERS: IT'S THE BEAST.*

"I love it!" Emma squealed, clapping her hands.

Opal shrugged, while Nico covered his eyes.

Logan wanted to be a businessman like his father, Sylvain Nantes—owner of Nantes Timber Company and a dozen other ventures in town—so he always kept an eye out for money-making opportunities. It seemed the lure of Beast-related cash had gotten to him, too.

"That's not what the Beast looks like," Tyler noted primly. "I would know."

Logan's expression soured. "It's a cartoon, dingus. Plus, you wouldn't know, anyway. That wasn't the real Beast you fought, it was a figment."

"There *is* no real Beast," Nico mumbled.

At the same time Tyler shot back, "Oh, *I wouldn't*, huh?" He glanced from face to face, a familiar glimmer building in his eyes. "Do I need to tell the story again?"

Everyone groaned.

"Why'd you set him off, Logan?" Opal whined. "He'll never stop now."

Logan raised both palms, grimacing. "You're right. I'm sorry, Tyler. We all know how—"

"*There I was*," Tyler thundered, swinging his arms wide. "Facing the dark sea horror of a thousand legends, Timbers' infamous and deadly Beast. I had nothing in my hands but raw courage, and maybe a knife, yet my friends were in danger and needed my help. So. I. Stepped. *Up*." He pounded a fist into his palm, ignoring the eye-rolls circulating the group. "I stared the hulking, razor-tooth monster—"

"Figment," Logan corrected.

"—dead in the eye, and said, 'Not this time, Beast! Today, *you shall not pass*!'"

"Someone kill me," Nico moaned.

Emma clapped her hands a second time. "Tell it again! Tell it again!"

"Don't encourage him!" Opal, Nico, and Logan blurted at once. Tyler was launching into a much more detailed version of his heroics when a commotion by the pier caught Nico's attention. "Guys, look. Something's up."

"Its fangs were *dripping* with poison," Tyler continued, but broke off as the others stared down at the waterfront. "Well, fine then. What is it?"

Opal squinted, shielding her eyes. "Some kind of . . . weird van is coming off the ferry. It's headed this way." The vehicle pulled out of the unloading area and began climbing up Main Street toward them. The dockside crowd turned as it passed by, a few people pointing and chattering excitedly.

"What the heck?" Nico whispered.

The van was painted a deep blue with jagged orange letters on its side. Several thick, stubby antennas jutted from the roof. As it pulled close, Emma gasped, and Nico could finally make out the words emblazoned on the vehicle's sliding door.

"Freakshow," Nico read aloud, scratching the back of his neck. "What in the world is that?"

Emma popped up from the bench and started bouncing up and down. "*Ohmygosh ohmygosh ohmygosh!*"

The others spun to look at her. Emma was staring wide-eyed at the vehicle, covering her mouth with both hands. "You *guys!*" she shrilled, dropping her arms to reveal an ear-to-ear grin. "That's a famous online show! It's the number one streaming-investigative-paranormal-news program on YouTube!"

"Excuse me?" Nico asked.

Emma ignored him. "*Freakshow* is the *best*."

"*Freakshow*?" Tyler made a face. "That title's not very nice."

"They investigate weird and inexplicable things," Emma explained, talking a mile-a-minute. "It's super professional and scientific, plus they do these amazing reenactments. Like last year they *proved* that Bigfoot uses this laundromat in Spokane at least once a month. They had night vision footage and everything."

"Oh man, *that* show?" Tyler pursed his lips, shaking his head as he glanced at the others. "Emma made me watch a few eps last year. They don't do real news, just shock stuff with fake special effects."

"That's not true!" Emma huffed, as the van rolled to a stop in front of White Pines, the nicest bed-and-breakfast in town. "They do serious detective work, Tyler. Verifying that paranormal things really do happen in remote places." She tapped her chin with an index finger. "They must be here to investigate the Beast."

Nico felt a chill creep down his spine. He glanced at Opal, who was chewing her bottom lip.

"We don't want any paranormal investigations in Timbers," Opal said quietly. "For obvious reasons."

Logan dropped his Beast shirt onto the bench. "Who's that getting out of the van?"

A short, wiry man wearing a Yellowstone tee, jeans, and hiking boots stepped from the vehicle. Yawning, he pulled off a wool ski cap, running a hand through his dark brown hair as he examined his reflection in a window. *He looks like an ad for Ultimate Frisbee or something.*

Nico caught Emma and Opal exchanging a glance. "Is that the host?" he asked.

"Yes!" Emma said, barely able to contain her excitement. "Colton Bridger. He has a film degree from USC and used to be a professional bird-watcher, and before that he shot back-country skiing videos. He lived a *year* in Tibet to learn meditation. Bridger's not afraid to go anywhere. He does all the writing, directing, and editing for *Freakshow*."

"A professional hipster," Tyler murmured. Logan snorted, but Emma didn't seem to hear.

"Colton Bridger has won *seven* Web Breaker click-count awards," she continued breathlessly, "and last year he was named 'Most Downloaded' by Online Magazine. You guys, he's a star. In *our* town. I can't believe it!"

Bridger was rotating in a slow circle, taking in the neighborhood as two men and a woman unloaded a set of battered trunks behind him. When his inspection reached their bench, he paused. Then, incredibly, he started walking toward them.

Emma stiffened like she'd been hit with a cattle prod. "He's coming. Over here."

Bridger approached, flashing an easy smile. "Hey, guys. I was wondering if you might be able to help me. My film crew and I are looking for a place called Fort Bulloch, somewhere near"—he held up a finger, pulling a scrap of crumpled paper from his jeans—"Razor Point? Any chance you could give us directions?"

Logan grunted. "Easy enough. Take Coast Street south out

of town and you'll run right into it. That way becomes a dirt road after a couple miles, but it doesn't go anywhere else."

Emma was blinking rapidly at Bridger. "Are you here to do an episode of *Freakshow*?"

His smile grew coy. "That we are. In fact, we hope to shoot a whole miniseries."

He extended a hand and Emma shook it, beaming.

"Colton Bridger. We've come to investigate the Beast rumors—how it wrecked your radish festival a few weeks back. The Internet is on fire about the attack. Everyone wants us to catch this devil in the act." His eyes twinkled, as if enjoying a private joke. Nico found himself disliking the man.

"The Beast isn't a devil," Tyler shot back. "It's just . . . the Beast. That legend has been around for decades."

"Right, right," Colton said smoothly. "You locals would know best, for sure. I'm here to show the world how real this monster is once and for all. That it's almost Halloween makes everything *perfect*." He nodded at the Beast-themed windows surrounding them. "The creature hasn't exactly been bad for Timbers, has it?"

"Why are you heading to Razor Point?" Nico asked, hiding a frown. "The old fort's out there, but not much else." That area was too close to Still Cove for Nico's comfort.

"Didn't you hear?" Bridger glanced around dramatically, dropping his voice to a conspiratorial whisper. "Some fishermen reported a Beast sighting there three hours ago. Today

32

I might capture footage of an actual sea monster." He straightened, pulling his ski cap back on. "Thanks for the directions. Hope to see you kids around soon. It's always great to meet our fans!" He strode back to his van and climbed inside.

"Nobody said we were fans," Tyler grumbled. "That dude thinks he's as cool as there is."

Nico was nodding in full agreement, but stopped short when he noticed Opal frowning at the pavement, a dull metal object clutched in her fingers. Nico thought he heard her whisper, "Fort Bulloch."

Opal abruptly straightened to face them. "We should check it out, too. Before the film crew gets there."

"What, Razor Point?" Tyler said, his mouth forming a scowl. "Why?"

"I don't know . . . I just . . . Here." She held up the object in her hand for everyone to see. "I found this medal back on the houseboat. I want to . . ." Opal trailed off. Nico thought she wore an odd expression, like something was bothering her. "Can we just go look, okay?" she finished awkwardly.

"It's a long bike ride out to the Point," Tyler complained. "We'd have to leave right now if we want to beat that van."

Opal folded her arms. "Then what are we waiting for?"

4

OPAL

Opal skidded to a stop beside the rusty fence.

She scanned the fort's parking area and found it delightfully empty. *We made it first.*

The others pulled up around her in a ragged semicircle, sucking wind as they studied crumbling Fort Bulloch over the next rise.

Tyler dropped his bike to the grass. "How much longer until we can use your four-wheelers again, Logan? I'm not built for all this bonus exercise."

"Who knows?" Logan's face glistened with sweat despite the low temperature. "They've been stuck in my garage ever since that giant cockroach wrecked them. I've got to keep them both out of sight until Sheriff Ritchie stops investigating Beast Night. He took pictures of the tracks, you know."

"They should be thanking us for saving the rest of downtown," Nico grumbled.

Opal agreed. They'd used Logan's ATVs to lure rampaging figments away from town square, but had left tire marks all over the sidewalks. If anyone connected them to Logan's vehicles, he could get blamed for everything.

Opal rolled her bike into a tangle of alder trees behind them. "Come on. We don't want anyone to know we're here."

"Why *are* we here, exactly?" Emma asked, stashing her bike alongside Opal's. Together they approached the fence and ducked through a gap in the chain-link. Nico, Tyler, and Logan followed, whispering among themselves. Inside the perimeter, a short, grassy field stretched to the foot of the deserted citadel. "I mean, I get that you found a war medal, but . . . what does that have to do with us?"

"I think it connects to the Torchbearers." Opal tapped her jeans pocket. "There must be a reason the medal was stored on the houseboat, right? Last night, I googled the image, and it's something called a Distinguished Flying Cross. From World War II. Fort Bulloch was active during that era. I just think we should check it out."

Opal frowned. *Weak, even to my ears.* But she couldn't explain it better than that. Something in her head insisted this search was important. The spark of an idea, buried deep inside. Opal had learned to trust her intuition, even when it felt . . . different than usual. She stuffed her doubts away. What could it hurt to look?

"There's lots of weird crap on the houseboat," Logan

pointed out. "That medal could be some random trinket an old Torchbearer kept as a souvenir."

"Maybe," Opal said diplomatically, but she thought Logan was wrong. She'd had another flash of insight back in town. *When Bridger said he needed to go to Razor Point. I don't know . . . something.*

Fort Bulloch sat on a high promontory overlooking the sea. Its cement buildings were set in two rows, with a thick curtain wall encircling the entire fortification. Below it, a sea cliff dropped to a sandy spit of lowland bordered by beaches on both sides. At the very tip of the peninsula—on lonely Razor Point itself—an old military cemetery was just visible in the overcast haze. An automated lighthouse still operated at its farthest reach, marking the dangerous rocks that gave the area its name.

Inside the curtain wall, bunkers faced the ocean, their bulky concrete shells covered in emerald-green moss. A line of storage buildings ran behind them, giving the paths in between a tight, mazelike feel. The military closed the base in the 1950s, but the location had been an important stronghold for two centuries before that, guarding the coastline and surrounding areas.

"We're not supposed to be here," Tyler fretted, pointing to a NO TRESPASSING sign. "This is restricted government property."

"What are we looking for, exactly?" Nico asked, hands in his pockets.

Opal heard the confusion in his voice, though she could tell he was trying to be supportive. "I'm not sure," she replied honestly. "We could try looking for anything that matches the medal's engraving. Airplane propellers?"

Nico nodded, but Opal caught him shooting a glance at Tyler, who shrugged. She ignored them and plunged deeper into the fort.

Rusty ladders ran up the outsides of the bunkers. Broken metal doors swung on raspy hinges. The walls were covered with graffiti, and broken glass crunched underfoot, left behind by teenagers who liked to sneak past the fences at night.

"There's gotta be info about Fort Bulloch in the school library," Tyler suggested. "We could do some research there. And *not* break the law."

"Yeah, maybe later," Opal said absently. But as towering clouds shifted in the Pacific sky—late afternoon sunlight slanting into her eyes—she kept thinking: *here*. The impulse had only strengthened. Something had to be learned, or seen, or found at the fort. *Here.*

"It'd make sense if a few Torchbearers were in the military," Emma said, her voice echoing as she poked her head into one of the gloomy bunkers. "I mean, their charge was to protect people from threats."

"Maybe," Tyler conceded. But Opal could tell he remained unconvinced. He kept looking over his shoulder, clearly more worried about getting caught than anything else.

"If we get busted here, I'll be grounded *again*," Logan complained. "And I will lose my mind. For real. I can't spend another minute in my house playing board games with my little sister. Not when figments are running through the hills."

"I can't believe no one's filmed here before." Emma's eyes twinkled as she examined every inch of the fortress. "Those *Freakshow* guys are going to get amazing footage, even without a Beast shot."

Opal stopped. They'd reached a small amphitheater—a smooth semicircular patio with cement benches descending to a raised stage. Spray paint and lichen covered the walls, but the floor was oddly clear of both.

"This must be where they performed the human sacrifices," Tyler said, nodding sagely.

"Gross." Logan tromped down onto the stage and spun in a lazy circle. "Well? Now what? Should I sing?" An icy wind swept through the hollow space, sending shivers down Opal's back.

Nico glanced at her, spoke in a neutral voice. "Should we go back?"

Opal shook her head. "Not yet."

Is it something I have to find? she wondered. *Like an object?*

"Yo." Emma pointed to the far side of the amphitheater. "More bunkers thataway."

"I'm not sure how much farther we should go," Nico began, but Opal strode forward without looking back. After a tense moment, she heard the others follow. They passed another row of storage buildings, descended a flight of steps, and reached an archway that cut straight through the outer wall.

"Wait." Logan stopped and held up a hand. "Do you hear that?"

Opal listened hard. At first, nothing. But then voices carried across the fort's strange concrete acoustics. "The *Freakshow* crew?" she whispered.

"Who else?" Tyler snapped. "Let's bail. We can sneak around them back to the fence."

"*No.*" Opal saw Tyler flinch. She took a deep breath and softened her voice. "Just a little farther. I want to see what's beyond this archway."

"Opal—" Nico began, but she darted ahead once again, her pulse quickening when she realized the archway was actually a tunnel burrowing into the stony hillside.

Daylight was barely visible at the opposite end, which exited to a forested glen at the base of the curtain wall. Opal thought the area might have been well groomed in the past, like a small park or garden.

There she froze, a tremor creeping up her spine. Opal turned around.

Beside the archway, a tarnished bronze plaque was bolted to the concrete wall.

Opal swept in close, brushed away some encroaching moss with her fingers, and read the words stamped there.

In Loving Memory of Our Lost Airmen.

A short list of names followed.

"What's that?" Emma asked, peering over Opal's shoulder.

"A war memorial," Tyler answered, hemming to Opal's side. "Looks like this one is dedicated to Timbers men and women who died fighting in World War II."

Each name had a raised symbol stamped beside it. Most looked like unit emblems, though Opal didn't know much about that kind of thing. Her eyes ran down the list.

There.

A name.

CHARLES DIXON.

Next to it, engraved in the flaking metal, was a hand holding a torch.

"The Torchbearer symbol!" Emma squawked. "Opal, you were right!"

Nico blinked in surprise. "Okay, wow."

"No, wait . . ." Opal reached out and traced the emblem with her finger. "Look. This is similar to the basic design we've seen before, but different. The flame on this one swirls in a circle instead of burning in jagged streaks." She stepped back and sucked in her lip. "What does *that* mean?"

Emma dug under her collar and removed her Torchbearer necklace. Logan had carved one for each of them. She held it up next to the plaque. "You're right. Close, but not the same. Huh."

Opal swung her backpack around and rifled inside for a piece of paper. She wanted to make a rubbing of the plaque.

"Almost there!" Colton Bridger called out to someone. "I want a shot of the ocean from up here, then we'll work our way down to the beach."

Opal's eyes popped. The film crew was nearly on top of them. She pulled out the first thing her fingers touched—the old leather-bound notebook. Opal flipped to a blank yellowed page and pressed it to the plaque, hurriedly running a pencil tip over the paper.

"A photo would be faster," Emma whispered. "Like, light-years faster."

"You take one." But Opal had to get it down like this. This was tangible. This, you could *touch*.

"We're out of time," Nico hissed. "Come on!"

He was right, but Opal kept at it. The plaque's hard edges appeared.

She heard a whistle.

Logan was farther along the base of the wall with two fingers to his lips. When they all looked, he pointed and whisper-shouted, "There's a second archway over here!"

"Done." Opal pushed back from the wall. Everyone

scurried after Logan and ducked into the gap, jostling like wild dogs in their silent rush to escape. The tunnel was humid and claustrophobic, and stank of things Opal didn't want to know about. Holding her breath, she hurried up the steep ramp, hoping it led somewhere safe.

They spilled from the passageway into another maze of bunkers, but here the path cutting back across the fort was fenced off and padlocked. Logan grabbed his head with both hands. "We're trapped!"

Voices carried from the tunnel mouth.

"Where does this one go?" Bridger asked, his voice echoing up. "I don't want to miss—"

Nico snagged Opal by the shoulder, then pointed to a rusty ladder running up the outside of the closest bunker. *Climb*, he mouthed. *Now.*

Opal studied the flaking orange rungs with serious misgivings, but the footsteps headed their way made the decision for her. She went first, climbing as fast as she could, praying the ancient ladder would hold. At the top, Opal scrambled onto the bunker's mossy roof. Even in her panic, the view took her breath away. Rolling Pacific waves stretched endlessly toward the horizon.

Emma scaled the wall next, with Tyler right on her heels. Then Nico followed, with Logan, the heaviest, going last. He slipped over the edge just as Colton Bridger appeared in the archway.

"Now what?" Tyler whispered.

"This row of bunkers leads back to where we broke in," Opal said in a hushed voice. "We can walk along the tops of them."

"But how will we get down?" Nico asked, eyeing the not insignificant drop to ground level.

Opal shrugged. "Hope for another ladder." It was pointless worrying about it now.

They crept along like cats. Anyone looking up from the beach would've seen a line of hunched silhouettes moving across the top of the fort, paper-doll cutouts against the blue-gray sky.

Nico was in the lead when he stopped suddenly, causing a minor pileup. He whistled low.

"Look at *that*."

Opal followed his startled gaze. Out in the Sound, a giant band of seawater had turned bloodred, rippling in a huge swath around Razor Point. It reminded Opal of the oil slicks that gathered in gas station parking lots. The scarlet stain shimmered, iridescent in the afternoon light.

"Red tide," Nico said quietly, shaking his head in disbelief. "A kind of algae bloom. That's *not* good. I wonder why it wasn't on the news?"

They all stared down at the ocean. The bloom looked like a sunset spilled across the waves. Finally, they stopped gawking and shuffled to the far end of the roofline, which dropped to a cobblestoned courtyard. Ivy covered this end of the wall, green tendrils reaching up to spread beneath their feet.

"No ladder," Logan grumbled.

Emma knelt. "I bet these vines are strong enough to hold us."

"Better not be poison ivy," Tyler said sharply. "I'm not looking to collect any new rashes."

Logan sighed. "What choice do we have?" Using the vines as ropes, he slowly worked his way down the wall. Emma went next, skittering easily like a squirrel and jumping lightly to the ground.

"Seems fine!" she called up.

The others followed. Opal dropped last and faced the group. "Guys, I think we found something really important."

Nico nodded. "That red tide is nuts. I've got to ask my dad about it."

"Not that. *The plaque.*" Was she the only one who thought this mattered? "Someone engraved a version of the torch on a public war memorial, where anyone could see. We have to check for the name Charles Dixon in the Torchbearers records."

"Let's get out of here first, okay?" Logan led everyone back to the fence, where they wiggled through the breach once more. On the other side, he smiled and rubbed his hands together. "Okay, back to business. Field trips are fun and all, but I've got T-shirts to sell."

Tyler snorted. "Because *that* matters."

Opal pulled her bike from the trees, silently fuming.

This discovery meant something. It *had* to. Why else would she have felt so drawn to it?

But she had no idea what the meaning could be.

5

NICO

Nico's race car sank into a crocodile-filled swamp.

Sighing, he put down his controller. "I concede defeat."

"Dumb game being dumb," Tyler mumbled, watching his monster truck burn on-screen. His glare snapped to Emma. "How'd your motorcycle get a flamethrower, anyway?"

"Trade secrets," Emma replied smugly. "Now, don't you boys have something to say?"

Nico groaned. Tyler covered his eyes and huffed. They were trapped on the couch with no possibility of escaping.

"I'm *wait-ing*," Emma said in a singsong voice, cupping her chin in one palm as she sat cross-legged on the oversized chair in her basement. They'd been playing video games there all morning, celebrating the glory of a fall Thursday off from school.

"Better get it over with," Emma warned. "Before my mom brings lunch down and you have a bigger audience."

Nico and Tyler met eyes. Rolled them. Then, like prisoners of war, they spoke in slow, dreary unison.

"Emma Fairington is the greatest gamer in Timbers. Tyler and Nico are lucky to be her friends. Tyler and Nico bow down before the amazing and talented Emma Fairington."

Both boys paused. Nico squeezed his eyes shut.

"Come come, now," Emma chided, clasping her hands together and batting her eyelashes. "Big finish!"

"Kill me," Tyler murmured.

"Me first," Nico said.

Emma clapped twice sharply. "Those aren't the words, gentlemen."

More sighs.

"All hail the Xbox queen and our personal hero, Emma Fairington."

Emma sank back in the chair and put her hands behind her head. "Yes. That was nice."

"Rematch!" Tyler barked, but he stopped short of restarting the game at Nico's headshake.

"Dude, if we lose again, we're up to level *three* humiliation," Nico hissed. "We'd have to do the dance."

Tyler dropped his controller as if snakebitten.

Emma giggled, digging into a bowl of chips. The trio was hanging out like old times, since Opal was helping her dad at the post office and Logan was working on a new T-shirt design. Torchbearing was obviously an around-the-clock responsibility, but they couldn't sneak out to Still Cove every single minute. People would notice.

"A wise choice, sirs." Emma bounced her eyebrows, but then her expression grew serious. "Plus, I want to ask you guys something."

"Uh-oh," Tyler muttered, squeezing his forehead.

Emma pursed her lips. "What? I haven't even said anything yet."

Nico grinned sourly. "Emma, you never say you want to ask us something unless you already know we're not going to like it. Otherwise, you'd just spit it out."

Emma opened her mouth indignantly, then closed it. "Okay. Fine." Her eyes dropped. "You're not going to like it."

"Lemme guess," Tyler grumbled. "You signed us up for the school play again, didn't you? What do I care about some orphan named Annie?"

"No, no, nothing like that." Emma shifted awkwardly. "This is something I want to do."

"Is it the trick-or-treating thing?" Nico asked, trying to be diplomatic. "Maybe we could hand out candy this year instead. I'm sure most of it could accidentally fall out of the bowl."

She shook her head. "It's not that either, although I still think you're crazy."

Nico shrugged. "Well? What is it?"

Emma took a deep breath, then squared her shoulders. "I saw a flyer for an unpaid grip position with the *Freakshow* crew. I want to apply for it."

"Emma, *no*," Nico blurted, just as Tyler said, "What's a grip?"

"Technically the posting reads more like a production assistant gig, but I'll make them call me a grip. That's the job I want. A grip is someone who sets up, fetches, and carries things for a camera crew in the field, and also helps organize their gear." Emma smiled. "I'd be great at it. And think how much about filming I could learn!"

"Emma, the stated mission of that show is to expose monster legends." Nico spoke as patiently as he could. "You understand that as Torchbearers, we're specifically tasked with *hiding* a giant *monster factory*, right? That our whole purpose is to keep people like that away from figments and the Darkdeep?"

"*Yes*, Nico. I know that," Emma replied testily. "But shouldn't we be keeping a close watch on what Bridger and his crew are doing? Name a better way to accomplish that than having an informant on the inside."

Nico was about to argue further when Tyler spoke up. "That's actually a solid point, Nico."

"Don't *you* start!"

"Well, think about it," Tyler said quietly. "We can't keep

49

up with a van on our bikes, and we won't know where they're going until they're gone. What if they decide to check out Still Cove one afternoon? At least this way, someone in our group will hear about it."

Nico shook his head, still refusing to admit the logic in Emma's plan. "That show is a total joke. I watched a couple episodes last night, and they made me sick. *Freakshow* isn't interested in finding the truth about anything. They use shock tactics and sneaky effects to make people think they've seen weird things. The locals always end up looking like clowns. Colton Bridger is going to make Timbers seem ridiculous. Or worse, what if he actually *finds* the Darkdeep? Can you even imagine?"

"All the more reason for me to get close," Emma insisted. "Maybe I can talk them out of mocking people, or steer them away from anything that matters."

Nico fell silent. He hated the idea of Timbers becoming a punch line. Even the Beastmania made him uncomfortable. Every morning he glowered at the boatloads of bucket-hat-wearing tourists pouring off the ferry, hoping to snap a pic of a magical sea creature on their iPhone. Who needed them?

"You're dead set on this?" Nico asked.

Emma shrugged. "I'm a Torchbearer first. I won't apply if you guys don't want me to. But I think it's the smart move."

Nico exhaled deeply. "You're right. I'm being dumb."

Rising, he stretched with a yawn, then swept his jacket off the back of the couch.

"Where are you going?" Tyler squawked.

"Town," Nico said, heading for the stairs. "If that flyer's been posted for long, Emma won't be the only one interested. We need to act fast. Come on."

Nico smiled as Emma's howl of delight chased him up the steps.

Emma sprinted across the torn-up grass of town square, screaming and waving a form over her head.

"I'm guessing she's hired?" Tyler said dryly, blowing into his fist. He and Nico were standing on a street corner, the same one where Nico had started the wild figment chase on Beast Night. Damage was still visible in dozens of spots around the little park, from its demolished fountain to the broken lampposts and gouged lawn.

Emma bowled into Nico and Tyler and wrapped them both in a ragged hug that was more like a double headlock. "I got the job!"

"Take it easy!" Nico laughed, stumbling backward.

"How is she so strong?" Tyler wheezed, unable to free himself.

Emma ignored their complaints, talking at warp speed. "There were a dozen applicants to start with, but most wanted money and bailed when they found out it's unpaid. Of the people left, I scored highest on their test and they picked me!"

"Test?" Nico's brow furrowed. "What'd they ask you?"

"Simple stuff, really." Emma released them and stepped back, looking pleased. "Diagramming a lighting rig, coiling AV cables, naming the secret numbers on *LOST*. That kind of thing."

"*LOST* numbers?" Tyler shook his head. "Didn't that come out before we were born?"

"That's what online streaming is for, you dip. For the record: 4, 8, 15, 16, 23, and 42."

"So that's it?" Nico said. "You're in?"

Emma nodded. "I just have to get this permission slip signed, but that's no problem. My parents are super tied-up at the shop selling ponchos to soaked tourists, so they'll be glad I have something to do. Colton said he's filming here through at least Halloween. It's perfect!"

Nico scratched his temple. "Wonderful."

"One thing, though," Emma said, her cheeriness fading. "They've been interviewing every local they find interesting, asking questions about the Beast. Basic stuff, mostly—where it came from, how long the legend's been around, that kind of thing. But then Colton asked *me* about Still Cove."

Tyler cringed. Nico's head flopped back.

"Define *interesting*," Tyler said. "Who are they talking to?"

Emma frowned. "Colton seems to prefer our town's more

colorful characters. Or those willing to go along with whatever he's driving at."

"Gaaaaah," Nico moaned, still staring at the sky.

Tyler ran a hand down his face. "And Still Cove?"

"People keep telling him that's where the Beast lives," Emma said, wincing slightly. "I bet he'll try to film there."

Nico shook his head. "We just have to take it one day at a time. Stay ahead of them."

Emma shifted uncomfortably. "There's something else, too."

Tyler pressed both palms to his eyes. "Let's hear it."

"They're also asking about Beast Night. Mayor Hayt overheard Colton interviewing Megan Cook, from third period, and she claimed there was Beast slime all over the fountain the next day, but the rain washed it away before anyone else saw. The mayor didn't look happy. I heard her tell a staffer that she expects an update on the sheriff's investigation." Emma swallowed. "She wants to know where every kid in Timbers was during the vandalism."

Tyler blinked in shock. "I thought the case was winding down."

Nico gripped his hair in frustration. "This is getting out of hand. We need to make sure we all have our stories straight. My dad will skin me if he thinks I had anything to do with the destruction of town property."

"*Your* dad?" Tyler shivered. "My dad'll ship me off to

military school on the next ferry. He's already got a brochure tacked up in our kitchen, from when my sister threatened to get a belly ring."

Emma turned to Nico. "Did you ask your dad about the algae bloom?"

He shook his head. "I haven't had a chance. But that's another thing keeping me awake. First, a sulfur cloud bubbles up through our pond, and then a red tide appears out of nowhere at Razor Point. It's like our whole ecosystem is spazzing. Meanwhile, we've got stray Pokémon running through the woods and a film crew breathing down our necks. It's all falling apart."

Tyler squinted at Nico. "You think the nature hiccups have something to do with figments?"

Nico tugged on his sleeves. "I don't know. It's just a lot of weird things at once, which makes me nervous."

Tyler nodded. "I hear that. So what's our next move?"

"Let's find Opal and Logan," Emma suggested. "They need to hear the news about the investigation before anyone starts asking more questions."

"We have to be careful," Nico cautioned, glancing around to make sure they were still alone. "We can't let any of this other stuff threaten the Darkdeep. That's what matters most."

"Truth." Tyler looked at his watch, then snapped off a crisp salute. "Orders, sir?"

"*Ha ha.* We both got creamed by Emma earlier, so I think she's in charge today."

"Thanks for remembering." But Emma's smug look was short-lived. "Let's rally everyone at the houseboat. Meet there in thirty?"

"Done." Tyler tapped a fist to his chest.

Nico nodded. A cold wind swept the square, swirling dead leaves like the worries in his head.

His spirits sagged. So much could go wrong.

Which problem was going to bury them first?

6

OPAL

Opal swished through the velvet curtain.

The others were waiting in the showroom, with varying degrees of impatience. And holding their noses—though pitch-black again, the pond still reeked of sulfur, and a rotten-egg stench was suffocating the houseboat. Opal tried to ignore it.

"There better be a good reason for this meeting," Logan grumbled, arms crossed as he stood beneath the spiraling, snakelike skeleton that hung from the ceiling. "I was making a killing on Beast merch today. Did you guys hear they're running an extra ferry now, to handle all the traffic?"

"Yeah," Tyler said. "My dad said the harbor's crazy with private boats, too. Timbers is a hot stop these days."

"Timbers Cafe was packed with tourists when my mom and I went in yesterday," Emma said. "They're all ordering the new Beastburgers."

"*Ew.*" Opal wrinkled her nose. "What are those?"

"Same as regular burgers, but topped with grilled radishes and three kinds of drippy cheese." Emma's lip quirked. "Kinda good, actually."

"You ate one?" Nico rolled his eyes. "So you're buying into this nonsense, too?"

"I like cheeseburgers," Emma said defensively. "And when was the last time the cafe offered something new?"

"*I'll* be trying one ASAP." Logan scooped his duffel bag off the floor and reached inside. "And check *this* out—I've got two hundred of these puppies shipping in tomorrow." He held up a sea-green football jersey with an image of the Beast on its hind legs wearing boxing gloves. Above it were the words *BEAST MODE*.

Tyler covered his face with both hands. "You've got to be kidding me."

Logan stretched the jersey to admire it. "These might even outsell *TIMBERS IS THE BEAST.*"

"Guys, *focus*," Nico said. "We have bigger problems. Colton Bridger is asking people about Still Cove."

Opal's heart skipped a beat. "What? Why?"

"Because everyone keeps telling him that's where the Beast lives," Nico said. "He's also asking a ton of questions about what happened on Beast Night, which is stirring up the mayor and Sheriff Ritchie."

"Oh no." Logan's eyes widened. "My four-wheelers."

Tyler made a false smile. "Any chance your dad could sell them to some Australians heading home?"

Logan shook his head grimly. "They're too busted up to even start right now, and their tires are still caked in dirt from town square."

Opal groaned. "Not good." And that was nothing compared to the threat the film crew posed.

What if Bridger found the island while investigating Still Cove? Or worse, the houseboat?

The Darkdeep seemed to be in sleep mode—so it didn't look *too* unnatural—but Bridger might stick an arm into it for pure shock value. She'd watched a little of *Freakshow* to see what it was like. In one segment, Bridger crawled inside a Transylvanian bat cave looking for Dracula artifacts, while gripping a clove of garlic for protection. He loved for his viewers to think he was in danger.

"There is some good news," Emma said. "I'll be infiltrating *Freakshow* starting tomorrow."

Logan made a face. "Since when are you a spy? Or working with those losers?"

"Since an hour ago." Emma beamed. "I got hired as a grip. I'll monitor what they're up to and report back."

Logan squinted at her. "What do you . . . grip, exactly?"

"Think of me as a gofer."

"The rodent?"

Emma blinked. "I'm a production assistant, Logan. I'll do odd tasks."

"That's great," Opal said. She was pleased they'd know what Bridger was doing in real time. Plus, she knew Emma would love the work, even if it was for such a trashy show.

"Just keep them away from Still Cove," Nico said, nervously rubbing his chin. "Distract them in Timbers if you can. Tell Bridger that those Beastburgers are made from real Beast."

Emma nodded. "I'll try to send them west, into the woods over by Nantes Timber. They'll probably believe whatever I say about local legends." Her eyes twinkled. "This could be fun."

Opal went to the chest where they stored the slime-covered books from the tunnel chamber. Setting aside the special dagger with the key in its hilt—the one they'd found in the stone cylinder, which allowed access to the hidden vault—she pulled out the *Index of Torchbearers*. The volume recorded every member of the secret society since its founding in 1741. Hoping against hope, Opal placed her fingertip on the last one listed—Roman Hale, the poor soul whose skeleton they'd discovered on the island—and traced up the page, searching for Charles Dixon.

"Looking for the name on the plaque?" Nico asked quietly.

"Yes." Then Opal exhaled loudly in frustration. "But it's not here."

Nico scrunched his shoulders. "Well, half this roster is ruined by slug-slime. He could be under there somewhere."

"But it's legible starting in the 1920s. The plaque said Dixon flew missions during World War II—in the 1940s—and I'm assuming the medal belongs to him. So his name should probably be in the visible part." Opal gently closed the splintering book, but her mood had turned foul. "I feel like something's missing." She glanced at the wall where photographs of old Torchbearers hung. "Like, maybe there's a part of being a Torchbearer that we're not doing. It can't just be hunting down stray figments as they appear. We could miss one, or someone might see us. And we don't *really* know how to monitor the Darkdeep."

Nico followed Opal's gaze to the line of picture frames. "Too bad everyone who could explain things is gone."

"And their best records are slimed," Tyler grumbled, scowling at the flaking *Index*. "I've been working through every book on this boat. I even snuck a few home to read in my closet at night. But it seems like the Torchbearers didn't write much about themselves."

Nico scowled. "How could they be so irresponsible? They didn't have a plan in case something like this happened?"

"We could dig up Roman Hale," Logan joked. "Ask *him*

what we're supposed to do." When everyone glared, he put his hands in the air. "What? Sorry."

"He was a real person, Logan," Emma scolded. "It's sad. I'm glad we buried him."

Tyler shuddered. "I never want to see another skeleton."

Nico's irritation seemed to boil over. "How is it possible that on this entire freaking houseboat there's not a single hint about what we're supposed to do?"

"We have the medal," Opal said quickly. "And a name connected to the Torchbearers: Charles Dixon." She removed the leather sketchbook from her backpack and opened it to her rubbing of the plaque.

Nico shook his head sharply. "That's neat and all, but how does it help us?"

Opal turned away. She knew he wasn't trying to make her feel bad, but none of them seemed to think her discoveries were important. And after failing to find Dixon in the *Index*, she couldn't really argue with them.

Opal dropped the notebook onto a bookcase. It flopped open, and she noticed a drawing in the bottom right-hand corner of one of the pages. She picked the book up and inspected the image: a single, spiky flower sketched in pencil. Flipping through the rest of the pages, Opal saw that, while blank otherwise, each one bore an identical illustration in the same place. *Almost like a signature.*

Logan grunted, tugging the back of his neck. "I mean, it's cool how the things Opal found fit together—and Dixon *definitely* has some connection to the Torchbearers—but I'm not sure it adds up to anything we can use, you know?"

The others went back to arguing about *Freakshow*. Opal removed the medal from her pocket, hefting its tiny weight in her hand. She could try drawing it in the sketchbook herself. *I could keep notes in there. Track our progress.*

But what progress? The tarnished medal had led her to the fort, where they'd found a plaque with the odd torch symbol and the name Charles Dixon. But did it matter? Did those things connect at all?

She glared down at the medal in growing annoyance.

Tell me something.

Opal slapped the notebook closed. Squeezed her eyes shut.

The medal's propellers lingered in her mind for a moment, then melted away, re-forming in the shape of the bronze plaque on its lichen-covered wall. Opal felt a wave of dizziness but didn't open her eyes, possessed by a sudden urgency she couldn't explain. The image in her mind shifted from the plaque to the military cemetery far below, at the tip of Razor Point. Opal didn't remember examining it closely while at the fort, but suddenly she could picture every detail.

The cemetery.

Where they bury soldiers lost in combat.

A second image flashed into her head—a white marble

crypt with flower-carved entry columns. Then her brain blanked, something like radio static screeching in her ears.

Opal's eyes flew open. She glanced down at the notebook. Her finger was wedged between two pages. The tiny flower drawn in the corner matched the carvings she'd just envisioned on the crypt.

"Guys," she gasped, but no one heard.

The others hadn't been watching, or noticed her distress. Logan was helping Emma try on a BEAST MODE jersey, prattling about product placement now that she was a member of the *Freakshow* crew. Tyler was leafing through the *Index* with his nose screwed up. Nico stood beside him, intent on the damaged parchment.

Opal felt eyes on her back.

She turned. The only object behind her was the glass jar on its pedestal.

Thing floating in its viscous cocoon, making no movement, as still and insensible as always.

A chill ran up her spine.

"Hey! Guys!" she called out.

Everyone turned, looking surprised. Logan wore a *What now?* expression, which ticked Opal off. "The military cemetery on Razor Point," Opal said impatiently. "We should go and search for Charles Dixon."

Tyler grimaced. "I went there once with my mom. It's super creepy. At the front are rows of white headstones that

63

all look the same, but deeper in there's an area with old crypts and all kinds of gnarly stuff. Some of the markers don't even have any names or dates on them anymore. Worn down to nothing."

"It's the next place to check out," Opal said firmly. "We need to keep on this." She didn't want to elaborate, or explain the weird vision she'd just had. *Am I crazy? Where did those images come from? Am I making up a story out of nothing, because I want this all to make sense?*

Opal crossed the room and pulled on her jacket and backpack, refusing to look at the green blob in its jar. "I'm going now. Come with me or don't. Up to you." Steeling her nerve, she strode for the curtain. Before swishing through it she heard footsteps trailing her.

Opal turned. Emma linked an arm with hers. Opal gave it a squeeze.

They spun around to face the boys, who were rooted to the floorboards in surprise.

Emma glared. "Anyone else joining us?"

Opal raised an eyebrow. The showroom held its breath.

"*Fine.*" Logan began stuffing jerseys back into his bag. "You don't have to be so dramatic."

"Stop whining, Nantes." Emma snorted a giggle. "It's not very BEAST MODE to chicken out on a cemetery trip."

Opal's gaze flicked to Tyler, who looked nervous. "The cemetery?" he said. "Now? For real?"

"It's not even dark yet," Opal assured him. Tyler's eyes rolled skyward, but he nodded.

Some of the tension eased in Opal's chest. "Nico?"

He held her gaze for a beat. "All right, Opal. But after this trip, we focus on the *right now* stuff. Rogue figments and annoying film crews. Red tides and smelly sulfur farts. Deal?"

"Deal." Opal felt a burst of relief. They would follow her. "First, graveyard. Second, er, those other things."

"Third, a grocery-store run," Tyler said. When the others glanced at him, he shrugged. "What? We're out of cupcakes."

Logan got a speculative look. "I wonder if anyone's making Beast-cakes yet?"

"Absolutely not," Nico snapped. "What's next, Beast-cicles?"

"Not a bad idea," Logan murmured to himself. Emma and Tyler both laughed.

"Come on, Torchbearers," Opal said, a renewed confidence flowing through her. "Let's solve this riddle once and for all."

7

NICO

The sun sank into the ocean like a ball of molten lava.

Nico shivered on his bike, watching the dying rays reflect off the bloodred swells encircling Razor Point. He backpedaled lazily, coasting along a gravel trail that angled down off the bluffs in a long bumpy ramp. The beach was dead ahead. Beyond it was the narrow peninsula where the old cemetery lurked, in the shadow of Fort Bulloch.

Nico was worried.

The algae bloom was bad enough—those didn't usually happen in Washington, and the scientists on the news seemed baffled by this one—but he kept thinking about the sulfur cloud that had sizzled up in the pond. Where had *it* come from? Why did the horrible smell still linger? Nico worried there was more going on in those fathomless black depths than they understood.

Did the Darkdeep extend down to a physical place, or was

it just some kind of break in reality? For that whole first week, every time Nico jumped into the Darkdeep it would spit him out in the pond's freezing waters, right there on the island. But on the night it overloaded completely, the well transported him to a *different* place—a limitless black void that definitely wasn't underneath the houseboat. So where did it go, really? Was the *Darkdeep* causing the rotten-egg smell?

Nico's tires hit sand, jarring him back to the present. The cemetery was a hundred yards ahead, occupying a grassy field sandwiched between two skinny beaches. The very tip of the peninsula was obscured by uneven patches of woods. Nico saw the automated lighthouse come alive and begin its nightly patrol.

Opal was slightly ahead of him, her long braid bouncing as she zipped toward Razor Point.

What are we doing out here?

Nico didn't understand Opal's obsession with the medal, or the rest of it. Sure, it'd been cool when they found that swirly torch design on the plaque at Fort Bulloch. Nico was impressed her instincts had been right—Charles Dixon was clearly either a former Torchbearer or connected to them in some way. But that was just history. Trivia. Something they could explore when they had free time.

Which wasn't now. The sheriff's investigation. Rogue figments. Environmental glitches. An unscrupulous film crew nosing around, prying into their secrets. They had several *serious* fires to put out, so what were they doing breaking into a cemetery at night, on nothing more than a whim?

He ground his teeth but kept pedaling.

It's important to Opal.

They reached the front gates—two sections of wrought iron posts padlocked together in the middle. The grounds had closed hours earlier. A low wall ran around the perimeter, but it wasn't something to keep determined people out. And after all, who'd break into a military graveyard?

Logan tested the gates and found them secure. "Over the side?" he suggested, but without enthusiasm.

"This wall should be easy to scale," Opal said, propping her bike against it. "Come on."

Nico suppressed a sigh but followed as she moved a few yards farther down. Opal was right—the gates were the only part of the boundary difficult to climb. The rest of the wall was only five feet high, made of brick and dressed with granite slabs running along its top. In moments, all five of them were on the other side, staring at neat rows of white headstones.

"This front section is where anyone in Skagit County who served can be buried," Tyler said, flaunting his knowledge of local history. "If you're a soldier from Timbers itself, there's a smaller section in the back you can choose."

"Pretty," Emma said, taking in the silent rows as the stars came out. "It's peaceful here."

A wooded area stretched toward the lighthouse. Nico

spotted a few squat stone structures nestled among the ancient trees. A lonely angel statue, draped in vines, peeked above a clump of wide-leafed maple trees. The last memory of daylight cast purple blotches across the sky, then faded completely. The temperature dropped from cold to colder. Nico zipped up his jacket.

Opal shrugged off her pack and began handing out flashlights—he'd watched her add extras before they left the houseboat. She clearly didn't want anything to get in the way of her search for Charles Dixon's final resting place. Nico couldn't understand where all this urgency was coming from, but he wasn't going to ask.

"That's where the crypts are." Tyler pointed at the woods, then cleared his throat. "It's creepier back there."

"That's the place," Opal blurted immediately. She seemed about to say more, but looked away instead. When she spoke again a few beats later, Nico was sure it was about something different. "I mean, Dixon was probably local, right?" Opal slung her bag back onto her shoulders. "If connected to the Torchbearers? So let's search that area first."

"Makes sense," Emma said. She and Opal powered their flashlights and started walking down a crushed-shell path toward the trees.

"Why are these girls insane?" Tyler muttered, flicking his beam on. "They act like dead people aren't all around us right now. Don't they know it's almost Halloween?"

"No one said we have to follow," Logan suggested. "We could do our searching right here by this comfy wall."

Nico turned on his flashlight. "Come on, guys. The quicker we find Dixon, the quicker we can leave." He strode after the slim beams of light ahead. Grumbling, Logan and Tyler followed on his heels.

The local section of the cemetery was smaller—less than a dozen rows arranged in a grid, and bound by a spiky fence. Most of the graves were modest stones set into the ground, but a few larger memorials dotted the wooded meadow. Opal, apparently, only had eyes for those.

"Why do you think Dixon has a crypt?" Nico whispered, the darkness lowering his voice even though they were clearly alone. He could hear heavy surf pounding Razor Point's namesake shoals not far away.

"I just do," Opal snapped. Then she exhaled deeply. "I have this . . . feeling. Look for a white tomb with flower carvings along both sides. Don't ask me why . . . Just trust me."

"O-kay." Tyler glanced at Nico, then put his light under his chin, displaying big, concerned eyes.

Nico made an exaggerated shrug. Opal clearly wasn't in the mood to explain.

They scurried from crypt to crypt, examining the marble exteriors. Logan and Emma hunted names, but even before calling them out, Opal would decide a structure was wrong and move along. Nico had the impression she knew *exactly* what she was looking for, but how was that possible?

Finally, they reached the last crypt, in the corner of a back row underneath a huge weeping willow tree. The exterior was a stone rectangle about four feet high and six long, with twin pillars flanking a tiny, templelike door.

Tyler aimed his flashlight. Spiky, star-shaped flowers with long thin petals were carved along each column.

"This is it!" Opal said excitedly.

"Fact," Logan confirmed, illuminating a line of block letters engraved above the door.

CHARLES DIXON

"There's writing on the side, too," Emma said excitedly. "*Forever Watchful.*" She scanned the rest of the crypt with her flashlight. "No years, though. That's weird. I wonder how old he was?"

Nico felt a hand snag his shirtsleeve tightly. Tyler was staring at a carving on the lintel above the door. "Check it out."

An upthrust hand, holding a swirling torch.

"Bingo," Logan breathed. "That matches the plaque." Then he scratched his face. "So, um . . . now what?"

No one spoke for several heartbeats.

"We open it," Opal said finally.

Tyler groaned and covered his eyes. "Why did I know she was going to say that?"

"Just hold on!" Nico ran a hand through his tousled brown hair. "We've established Dixon was probably a Torchbearer. Why do we need to break into his crypt?"

"His *grave*!" Tyler hissed, slapping his thigh in agitation. "You want to disturb a soldier's final resting place?"

Opal turned to face the others. The rising moon sparkled her hazel eyes.

"All of the clues led here," she said intently. "To *this* door. That can't be an accident. I think we're supposed to find something, or *learn* something, from inside this crypt." She glanced at the simple name carved into stone. "I think Dixon would want us to open it."

"I agree," Emma said suddenly.

When Tyler turned on her, she met his glare. "We can do it respectfully. Let's just look inside."

Tyler hid his face, but Logan was already examining the entrance with curiosity. Opal looked to Nico. He nodded heavily. "We open the door, take a quick look, close the door. Touch nothing. That's all."

Opal's hand brushed his. "Help me open it."

Together they approached the front of the crypt, ignoring Logan's annoyed grunt and Tyler's mumbled prayers for forgiveness. There was no lock, and the hinges looked sound.

Pulling as one, they were surprised when the heavy marble swung outward without resistance.

"We're not the first to do this!" Opal said excitedly. "It's *meant* to be opened."

"Okay, that's interesting," Tyler muttered, pinching his temple. "What in the world?"

Five heads peered through the doorway as Opal and Nico aimed their lights. Inside was a smooth rectangular space with blank walls like a bank vault. No alcoves or visible niches. No coffin or sarcophagus, either. The crypt was totally empty.

"Welp." Tyler straightened with a suspiciously relieved sigh. "That was a letdown. We can go now."

"You think someone cleared out the crypt before us?" Emma wondered. "It looks . . . well maintained in here." She sneezed. "Except for the dust."

"No no no," Opal was murmuring to herself. "This can't be right. I was *sure* . . . There has to be . . ." Ignoring Nico's hiss of warning, she crawled headfirst into the crypt.

"Opal, *no*," Tyler said in a choked voice, so shocked he could barely get the words out.

"Bad idea!" Logan spat. "Bad *bad* idea!"

Opal ran her hands along the marble walls. Her head dropped, and she pressed an ear to the floor, rapping it with a fist. Then she flipped over onto her back and stared up at the ceiling.

"Opal, please," Nico said in a flat voice, trying not to reveal how creeped out he was. "It's okay. We'll look up Charles Dixon at the library. I'm sure we can find out more."

But Opal wasn't listening. She rose to her knees and pressed a palm against the ceiling. Astonishingly, her hand disappeared into the stone. "There's a hidden shelf!" she squealed.

Nico watched her remove something and wriggle back out of the crypt. He released a pent-up breath as Tyler scampered around behind Opal and shut the crypt door. "That's done with!" he said fiercely, hastily stepping away from the tomb.

"What'd you find?" Emma asked, staring at a small leather bag in Opal's hand.

"I don't know." Wedging her flashlight into the crook of an elbow, Opal started to unbuckle the snap.

Branches crunched in the night.

Everyone froze.

Tyler spun, aiming his beam down the path. "Did you hear—"

High-pitched, cackling laughter echoed from somewhere overhead.

Nico looked up, then stumbled backward in alarm, tripping awkwardly and landing on his butt. "Guys, look out!"

Standing on top of the crypt, just above the swirly torch carving, was a green-skinned creature with wiry limbs and wide, flaring ears. Unblinking red eyes peered down at Nico, above a grinning mouth bristling with sharp, pointy teeth.

Nico stared, his heart rate speeding to a gallop.

Emma screamed and slammed back into Tyler, who was gaping at the creature in horror. Logan dropped into a crouch, while Opal backpedaled, shoving the leather bag into her pocket.

"What is *that* thing?" Opal gasped.

"You mean things!" Tyler pointed at the weeping willow looming behind the crypt. Two more reptilian creatures lurked in its branches, gazing down at them with malevolent scowls. One started laughing uproariously—a piercing, chattering sound that froze Nico's blood.

"Gremlins," Logan whispered, his voice cracking. "They must be figments that escaped the Darkdeep. But how'd they get here?"

Before anyone could respond, one of the tree gremlins swung down on a vine with a gleeful howl, forcing Logan to dive for cover. His companion dropped to the ground and charged at Emma, arms spread wide. She lurched backward and tripped over Logan, collapsing on top of him in a heap.

"*Oof,*" Logan wheezed. "Get off me!"

The lead gremlin laughed from his perch atop the crypt. He seemed to be enjoying the show. Nico clambered to his feet, his anger rising. "They're just figments," he yelled. "Spread out!"

Reaching into his jacket, Nico removed a Torchbearer dagger and held it up for the gremlin to see. The creature stuck out his tongue, cackling maniacally. The other gremlins feinted at the group, making everyone jump back. Then they scurried onto Dixon's tomb to stand beside their leader. All three made a rude gesture in unison.

"Oh, that is *it*," Opal snarled. She pulled out her dagger as well. "Try that vine trick again, tough guy. I dare you."

The gremlins were capering in a weird dance that Nico felt sure was some kind of calculated insult, but they suddenly froze. Their leader sniffed the air. Eyes widening, he spun and chittered something to his companions. As one they scampered into the willow tree, making whimpering noises as they scurried from sight.

Logan smiled, nodding sharply at Nico and Opal. "Good job. You scared them off."

A loud thump echoed in the darkness. Nico felt its vibration run through his legs.

He stopped breathing. Slowly turned around.

"Um, guys?" Tyler whispered. "You hear that?"

A second thump sounded, closer than the first. Nico felt it in his bones.

"I don't think they ran from *us*," Emma breathed.

Hands shaking, Nico aimed his flashlight down the path. Two huge, glowing eyes stared back.

8

OPAL

The enormous gleaming eyes met Opal's.

An overwhelming scent—that of deep ocean, of ancient salt and seaweed—assaulted her nose as something *massive* stalked into the glow of their flashlights. The creature reared up, towering over Opal and the others as they cowered beside Dixon's crypt. A roar shook the ground.

The Beast.

It's real. Really, really real.

"How is it back?" Emma squeaked, recoiling beside Opal. "Tyler dispelled this figment weeks ago!"

The sea monster was blacker than the night behind it, except where their lights touched its body, revealing sleek indigo-blue scales. Opal heard its lungs bellowing in and out, then another sound crowded her ears—a rapid pounding, like a jackhammer. She realized it was her own heart beating out of control.

"This isn't a *figment*," Nico warbled, his shoulders quivering with fear. "It's the real deal."

"But the Beast doesn't actually exist!" Logan yelped, denying the evidence in front of his own two eyes. "It's just a story!"

The monster stamped a massive foot, dragging thick claws through the hard-packed earth.

Nico swallowed. "I think it's . . . angry."

"Really?" Tyler shrilled. "What tipped you off?!"

The Beast thundered a second time. Moved closer toward them.

Everyone took a step back.

Tyler stammered in nervous terror. "I was r-right, by the way. About what it l-l-looks like. What are the odds, h-huh?"

Opal backed up another step, afraid to move too quickly and trigger a reaction. She noticed a few small differences between the figment Tyler had conjured inside the Darkdeep and the creature in front of them—this Beast's head was slightly narrower, its legs bulkier under a sinuous body—but not much. The monsters were largely identical.

How is that possible? How did Tyler know what it really looked like?

The Beast lowered its head, regarded them with all-too-intelligent eyes. Then it turned to look at something on the path. For a brief moment Opal thought it might return to the ocean only a short distance away, but the awful head swung back. The Beast's mouth opened to reveal twin rows of razor-sharp teeth. Lashing its tail against the ground, the monster began closing in again.

"Run!" Nico shouted.

Everyone scattered among the crypts and tombstones, yellow beams bobbing madly as they scampered for cover. Opal ducked behind Charles Dixon's tomb and switched off her flashlight, fingers shaking as she peeked around the corner.

The graveyard had fallen deathly silent—even the insects were quiet—except for the thud of the Beast's lumbering treads. The creature moved slowly, pausing to snuffle the air as if searching for something. *Or hunting dinner.*

Then it exploded forward, impossibly quick for something so large.

A scream, then sounds of struggle.

"Help!" Logan shrieked in terror.

Pulse racing, Opal switched on her light and swung it around the crypt. The Beast had snagged Logan by the hood of his jacket and was shaking him like a dog with a rat in its mouth.

"Logan!"

Opal darted into the open space before the crypt, only to stare helplessly, unable to do anything as the creature began dragging Logan toward the sea. Nico charged out from behind a tombstone, waving his flashlight, Emma a short step behind him. The Beast paused, a low growl escaping its jaws.

Logan managed to twist, turn, and shrug out of his jacket. He hit the ground and scrambled toward his friends.

"Scatter!" Opal yelled. "Don't be an easy target!"

The Beast's vast bulk was blocking the path back to the wider cemetery beyond. They'd never sneak past it and escape. So Opal switched off her light again and the others followed suit, plunging the older graveyard into a gloomy moonlit haze. She peered nervously at the pointy fence surrounding this section—they could try to climb over, but it'd be tricky and leave them exposed. Could they scale it in time?

Someone bumped into her in the dark, whispering, "It's real, it's real, it's real, it's real."

Opal calmed her nerves enough to whisper. "Ty?"

Silence, then a shaky voice replied, "Yeah."

"Can you think of anything that might help us?" Opal hissed. "A way to fight back?" Tyler had been terrified of the Beast his whole life. *He has to know something useful about it, right?*

But Tyler didn't answer. Opal was afraid he'd locked up completely.

The Beast approached, sniffing Dixon's tomb. Pushing Tyler before her, Opal slipped around a corner just as a giant eye appeared right where they'd been hiding. They scurried around the next corner and put their backs to the crypt door. Opal gasped as the Beast's long, muscular tail swung close. The monster's head appeared above the crypt, but it didn't look down to see them.

Nico's voice cut through the night. "Who can hear me?"

"Me," hissed Logan.

"I'm here," Emma whispered.

"Tyler and I can." Opal shrank back against the marble as the Beast howled, eyes combing the darkness.

"We should all bolt together," Nico called out, still invisible in the gloom. "Try to lose it in the woods. Ready?"

Various grunts sounded. All seemed to agree.

Opal felt her palms begin to sweat. Who would the Beast attack? *Don't think. Just go.*

"Now!" Nico yelled.

Opal heard pounding feet. Shadowy forms slipped behind the Beast and tore down the path.

"Go!" Opal pushed Tyler in front of her, but their feet got crossed up and they slammed into each other, collapsing in a tangle.

The Beast spun, roaring in triumph at winning the game of hide-and-seek. The monster loomed over them, exposing its teeth. Saliva dripped onto Opal's leg.

That's it. We're officially Beast chow.

A light flickered on the path. Nico was racing back toward them, eyes round as dinner plates.

"Over here!" he shouted, waving his flashlight. "Come get me, you big dumb lizard!"

Opal rolled away from Tyler, who was on all fours. Pulling her legs back, she kicked him with both feet, propelling him behind Dixon's crypt with a squawk. Then Opal powered her flashlight and aimed it directly into the Beast's eye. The creature jerked away with a startled snarl.

But it recovered fast. Growling in rage, the monster's jaws snapped toward her head.

Without another option, Opal dove back against the crypt, ripped its door open, leaped inside, and pulled the portal shut with a clang.

Something heavy smacked against the other side, shaking the whole tomb. Opal screamed. She heard a frustrated growl as the Beast hammered the crypt again, harder than before. *Was that its tail? Will the roof cave in?* But the door held, and the building didn't collapse around her.

Opal almost laughed. She was safe, but trapped. *What do I do now?*

FIRE.

The word blasted into her mind as if someone had spoken it.

Opal sat up straight, nearly slammed her skull against the low ceiling.

What was happening? Was that a voice in her head?

The Beast pounded the crypt again, and this time the walls

groaned ominously. Dust rained from between marble slabs in the ceiling, filling her eyes and making her cough and choke.

FIRE.

Opal was too scared to question what was happening. "Okay, sure. But where am I supposed to find *fire*?"

SHELF. LEFT SIDE.

Who is saying these things?! But Opal reached into the gap in the ceiling and felt around, this time running her hand along its sides. She touched a pair of knobby, elongated sticks. For a horrible moment she thought they were human bones, and snatched her hand back. Why *was* the crypt empty?

But another tomb-shaking thump settled it. Opal pulled down one of the objects—a length of wood with tattered, desiccated cloth wrapped around one end.

A torch.

Torches!

Opal yanked the other one down and hugged the ancient brands to her chest. *But how do I light them? And will they even catch?* The cloth-wrapped ends were stiff and crumbly, and smelled odd, like seaweed dipped in brine.

"Opal!" A voice yelled. "Are you okay?!"

Nico. *Why didn't he take off?* Opal could practically feel the Beast turning on him. She had to act quickly. "Why store torches with no way to light them?" Opal muttered darkly.

Then her eyes popped. Her backpack! She had the Zippo lighter from the tunnel chamber. Opal wriggled out of the straps, then dug inside until she found it at the very bottom. She nearly squealed in delight.

Outside, the Beast howled.

"*Oh crap*," she heard Nico blurt. Then, "Tyler, get back!"

No more time. Opal kicked open the crypt door and slithered outside. Dropping to her knees, she flicked the lighter and spun its wheel. "Please, please, please."

A spark kicked, then a flame. Without looking up, Opal held the lighter under the torches and watched the fire spread. In moments both were burning, giving off a weird, organic scent.

Opal whirled, only to find the Beast's face inches from hers.

With a terrified yelp, she swung the torches in front of her like two batons.

The Beast shrieked and pulled back a few feet.

"Nico!"

Opal darted to where he and Tyler crouched on the Beast's opposite side. Nico had his dagger out and was gripping it tightly, his face a mask of determination. Tyler was holding a rock as if he intended to peg the sea monster. His gaze cut to Opal, frightened but unyielding.

The Beast made a sound deep in its throat, regarding Opal with narrowed eyes as she shielded the boys behind her torches. She passed one to Nico, who took it and squared his shoulders, his face ghostly pale.

Opal took a tentative step forward, holding her torch high. "Leave us alone!"

The Beast's eyes glinted, its scales shimmering like deep ocean currents. With a last, spine-shivering howl, it spun and vanished into the darkness. Opal heard a crunch, then a loud splash. The monster was gone.

Opal's legs gave out, and she sat heavily on the ground. Tyler collapsed beside her. He was shaking all over.

"Where'd you find these?" Nico asked, staring at the torch in his hand. His features glowed in the fiery light.

Opal felt like hugging him. He and Tyler had come back for her, even with the Beast in their way. She took a deep breath, trying to slow her racing heart. "They were inside the crypt."

Nico nodded. "That's some quick thinking. How'd you know they would scare it off?"

"I just . . . did." Opal wasn't sure what to say. She could still smell the creature's musk on the breeze.

Tyler's head shot up. "The Beast. It's *real*. No question about it this time."

Opal waved in the direction the Beast had vanished. "I'd call that pretty definitive proof."

Footfalls echoed off the crypts. Emma and Logan appeared, running back down the path to join them. "Where were you guys?" Logan called out. "We lost you in the woods."

While Nico explained, Opal blinked in the torchlight. *How did I know these were there?*

She could try to play it off. She could say she'd rummaged the crypt and found them, and had guessed that a Beast from the ocean's murky depths would naturally fear an open flame. She didn't have to discuss the voice that had sounded in her head.

But that wasn't what happened. Some . . . *thing* had spoken. As clearly as the day she'd stared into a glass jar on its pedestal and saw the green blob inside smile at her.

Come, Opal.

Come and see what I have for you.

Opal rose, slowly pivoting to face the others.

"Let's go back to the houseboat," she said. "We really need to talk."

Thunder cracked behind her.

Then, suddenly, it began to hail.

PART TWO
TORCHBEARERS

9

NICO

Nico rubbed his forehead in exhaustion.

It'd been a crazy night. Outside, fist-sized chunks of hail rattled off the houseboat's roof. The moonlit sky had turned a weird green-black haze. Nico wanted to go home, slip into his bedroom, and fall dead asleep before his dad could ask him a bunch of questions. But Opal had *insisted* they return to the houseboat first. So here they were, even as the clock inched closer and closer to his curfew.

"So the torches were hidden inside the crypt?" Emma asked, drawing Nico's attention back to the discussion. They were sitting on the showroom floor in a ragged circle. Opal nodded, explaining again where she'd found the lifesaving brands. But as she spoke, her eyes kept straying over Nico's shoulder.

He glanced behind him, but there was nothing to see except the pedestal with its green jar and the secret wall-panel entrance to the Darkdeep, which now had a bookcase pushed in front of it for safety.

"It's truly amazing, isn't it?" Tyler was propped back on his elbows as he gazed at the ceiling skylights. "I'm so incredibly brave that I've battled both a figment of the Beast *and* the Beast itself. Who do you think will play me in the movie?"

"Please," Logan joked, pushing Tyler's shoulder until he flopped sideways. "What actor wants to hide behind a crypt for the pivotal fight sequence?"

Tyler sat back up, his brows arching indignantly. "Perhaps you didn't hear about my selfless rock-throwing charge, Logan. You were busy cowering in the woods while I attacked the deadly monster with nothing but my bare hands. And some rocks."

Logan closed his eyes and made snoring sounds.

"Those gremlins," Nico muttered, frowning at the floorboards. "*They* were figments, even if the Beast wasn't. And they're on the loose."

Tyler clicked his tongue. "Where do they keep coming from?" He glanced out the window and shivered. "Guys, I don't think I'm up for chasing monsters through"—he tossed a hand—"whatever this storm is right now. Frozen baseballs are falling from the sky."

Nico nodded sullenly. "The gremlins could be anywhere, it's pitch-dark out, and the weather is terrible. Our bike ride home is going to be ugly enough as it is. We'll just have to deal with them later."

Logan blew out his lips. "And hope they stay away from town."

"How'd you know to look for torches?" Emma asked Opal curiously. "You'd been inside the crypt once already, and only found that little bag."

The bag.

They needed to examine it, but Opal didn't seem in any hurry to do so. She didn't even seem to be listening to Emma, though coming back to the houseboat had been Opal's idea.

"Can we see what you found?" Nico prodded gently. "Might be a clue and all, you know?"

Opal's head jerked up. "Huh? Oh, yeah. Sure. Hold on."

She pulled out the faded leather satchel and handed it to Nico.

"Guess I'll open it, right?" he said. Opal was so distracted, he was getting a little worried. *It's been a tough night.*

The others nodded, so Nico undid the clasp. Inside was a single object: a thin bronze compass. Nico hefted the battered instrument and found that it still worked. The compass was about the size of his palm, with the cardinal directions engraved directly into the metal.

A *fifth* marking was also etched into the casing: the traditional Torchbearer symbol appeared at forty-five degrees east of south, equidistant from both points. Shrugging, Nico handed the compass around and everyone gave it a look. But when it reached Opal, she showed little interest, lost in her thoughts as she passed the artifact on without more than a cursory glance.

"Okay, Opal," Nico said loudly, startling her more than he'd expected. "Out with it. What's bothering you?"

"Huh?" Her gaze shifted up and to the right. "What? Oh, nothing. It's . . . never mind."

"Nope." Nico crossed his arms. "You wanted to come back here for some reason, and it clearly wasn't to inspect this bag or talk about the Beast. Something's on your mind. It's time to tell your friends about it."

Opal said nothing for a long moment, then nodded slowly. After a deep breath, she straightened and addressed the others. "I found those torches because a voice in my head told me where they were hidden."

Dead silence.

Opal's gaze moved intently from face to face, daring anyone to speak.

Finally, Nico cracked. "You mean . . . like . . . your intuition?"

"No. I mean, *something spoke inside my head*. It said where to look."

Tyler stiffened, his voice dropping. "Oh no. A ghost?" He wheeled on the rest of the group. "I *told* you guys we shouldn't have been messing around in a graveyard this close to Halloween. But did any of you listen?!"

"Not a ghost," Opal shot back. "At least, I don't think so." She went quiet again, as if debating something in her mind. Finally, "I think I know who it was, too."

Nico ran a hand over his mouth. This was *not* what he'd expected. Opal thought she was hearing voices?

Emma moved closer to Opal and took her hand. Opal barely seemed to notice.

"Well?" Logan said. "Who was it, then? Elvis? Casper?"

"Don't be mean," Emma snapped.

"I'm not," Logan said defensively. "It's . . . just . . . unusual. To hear other people. Talking. In your head."

Emma scooched around to catch Opal's eye. "Just tell us what happened, okay? Don't worry about how it sounds. We've been through enough bonkers stuff since finding this place that one more thing isn't going to blow our minds. I mean, we just got done *battling a sea monster*. The lid's kinda off for weirdness."

Opal took a deep breath, then her jawline firmed. She pointed to the pedestal behind Nico.

"That thing. The . . . Thing in the jar."

Everyone whirled to look. The little green creature was floating languidly in the viscous fluid.

"You think a dead green blob creature spoke inside your head," Tyler said slowly. "While we were in the cemetery."

"Does it sound crazy?" Opal replied sharply, pulling away from Emma and drawing her knees in tight. "Yes, it does. Believe me, *I know*. That's why I haven't said anything. But this isn't the first time I . . . I think it's . . . it's communicated with me. I've felt stuff before now."

Nico rubbed the back of his neck. *Tread carefully here.* "Tell us about . . . the . . . other times," he said, waving a hand vaguely.

Opal studied his face, then nodded. "The first contact was during our celebration, when we did the radish stuff. As the movie was playing, I felt eyes on me. I looked over, and I *swear* that Thing winked and smiled. Then I heard its voice in my head. It said: *Come and see what I have for you.* That's a message I'd . . . *felt* before. On the day we found the houseboat."

Nico nearly flinched. Opal's words jarred him badly. He'd had the same experience when they first discovered the pond together. *But it wasn't some voice inside my mind. Just a . . . feeling.*

"What else?" Tyler prodded. Everyone kept darting glances at the jar, but it looked the same as always.

Opal started chewing her lip. "Two days ago, I had a weird urge to open that lunch box, which is where I found the medal. It . . . I can't explain this very well, but I've never cared about that lunch box before, or really even noticed it. But suddenly it felt like I was being directed over there somehow. I got the same feeling at Fort Bulloch, and we found that plaque with Charles Dixon's name on it."

"Which is why you wanted to explore the cemetery so badly," Emma concluded, squeezing Opal's shoulder. "You were following a trail." Her blue eyes grew soft. "Opal, why didn't you tell us about this?"

"Because I wasn't certain it was real," Opal said immediately. Thunder boomed outside, but the pattering on the roof seemed to slacken. "It all seemed so ridiculous—a voice guiding me in my head? Then, later, I wasn't sure if you guys would believe me." Her eyes flashed. "Some of you don't believe me right now."

Logan winced. Nico kept his face neutral, but it felt like a guilty sign was hanging around his neck.

"I trust you," Emma said. "I know you'd never make something like this up."

"Nobody thinks *that*," Tyler said testily, shifting his weight. "But, still . . . you have to admit . . ." He glanced at the jar. "If that Thing's alive, and attacking your brain, why does it look so dead?"

Opal stared at him for a beat, but then her gaze dropped. "I understand. I'm not sure I'd believe me, either."

"Why just you?" Nico asked. "Can you think of any reason?"

Opal shook her head.

Logan popped to his feet. He walked over to the jar and began tapping the glass. "Hey. Thingie. Wake up!"

"Logan, don't!" Opal shouted, scrambling to her feet. "It isn't funny."

Logan spun and strode back to stand in front of Opal. "I'm not trying to be funny. I know you think this voice is real, but it isn't. A few weeks ago, when I first saw a figment, I thought I'd lost my mind. The stress ate me alive, and suddenly I was seeing and hearing stuff that wasn't there, and assuming all kinds of insane things. But there *was* an explanation." His voice grew gentle. "You helped me see that. Now I want to do the same for you."

Opal turned away. Nico stood and glared at Logan. Logan shrugged. Mouthed, *Do you believe her?*

Nico found he couldn't hold Logan's gaze. *Do I? I should, I want to, but . . .*

"Guys, it's getting late," Tyler said quietly. "Maybe we should tackle this tomorrow."

"That I agree with," Logan said, then forced a laugh. "We fought a sea monster tonight. Opal scared it away with a torch. We all deserve a break."

An olive branch. Nico waited to see if Opal would take it.

She turned back to the group, wiping quickly at her face. "Yeah, you're right. Let's go home. Thanks for listening, everyone. Maybe I'm just a little spaced right now."

Yet something flashed behind her eyes. Nico was certain Opal didn't believe what she'd said, but now wasn't the time to push harder.

"You were right about the cemetery," Nico said. "Charles Dixon definitely has a Torchbearer connection. Maybe we can figure out what it is." Opal nodded but didn't reply. Instead she dug that old notebook out of her backpack and ducked her head into its pages.

"At least the stupid film crew didn't show up," Tyler said. "If they'd caught me in action, I'd be stuck signing autographs for the rest of my life."

Nico smirked. Logan shoved Tyler toward the curtain.

"Tomorrow's my first day on the job," Emma chimed. "Don't worry, I'll keep them pointed in the wrong direction."

Everyone gathered their things. Opal put the compass into her pocket. Tyler grabbed a book from one of the trunks, muttering something about research. The girls walked out together, Emma giving Opal's arm a quick pat as they exited through the curtain. Nico was last to leave. He shot a final glance at the jar on its pedestal.

What are you, really?

With a shrug, he flicked off the lanterns, plunging the showroom into darkness. Nico hurried out after his friends, but found them standing on the porch wearing startled expressions. The hail had stopped, but dozens of the icy projectiles were piled on the front steps.

With the precipitation over, the sulfur smell crept back with a vengeance. Breathing through his mouth, Nico moved up beside Tyler. *What in the world?* He knelt and scooped a chunk of hail off the wooden riser.

"Someone explain that to me?" Tyler whispered.

Nico just shook his head. The ball of ice in his hand was the size of a grapefruit, perfectly round and solid all the way through. It was also tinged a dull red, and seemed to be glowing from its center.

"Someone *explain* that to me," Tyler repeated.

"The red tide?" Logan offered. "Maybe it got mixed into the hail somehow?"

"I don't think that's a thing," Emma said. "At least, I've never heard of it happening."

Opal was silent, but her eyes shone with questions.

Nico dropped the hailstone and stepped back, wiping his hands on his jacket. He glanced up at the eerie green-black sky.

"I have no idea what's happening," he said quietly. "But things are getting out of hand."

10

OPAL

Opal watched the interview with growing irritation.

"Would you say that living in Timbers *itself* is an act of bravery?" Bridger asked, arching an eyebrow.

"Yeah," Carson Brandt answered seriously, scratching his freckled nose. "I guess I would. We should probably, like, start doing Beast-attack drills at school. To be safe." He glanced at his buddy Parker Masterson, who nodded rapidly.

Opal rolled her eyes, tightening her hood against the light morning rain. She was standing at the foot of town square's tiny amphitheater, which was decorated with ghosts and spiderwebs for Halloween festivities the following day. The *Freakshow* crew had commandeered the space, capitalizing on the spooky setup. Bridger was asking people ridiculous questions on camera, no doubt hoping for dumb answers exactly like the one Carson had just given him.

A wet, chill wind whipped in from the sea, sending a few paper bats sailing. *I hope those crash on Bridger's head.*

Opal was in a bad mood and knew it. She wanted to talk to Emma—the only one who believed her—but Emma was busy assisting the crew. She'd ducked into the *Freakshow* van twenty minutes ago and hadn't come back out again.

Bridger was mostly a hit with the locals, firing off quips between takes that drew laughter from the small crowd watching the film crew work. But the whole thing felt like nails on a chalkboard to Opal. Couldn't her neighbors see he was mocking them?

Clouds hung low and gray in the sky as mist cloaked the surrounding hills. Opal had assumed filming would be cancelled on a day as ugly as this one, but the film crew seemed to love the added gloom. "It's so atmospheric," she'd heard the bearded cameraman exclaim in a satisfied voice.

The freaky hail had melted overnight, leaving no trace of the red glow inside it. Opal wondered if anyone else had even noticed. She shivered, rubbing her hands together, then grimaced at the old mittens she had on. Her cute new gloves were nowhere to be found, so she'd had to wear these kiddie ones. Their googly eyes and sewn-on smiles made her hands look like talking monsters. *I should tell Logan. Beast Mittens would sell like crazy.*

"Hey, kid," someone said behind her. "Do you know where they sell those *BEAST MODE* shirts?"

Opal turned to find a skinny college guy wearing earbuds standing right next to her. Sunburned and slightly wobbly, he was gawking around like he'd just arrived at Space Mountain. He spoke again before she could answer. "Oh man! Is that Colton Bridger up there?"

"Yeah."

Opal wished the guy would leave her alone. She wished all the out-of-towners would go home. Across the square, tourists were taking selfies in front of the *Freakshow* van.

"This place is the best," Earbuds said. "You're so lucky to live here." His ski cap rode high on his head, making him look like a gangly elf. "You *do* live here, right?"

"Uh-huh."

Opal spotted Carson and Parker walking away, chattering excitedly to each other as they high-fived. Bridger ran a hand through his short brown hair and glanced around. Plenty of townspeople were loitering near the amphitheater, hoping to be interviewed but trying to act natural. Bridger's eyes locked on Opal and he started striding over to her.

Oh great.

"You can find *BEAST MODE* jerseys at the hardware store," Opal told Earbuds, pointing to a pop-up shop under the green awning a half block down Main Street. Logan had added the second location this morning, stocking new merchandise while his dad called in favors. "They're designed by one of my friends."

"Awesome," Earbuds said. "I *always* shop local." He hurried away.

Opal's eyes darted for a plausible escape route, but Bridger smiled and waved, foreclosing the possibility. "Hey there, little friend!" he called. The cameraman and lone female crew member—who seemed to be in charge of lighting—trailed after him. Emma brought up the rear, grinning ruefully. *I guess she escaped van duty.*

"You gave me directions the other day, right? Can I interview you?"

Before she could respond, Bridger nodded to his team and began spit-smoothing his hair. "I can't guarantee we'll use anything, but I'm collecting footage, and you seem perfect. You've got a great outdoorsy-kid vibe."

Opal stiffened. A vibe? She wore a sweater, jeans, boots, and a rain jacket. *And these ridiculous monster mittens!* She stuffed her hands in her pockets. "I guess." Opal really didn't want to talk to Bridger but couldn't see a way out of it.

"Great. We'll worry about permissions and all that later." Bridger motioned for his crew to start filming and thrust a microphone in her face. "I'm here with—"

He paused, waiting for Opal to speak.

"Opal Walsh," she said.

"Opal Walsh, who has spent all her young life right here in Timbers." Bridger beamed—not at her, but at the camera.

Resentment surged within Opal. He just assumed she'd

never been anywhere else. That he'd pegged her exactly. So she smiled as the cameraman zoomed in on her. *I can play games, too.*

"That's right, Colton," she said, sugary-sweet.

"And have *you* ever encountered"—Bridger paused dramatically—"the Beast?"

He smirked, like he knew exactly what she was going to say: *No, sir, but I've heard a lot about it, and I think I saw its tracks once by my daddy's woodchuck nursery, and it's for sure definitely totally completely real!* Hopeful, cute-kid stuff, just happy to be on a TV show.

Yes, she'd been born here. He was right about that. But it didn't mean he knew her.

"Of course," Opal answered earnestly.

Bridger blinked. "Really?" He sounded surprised, but immediately went with it, his eyes lighting up as if imagining Dumb Kid Script Number Two: *Yessir, I swear I spotted the sea monster once, behind the chain-saw store at midnight. It tried to eat my dog, Sir Barksworth. Scared me to death!*

Colton leaned in closer. People had gathered to watch the interview, and Opal noticed a knot of her classmates standing a few yards away.

"What did the creature look like?" Bridger asked in a theatrical voice.

"Like this!" Opal jerked her hands from her pockets and snapped the monster mittens in Bridger's face. He jumped back with a startled yelp as laughter erupted around them. Emma went red-faced trying to keep it together.

Opal tucked her hands back into her pockets. "*Aww.* You scared them away."

"Ha ha ha ha ha!" Bridger bellowed loudly, smiling at the crowd. "That was great. Boy, do I love children." He made a throat-slash gesture at his cameraman, who stopped filming.

Opal hid a smile, shooting a glance at the giggling kids from school. She'd successfully concluded the interview.

"Jokes are the best," Bridger was saying, trying not to look annoyed. "Thanks, Olivia. Wonderful stuff."

"It's Opal."

"Anytime."

Bridger stalked away, muttering to himself. His cameraman grinned and shot Opal an amused wink before following. Emma caught Opal's eye and nodded toward Timbers Cafe, then mouthed *five minutes.*

Opal flashed a thumbs-up as her friend scurried after Bridger. She could use a hot chocolate, and wanted an update from Emma on what the film crew was planning. But as she started down the sidewalk, cute ninth grader Evan Martinez appeared out of nowhere and fell into step alongside her.

"That was hilarious," he said, tugging on the sleeves of his Messi jersey. "Did you wear those mittens on purpose?"

"Oh, yeah," Opal said. "Had it all planned out."

Evan's eyes twinkled. He smelled amazing, like cinnamon

sticks and . . . Gatorade? "Bridger's face—oh man, it was *priceless*. It's good to know at least one other person in town isn't falling for this *Freakshow* garbage."

Opal nearly missed a step. "You don't like it, either?"

Evan's mouth thinned. "I hate it. Plus, they're annoying everyone at my parents' B&B. They stay up all night, super loud, and Bridger keeps calling me *buddy*. He acts like we're all small-town hicks. I heard the sound guy making fun of our high school's mascot."

"Ugh," Opal said. Although, to be fair, she'd never loved the Eager Beaver.

Evan bumped a fist on her shoulder. "Well, anyway. Nice job. See you at school."

"Sounds good."

Opal lingered for a moment, watching him bounce away down the block, then ducked into the cafe. The place smelled incredible. She had enough cash for a hot chocolate and their signature blueberry scone, one of the few things that hadn't been renamed after the Beast.

She waited by the counter until Emma slipped onto the stool beside her, then leaned in close. The cafe was full, and Opal didn't want anyone to overhear. "How's it going?" she asked in a low voice. "Has the crew said anything about last night?"

Emma's nose was pink with cold. "Nope. I think we're good."

Opal exhaled. She and Nico had ridden to the cemetery super early—to see if there were any Beast footprints or tail marks they'd need to hide—but the hailstorm had removed most of the evidence. There were still a few traces if someone knew where to look, but maybe no one would.

"They *are* still talking about Still Cove," Emma said glumly. "Colton knows that a lot of Beast legends point there. I think he wants to charter a boat and see for himself."

"Crap." They'd have to do something. The film crew couldn't be allowed into the cove. "Are you on a break right now?"

Emma nodded. Then she beamed, eyes shining. "Colton lent me his *credit card*. He said to get three coffees for the crew and something for myself." Emma waved a Platinum American Express. "Can you believe it?"

Opal studied her friend's giddy smile. She knew being around a real film crew—no matter how or why—was a huge deal for Emma. She dreamed of making movies herself one day. It was natural she'd be excited about the job.

"That's great," Opal said, voice neutral. "But don't forget—tomorrow is Halloween. Bridger might be planning something big for the holiday."

Emma nodded, her expression growing serious. "I've been meaning to talk to you about this no trick-or-treating situation. I think the boys may have had their brains erased."

Opal snorted, then shrugged. "Logan got us all invited to

Azra Alikhan's haunted house party. That at least means costumes. Sound fun?"

Emma pursed her lips. "Well, I do like scaring people. And fake blood . . ."

Opal laughed. "Just keep your eyes open, okay? We need to be a step ahead of them."

Emma cracked her knuckles. "Absolutely."

Opal took a to-go cup and headed for the docks. She wanted to see if any of the film crew were trying to rent a boat yet. Plus, she loved being near the ocean in this kind of rainy weather, when the sea and sky seemed to merge with the ever-present mist.

Reaching the waterfront, she found the area largely empty—almost everyone was back up at town square, gawking at *Freakshow* and Timbers' Halloween preparations. With school out, many parents had taken the day off as well, like a town holiday.

Feeling an odd pull, Opal decided to walk out onto the pedestrian dock. Her thoughts kept returning to the pitched battle in the cemetery. The Beast. It was *real*. It had come up on dry land. But why? Because of them? Something they'd done? Or was it something they *weren't* doing, as Torchbearers?

Opal wondered what the Beast really was. What it wanted. *Is the sea monster connected to the Darkdeep somehow?*

And where had those gremlins come from? Where were *they* right now?

She glanced at the gray-green ocean lapping against the dock's wooden pilings. Was the Beast down there in the murky depths, all alone?

To her surprise, Opal found that she'd strolled halfway along the dock's length. An icy breeze brought her back to her senses. What was she doing out there? This was one of the coldest spots in Timbers. She turned to head back toward town, but found herself zipping her jacket tighter and striding all the way to the end instead.

The floor planks were old but well maintained, the dock's handrails bleached and pitted from years of exposure to the elements. Opal reached the far railing and leaned against it, facing the sea. She shivered, her breath making a small cloud around her face, but Opal didn't hurry away. Glancing down, she noticed a curious divot carved in the corner where the handrails met. The gap was round, with a few odd notches cut around its outside.

It looked . . . familiar.

Something clicked in her brain.

Opal nearly dropped her cup into the ocean. She dug into her pocket and pulled out the compass from Dixon's crypt. Carefully, she pressed the whole thing into the wooden circle.

It was a perfect fit.

11

NICO

Nico stared at the compass in the handrail.

The match was exact—he could tell it was meant to go there.

"You just *happened* to find this while wandering down the pier?" Tyler asked, frowning as he watched Opal closely.

"Yes," Opal snapped. "No one . . . *told* me, if that's what you're asking. I was out on the dock and noticed the gap, and the answer clicked in . . . in my brain." She glanced away, hugging herself against the whipping breeze.

Nico watched her brow furrow, as if Opal wasn't sure about her own answer.

Tyler raised both palms. "I was just asking. Because this is an incredibly lucky break."

Opal, Tyler, and Nico were huddled at the end of the walking pier. Logan was tied up with his Beast-shirt stands, while

Emma and the *Freakshow* crew had ventured into the woods north of town to get B-roll shots of giant trees and other Pacific Northwest staples. Emma had texted they'd be gone at least a couple of hours.

Nico watched Opal tug on her braid as she stared at the railing. "I came down to the waterfront to see if Bridger was nosing around for a boat," she explained peevishly, "and decided to walk out here." She waved a hand at the compass snugly ensconced in the handrail divot. "Suddenly, the answer was, like, *literally* right in front of me."

Nico nodded, relieved. He'd worried Opal would say this was another telepathic sending or something, and wasn't ready to deal with that right now. Stepping close to the railing, he tapped the compass on its face. "It definitely fits here. But what does that mean?"

"There are etchings in the wood around the compass," Opal noted. "Not just at the four directional points, but this slash here"—she pointed to a cut on the outside of the circle—"matches up with the torch engraved on the compass."

Nico straightened as a new thought occurred to him. "Look dead south. It's aiming exactly at Fort Bulloch."

Tyler spun to face the opposite direction. "North lines up with the old lumber mill. You see?"

Nico shaded his eyes. Tyler was right. Directly north of where they stood loomed the very first timber factory, the original one around which Timbers was founded. The hulking building was now a museum displaying historical exhibits about the Nantes Timber Company and the town's wild and lawless early days.

Opal had caught on as well. "Due west is out to sea," she said, chewing her lip. "And east . . ."

As one, they wheeled to face Main Street as it climbed toward downtown. Due east—straight as an arrow—sat Town Hall on its corner of town square.

Tyler began bumping his fists together in excitement. "The old mill, Fort Bulloch, and Town Hall are by *far* the three oldest buildings in Timbers. That fits too perfectly to be a coincidence. And Opal's right about the torch symbol—it lines up with this cut in the railing, so we know the compass is positioned correctly." He stopped moving and pressed his lips, thinking hard. "But what does that mean? It's almost like . . ."

Nico straightened suddenly. "Could the slash mark indicate a place, too?"

"Yes!" Tyler hissed, grabbing Nico by the shoulder. "Look—it's pointing exactly southeast. What's over there?"

They all peered in that direction, which ran back over the waterfront. Three gasps sounded at once.

"How have I never noticed those before?" Tyler breathed.

"Don't beat yourself up," Nico said with a laugh. "I knew they were there and didn't think of it, either."

Opal grunted. "Well, you can't miss it now."

A hundred yards from where they stood, the old Custom

House rose in the center of Coast Street, topped by a cupola with a copper bell that had oxidized to a pretty lime green. Once the place to weigh a fisherman's daily catch—under the watchful eye of a tax collector—it was now a busy office building housing several departments of government, including the National Park Service where Nico's dad worked.

Carved along the outside of the cupola were tiny starburst flowers.

"Asters!" Opal blurted. When both boys looked at her, she pulled out her phone and opened its search history. The last link was to a botanic website called *Famous Flowers of Washington*. "I googled the flowers carved on Charles Dixon's crypt." She showed them a pic. "See? They match the ones up there on the Custom House." Opal pulled out the leather notebook she'd been carrying everywhere and pointed to one of the tiny flower sketches. "*And* there are dozens of asters drawn here, inside this book I found on the houseboat." Her voice carried a triumphant ring.

Nico scratched his cheek. "The Custom House, huh?"

"It's really old, too," Tyler admitted. "Probably next after Town Hall."

"Let's check it out," Opal said firmly. "Look for any sign of the Torchbearers."

"My dad works in there." Nico ran a hand over his mouth. "He's not a fan of surprise visits."

"Then we'll leave him out of this one," Opal said. "Make it a stealth mission."

Nico stared at the old building, and the dozen or so people going about their day around it.

"Better make it extra stealth," he muttered.

"This isn't gonna work," Tyler muttered, shifting uncomfortably in his brand-new *BEAST PRACTICES* hoodie.

"Of course it will," Opal shot back. She wore big tourist sunglasses and an itchy-looking *YOU'RE THE BEAST* sweater. They'd borrowed the clothing from Logan, who warned them not to get anything dirty or they'd have to pay for it. He'd been highly skeptical of their mission—and didn't want to miss out on any sales—so he hadn't come along.

They were huddled on a bench one block away from the Custom House. Nico wore Logan's most ridiculous design—a black *UNLEASH THE BEAST WITHIN* windbreaker that came with matching Beast-logo track pants.

"It's usually slow around this time, especially since it's Friday." Nico tugged at the pants, trying to get them to cover his socks. Had Logan given him a too-small pair on purpose? "But that doesn't mean the security guard won't bounce us if he thinks we're screwing around. They keep a close watch on the place."

"Then why do this now?" Tyler said. "We could come back when everyone's gone."

"Because we're already here," Opal replied matter-of-factly. "I don't want to waste any more time, or have to break in later when the building is closed. Now quit whining and act touristy."

Tyler scolded. "And how is that, exactly? Pretend I'm lost and start yelling 'Go Beast!' every twenty steps?"

"Come on," Nico hissed. "The way is clear." They rose and scurried across the street, peering all around in curiosity like three out-of-towners trying to catch a sea monster. As they drew level with the building Opal snuck a pic, then zoomed it on her phone to see details. "Nothing else on the outside looks interesting."

"What'd you expect?" Tyler grumbled, lagging behind. "A giant hand holding a torch like the Statue of Liberty?"

"I'm just being thorough," Opal snapped. "You could help instead of being snarky."

Tyler crossed his arms. "We won't learn anything on the street. Someone has to go inside."

He and Opal both turned to look at Nico.

Nico frowned at them. "Did I mention my dad works in there? Pretty sure he'd recognize me."

"He'd recognize any of us," Opal countered. "But you've been inside before. You know the layout, and you've got an excuse if you get caught. Just pretend you need to ask him something."

"Because that'll go over well." Nico closed his eyes, then sighed. "Wait here."

Steeling his nerve, he marched for the front door. Heat enveloped him like a warm fist as he entered the lobby, looking for anything that hinted at the Torchbearers.

Footsteps echoed down a wide staircase to the second floor. Some instinct made Nico slip into the shadowy alcove beneath them. A second later, Warren Holland strode across the tiles, a stack of papers tucked under his elbow as he balanced a mug of coffee.

Nico stopped breathing. Humming to himself, his father began pinning documents to a bulletin board directly across from where Nico hid, no more than a dozen feet away. Heart pounding, Nico willed himself invisible. If his dad turned around, he couldn't miss his own son lurking underneath the Custom House staircase with zero reason to be there.

Warren finished with a grunt and began to pivot, but paused as the antique elevator beside the bulletin board chimed. The gate opened and a woman in a business suit stepped out. She nodded pleasantly to Warren and held the sliding door ajar.

"Hi, Warren. Going up? I know you prefer taking the stairs to waiting."

Nico's dad grinned back. "Sometimes you get lucky. Thanks, Brenda."

Warren Holland stepped inside the cage. Moments later, he was gone.

Nico closed his eyes. Slumping back against the wall, he whispered a prayer of thanks, resting his head against the cool marble. The surface was oddly bumpy. Nico pulled back, turning around to examine the wall behind him. And nearly choked. A compass identical to the one they'd found in Dixon's crypt was carved into the stone, with its arrow pointing straight down.

Nico slipped from the alcove and hurried outside. On the front steps, he glanced around, then waved frantically for Tyler and Opal to join him. He rushed his friends inside, crowded them into the narrow space beneath the stairs, and pointed.

"Wow," Tyler whispered. "Good work, Nicolas."

Opal squeezed his hand. "How'd you find this?"

"Oh, you know. Being observant. Careful analysis."

"I bet he hid from his dad back here," Tyler said, eyes still glued to the carving.

"Definitely," Opal agreed. Nico scowled at them both.

"Okay. I think this is saying to go . . . down." Tyler turned to Nico. "How do we get down?"

"Is there a lower level?" Opal suggested. "Like a basement?"

Nico shook his head. "Just an old boiler room with a giant electrical closet. Nothing else."

Opal ground her teeth. "Then we're missing something."

Footsteps in the hallway silenced their conversation. They held still as a group of office workers strolled through the lobby, gossiping about *Freakshow*. Then a more deliberate set of footfalls sounded across the tiles. Nico peeked out, saw the security guard testing a storage room doorknob to make sure it was locked.

Nico pulled back in a mild panic. "The guard will find us here. What do we do? He knows my dad!"

"Against the wall!" Opal whispered, suiting action to words as she flattened to the marble.

Then, in a blink, she disappeared.

Nico and Tyler gaped in shock. The footsteps drew closer.

"Guys!" Opal's voice echoed up from between Nico's feet. "Down here!"

Nico saw that one of the floor tiles had dropped open on a secret hinge. Opal was sprawled on the ground in a narrow, dusty hallway six feet below them.

"I found the way down," she mumbled, rubbing an elbow.

The footsteps were right on top of them. Nico looked at Tyler, then pushed him toward the gap. He dropped through just as Opal rolled out of the way.

A cranky voice called out, "Is someone there?"

Swallowing a lump in his throat, Nico jumped down after

his friends, then sprang up to push the tile back into place. It closed with a soft click. They held their breaths for several seconds, but nothing happened. Finally, Nico felt certain the guard had moved on, or at least hadn't found the trapdoor. He slowly looked around.

"I felt something on the wall up there," Opal said, still breathing hard from her abrupt fall. "When I backed against the carving, I must've triggered a hidden catch."

"Where *are* we?" Tyler whispered.

"Right where we wanted to be." Nico's voice thrummed with excitement. He pointed. "Look!"

At the opposite end of the corridor was a heavy-looking wooden door. A symbol was carved on its surface.

An upthrust hand, holding a flaming torch. *ACCIPERE VICTUS* was chiseled right above it.

Accept to Overcome.

The Torchbearer motto. Same as on the table in the secret tunnel chamber.

"We found them again, you guys," Nico said. Opal and Tyler grinned in delight.

They strode down the hall. Nico tried the door. It opened easily, and they stepped inside.

12

OPAL

Opal sneezed as dust swirled up from the floor.

"How many of these places *are* there?" Tyler said, his voice strangely muffled in the dim, musty room.

Seriously. They'd found an abandoned houseboat on an island in Still Cove. They'd found the Torchbearers' vault inside a hidden underground tunnel. The Darkdeep lurked behind a trick wall panel, and now they'd literally fallen through the floor of the Custom House into *another* secret room. Opal was starting to believe she didn't know her hometown at all.

But now we know more about Timbers than anyone. And not just its secret spaces. All of the crazy things she'd dreamed about as a kid—magical creatures, supernatural portals, other worlds—they seemed more than just possible now. They hid around every corner, if you knew where to look.

Which is why it drove her nuts that the boys doubted

whether Thing could actually be speaking inside her head. Why was *that* the impossibility they couldn't accept, after everything else they'd experienced together?

"What is this?" Tyler asked, eyes scanning the walls.

Nico shook his head. "It feels different from the other Torchbearer hideouts. Less . . . formal?"

This room wasn't damp and slimy like the tunnel chamber, though it *was* covered in cobwebs. And dust. Like, *so many cobwebs* and *so much dust*. Opal sneezed again, then machine-gunned another eight more.

"Bless you," Tyler said, a package of tissues emerging from his pocket.

Nico was running his hands along the wall, stirring up more particles. Opal blew her nose as he flicked a switch. An old fixture on the ceiling came alive, throwing a tired yellowed glow across the room.

"There's a light over here, too." Tyler left footprints as he crossed to a small table and fumbled a lamp on.

"The tunnel chamber must be the Torchbearers' old-school ceremony place." Nico waved a hand. "This feels more like . . ."

"An office?" Opal supplied. "Or maybe a boardroom?"

"Offices have *records*," Tyler said excitedly. He rubbed his hands together.

A paisley-patterned rug covered the floor. Two moth-eaten loungers flanked the lamp on its wooden table. There was an old desk at the far end of the room, and in the center sat a large oval table surrounded by chairs. A pair of bookshelves stood against one wall, with a massive bureau wedged in between. Filing cabinets made of industrial-looking steel lined another. The dim lighting gave everything an old-fashioned sepia tone.

"I guess they didn't believe in computers," Nico joked.

A large wall clock had stopped at 12:31. Opal wondered if there was any significance to the time, or if the battery had simply run out. Bolted directly below it was a square metal box, with a sign that read: *IN CASE OF EMERGENCY— BREAK GLASS*. The glass *was* broken, but the shards were mostly cleared away and whatever had been inside—a fire extinguisher?—was gone.

Nico pulled a volume from one of bookshelves and opened it. "Nice. No slugs on these. Maybe we can actually learn something."

Tyler began rifling the desk. "Lots of good stuff in here. Pencils, paper clips, glue . . ."

"Always with the office supplies," Opal muttered. Tyler huffed primly and resumed his search.

She wandered to the bureau and tried its handle. The top section opened with a creak. A few nautical flags were stacked inside, similar to the ones they'd found in the tunnel chamber. A painting hung above them, its frame nailed to the back of the cabinet.

Opal had taken enough art classes to have some idea what might be considered "good." This definitely wasn't. Her mother would call it "greeting card art"—super cheesy and fake while aiming for realistic. Cats or fields or flowers or cottages or misty castles.

This particular picture was a seascape. Opal could almost hear Kathryn Walsh picking it apart in her bank manager's voice. *Where's the light coming from? Where's the shadowing? That's how you spot amateur work—the artist doesn't define a light source in the scene.*

Opal chewed the inside of her cheek. The painting's subject was the Timbers coastline—the distinctive triple-striped base of the old harbor lighthouse sat prominently in the foreground. The sky above it was stormy in a heavy-handed, swirling cloud manner. The colors were saturated and unrealistic—bright reds and blues and deep black.

Opal smirked. Then the smile slipped from her face.

It was bad. *Very* bad.

So why was it there?

The red wash of an impossible sunset spread across the water, looking a little like the algae bloom off Razor Point. And in the far corner, way out to sea, something dark had been rendered in vague, haphazard strokes. Opal drew close, her nose nearly touching the canvas. At first glance, the shape resembled an alien spacecraft on spindly legs, but then Opal realized what she was seeing.

An old oil platform. The rickety, shallows-bound kind used in early offshore drilling.

Opal felt a jolt travel her body.

Two words thundered into her mind.

GO THERE.

She leaped back from the painting in surprise.

"Hey, guys!" Tyler called out, staring into a desk drawer. "I think I found something!"

Opal heard Nico cross to where Tyler was standing, but she couldn't tear her eyes from the painting.

Those words.

Go there.

That hadn't come from her.

"Do you think this is for us?" Nico asked Tyler. "Like a message for whoever came next?"

Who are you? Opal thought back, trying to communicate. Her hands shook as she lifted them to the painting and touched its frame.

Nothing. No response.

"Opal, check it out." Nico's voice was full of caged excitement. "I think this is what we've been looking for!"

Opal tore her eyes from the canvas. "Huh?"

Tyler was holding a weathered manila envelope with neat black letters printed across its front: *IF THE WORST SHOULD HAPPEN.* Below that ominous warning, spelled out in flowing calligraphy, was the word *TORCHBEARERS.*

"It's sealed." Tyler wiped dust from the envelope with the corner of his Beast shirt. "Should we open it?"

Nico shrugged, looking uncomfortable. "We found Roman Hale's skeleton in a ditch on the island. He's the last Torchbearer we know about, and the worst *definitely* happened to him."

"It says Torchbearers," Tyler said. "Plural."

Pushing her panic aside, Opal hurried to join them. "Maybe Hale wasn't the only one."

Nico frowned. "But the houseboat was clearly empty for years before we found it. If there were other Torchbearers, why would they abandon the Darkdeep?"

A thud sounded above their heads, causing them all to jump.

Nico glanced at his watch. "Oh crap. We'd better go. If they lock up for the night we could get stuck sleeping down here. Bring the letter. We'll open it with Logan and Emma."

"I wanna come back soon, though." Tyler shoved the envelope into the pocket of his hoodie. "Lots of cabinets to search." He followed Nico to the door.

Opal didn't move, eyes locked on the painting once again. *Go there? To an ancient oil platform in the Pacific Ocean?*

"Opal?" Nico asked. "You okay?" Something in her expression must've startled him. He took a step back into the room. "Did you find something else?" Tyler was watching her now, too.

Opal thought about how they'd reacted the last time she mentioned the voice. She didn't want to see those skeptical expressions again. Not until she knew more. *Not until I'm sure.*

"No," she said quietly, switching off the table lamp. "It's nothing."

Opal walked past them both on her way out of the room.

13

NICO

A voice caught them on the front steps.

"Hold it right there."

Opal and Tyler froze. Nico turned, heart in his throat. They'd found a cleverly concealed door at the other end of the secret Torchbearer corridor—one that opened into the Custom House's ancient boiler room—and had hurried out of the building. *If the security guard spotted us sneaking up from the mechanical area . . .*

But an even bigger nightmare stepped from the building. Warren Holland strode down toward the sidewalk, tree-trunk tall with a stern look on his face.

"He looks mad, bro," Tyler whispered.

Nico swallowed. "You think?"

"Hi, Mr. Holland!" Opal said hurriedly, smiling wide. "Is this where you work?"

Warren nodded amicably. "Hello, Opal. Hello to you also, Tyler. I hope your families are doing well. Yes, Opal, the park service has an administrative office on the third floor. I don't spend much time here, as I prefer working in the field, but it's nice having a place to file paperwork close by."

Warren's gaze shifted to Nico, and his voice dropped several degrees. "Why are *you* here, son? This isn't a part of town kids should play in. People are trying to work."

Nico opened his mouth, but no ready-made excuse came out. Warren nodded as if confirming bad news. "Opal, Tyler—Nico will speak with you again later. Have a good evening."

Dismissed by a parent, Nico's friends could do nothing more than say goodbye and head back toward Main Street. He was left to fend for himself.

"Nico, this isn't the time for games around my office," Warren scolded, when the others were out of earshot. The sky around them was darkening, heavy gusts sweeping pine needles down the sidewalk. "I told you, the issue of my reassignment hasn't been decided. I know you want to stay here in Timbers—so do *I*, as it happens—which means we can't have any irregularities that might reflect poorly on me. Do you understand?"

"Yes, sir," Nico mumbled.

"Good. Now tell me what you're doing nosing around the Custom House this late in the day."

Inspiration struck Nico. "I wanted to ask you about the red tide."

Warren straightened with a frown. "The algal bloom? What about it?"

Nico improvised. He really *was* curious. "Well, my friends and I all saw that big red streak in the ocean. When we were . . . out riding bikes." *Don't say breaking into Fort Bulloch.* "From up on the bluffs, I mean. Are red tides common around here? I've never seen one before."

Warren Holland's shoulders eased. "No, as a matter of fact, they aren't. I was just researching the issue myself. Outbreaks of this nature are exceedingly rare in these parts. There hasn't been an *Alexandrium catenella* bloom in Skagit Sound for over two decades."

"What do you think caused it?" Nico asked.

Warren's heavy brow knitted. "No one truly understands why red tides occur. They usually happen in warm, calm oceans with low salinity, often after days of heavy rain followed by a lot of sunlight. None of which happened here. But an algae bloom can be carried by the wind or spread by storms. Or an excess of certain elements—like iron, or runaway phosphorus and nitrogen—can establish water conditions favorable to explosive algae growth. Personally, I think ships have been dumping chemicals into the Sound, and the tide sprang from that. And when I find out who, they're going to regret it."

Nico thought for a moment. "Do algae blooms release sulfur?"

"Sulfur?" Warren squinted at his son. "I don't think so. Red tides deplete oxygen levels in the sea, threatening fish and other wildlife, and this particular species also releases a harmful toxin. It's an unfortunate problem we just have to wait out. Thankfully, the bloom doesn't seem to be growing and is staying put around Razor Point."

Nico considered the terrible stench lingering around the houseboat. He'd done a few searches and was almost certain the rotten-egg smell was sulfur. He risked one more question. "What might give off a big, nasty sulfur fart?"

Warren clicked his tongue at Nico's language, but his expression grew concerned. "Are you saying you smelled a large expulsion of sulfur somewhere? Because that's *also* probably illegal pollution."

"No, it wasn't in the ocea—" Nico caught himself, and faked a cough. His father eyed him curiously. "We started watching a movie in physical science class," Nico continued quickly, "but only got halfway through, so I never learned what causes them."

Warren took off his ranger hat and began idly turning it in his hands. "A sulfuric outgassing is usually volcanic. They can be poisonous, even deadly. I'm very glad to hear you didn't encounter anything like that around Timbers."

Nico felt ice leak down his spine. *Volcanic? In Still Cove?*

Warren replaced the hat on his head. "I need to drive out to the field station on Gobbler Ridge and check its propane supply. Can you feed yourself tonight?"

A rhetorical question. Nico fed himself most nights, unless his older brother, Rob, was visiting from college. "Sure thing."

"Head home now. I'll be back before too late." Warren hesitated a second, then squeezed Nico's shoulder. "Tomorrow I'll download some research articles about red tides. They're kinda fascinating when you get into the details."

"Sounds good." Nico turned up the block. With luck he could still catch Opal and Tyler.

"One last thing," Warren called.

Nico halted. Glanced back.

"I had a visit from Sheriff Ritchie this morning. He wanted me to account for your whereabouts during the radish festival fiasco. I told him you were at home, in bed, sound asleep." Warren looked hard at Nico. "That's true—right, son? You *were* home that night?"

Not so much, Dad. I was battling Bigfoot and his insane figment buddies over on town square. Probably saved Timbers.

"Of course." Nico forced a laugh. "Where else would I be?"

Warren regarded him for a moment longer than was comfortable, then nodded. "Go on, then."

Nico strode calmly back toward downtown. His father watched him go. But the minute Warren Holland turned to locate his battered Range Rover, Nico cut down a side street and began jogging uphill. He wanted to find the others quickly. Five blocks of zigzagging hustle brought him to town square. Opal and Tyler were nowhere in sight, but he spotted Emma sitting on the rear bumper of the *Freakshow* van.

Emma waved as he hurried over. "Hey, Nico!" she said in an overloud voice, her rounded gaze cutting to the van's open sliding door and back. "So good to see you! I've had an *amazing* day out looking for the Beast."

Nico gave her a puzzled look, but then his eyes widened in understanding. "That's great, Emma!" he replied, just as loud. "How is the film crew liking Timbers?"

Colton Bridger stepped from the van, holding a clipboard. He was glaring at whatever he read there, but looked up and nodded. "Oh, hey," he said. "Nico, isn't it? The ranger's son? We've shut down production for the day, but I'd like to interview you later." A frown drooped his lips. "I've run out of useful people to speak with, and our footage is . . . a bit spotty in places."

"We're going *all the way out* to Still Cove tomorrow," Emma said, staring intently at Nico as she spoke. "I told Colton it's the most boring place in the world, but he already rented a boat."

"Still Cove?" Nico gave a shaky laugh, watching Bridger from the corner of his eye. "What a waste of time. There's nothing in that backwater but rocks, fog, and sunken boats."

"So my new grip has told me," Bridger replied sourly. "But I'm out of better options, and the story hasn't come together like I'd hoped. No one actually *saw* anything during the Beast Night attack, and I haven't located a single grainy photograph of this so-called legend. There are no bite marks on surfboards, no heart-pounding survival stories, nothing even remotely interesting enough to put on camera. It's like your monster is a polite little seahorse who doesn't trouble anyone."

Nico almost laughed out loud. *Yeah, no.*

The female crew member hopped out of the van wearing a puffy North Face jacket. She said something quietly to Bridger, then gave Emma a friendly nod before turning to regard Nico.

"This is Jacqueline," Emma supplied. "Lighting pro extraordinaire." She glanced up at the tall woman. "Everything prepped for a rough ocean voyage? It's super choppy out by Razor Point. *So* easy to get seasick."

"We'll manage," Jacqueline said, a wry smile tilting her lips. "Colton's taken us on some dicey shoots in the past, and we always come out okay. What's one more?"

Bridger scowled. "Tell Jake to bring a Steadicam. And plenty of barf bags. You know he's useless on the water."

Emma glanced at Nico, but his brain glitched. He had no idea what to say. *This is a disaster.*

Bridger yawned into his fist. "I'm going to take a nap. Nice to meet you, Nico. A friend of Elizabeth's . . ." He waved absently, trudging toward the bed-and-breakfast up the block. Jacqueline said goodbye and climbed back inside the van.

Nico glanced at his friend. *Elizabeth?*

Emma rolled her eyes. "Come on, I'm done for the day." Together they crossed the street and walked up the west side of the park, stopping at a bench that faced the ocean.

"You're supposed to keep them *away* from Still Cove," Nico said immediately.

"I'm *trying*, Nico." Emma blew a loose strand of hair from her mouth. "But it's not gonna work. Bridger can be a pretentious showboat, but he's also a thorough researcher. He knows the Beast is rumored to live there, and he's not going to leave without at least checking it out."

"Emma, if he finds the island—"

"I know! But I can only do so much. They aren't taking any marching orders from the seventh grader who coils their AV cables."

Nico's hands curled into fists. He had to come up with a plan to keep *Freakshow* away from the Darkdeep. But how?

A streak of yellow lit up the sky, startling them both.

Emma blinked. "Did you see that?"

Nico nodded. "Storm coming in, I guess. Maybe it'll break up the algae bloom."

Emma wasn't listening. She was staring out to sea. Flashes of light reflected in her eyes as they widened in alarm.

Nico turned, and his jaw dropped.

Lightning. Dozens of strikes. The blinding slashes hammered down on a murky, fog-shrouded patch of ocean several miles off the coast. Closer to shore, a thin band of glowing blue-green algae appeared, stretching across the horizon and reflecting the brilliant flashes in the sky. A hot, charged wind swept the square, scattering Halloween decorations and knocking over cheap plastic chairs. The sizzling cascade continued for a full minute, then abruptly ceased.

"What was that?" Nico breathed, his pulse racing like he'd just run a mile.

Emma grabbed his sleeve. "There was no thunder, Nico. Just bolts, over and over. And did you see that algae float up in response?"

Nico nodded, swallowing a lump in his throat. His anxiety level was spiking through his scalp.

"Let's find Opal and Tyler. Logan, too. *Fast*. I've got a bad feeling there's way more than figments to worry about."

Together they raced away.

14

OPAL

Opal rushed back from the cash register.

"Did you guys *see* that?" she gasped.

"You mean the cataclysmic superstorm that just electrified the Pacific?" Tyler said, still staring out one of the windows at the Timbers Cafe. "Um, yeah. We saw it."

Logan was blinking like a mole. "I shouldn't have looked right at the bolts."

Opal sat down and glanced at the front door, hoping Nico or Emma would show up. She and Tyler had grabbed Logan at his Beast merchandise stand and dragged him along with them. There was *a lot* to talk about, but Opal wanted everyone together. She hoped Nico's father hadn't ordered him straight home.

The cafe was full of people—tourists and locals alike. Many had ducked inside to dodge a sudden squall that was blowing through downtown. "Never seen anything like this weather," a man at the counter said to his wife. They both shook their heads.

Servers were scribbling down Beastburger orders left and right. Bridger's bearded cameraman was shaking off his windbreaker over by the restroom, smiling like a loon because he'd caught the lightning on film. "Exactly what we needed!" he told anyone who'd listen.

The door bells jangled. Opal spotted Nico and Emma entering and pumped her fist. "*Yes.* Come on, you guys." All three shot to their feet. While Logan left cash on the table, Opal wormed through the crowd and snagged Emma by the arm. "You saw, right?"

"The outdoor laser show?" Emma nodded, heaving an anxious breath.

Nico snorted. "I'm pretty sure they saw it in Vancouver."

"Where can we talk?" Opal said. "I . . . I've got more stuff to tell you all."

"My house?" Tyler suggested. "My dad's in Astoria, and my mom and Gabrielle should be at hot yoga by now. My sister drags her there every week."

"Perfect. Let's go."

———————

"Are you sure no one's here?" Opal asked, sliding into a chair at Tyler's kitchen table. A stinging rain had chased them the entire way to the Watson household, just north of downtown and one neighborhood over from where Nico lived with his father.

"Positive," Tyler said, dumping cookies into a bowl. "We've got at least an hour. After yoga they always get gelato."

Emma was busy rooting through Tyler's fridge, pulling out dips and giving them the smell test. She settled on French Onion, grabbed a bag of chips from the pantry, and then dropped into a seat between Logan and Nico. "So what's up?"

Nico was eyeing Opal strangely. Logan shoved a Double Stuf Oreo into his mouth.

Opal hitched closer to the table. "You all saw the storm, right?"

"*Yes*, Opal." Four voices at once.

She ignored their exasperated tones. "And before that the algae bloom, and also the gas that escaped from the pond."

"Plus glowing red hail and some wild skies," Tyler said. "You gonna recap the whole week?"

"Did I miss something while out on location?" Emma said innocently, then flashed a grin. "I've always wanted to say that."

"Oh, not much," Opal replied. "We found a hidden Torch-bearer office in the Custom House."

"What?" Emma and Logan blurted in unison. Their eyes met. Looking baffled, Logan gestured for Emma to speak first.

"When?" she asked in shock. "How? What was inside?"

"An hour ago," Opal answered patiently. "There's a trick

flagstone behind the main staircase—I'll show you later, I promise. We found a room we think the Torchbearers used for meetings, but had to leave right away to avoid getting locked in the building. The good news is, we also found a letter that might help us finally understand some things. Show them, Ty."

Tyler placed the beat-up envelope on the tabletop. They all stared at the lettering.

IF THE WORST SHOULD HAPPEN.

"Okay, I definitely should've come along." Logan frowned at Opal and Tyler. "Thanks for telling me about this earlier, by the way."

Tyler gave him a guilty shrug. "Sorry. We didn't want to explain it all twice."

"But we haven't opened it." Opal was staring at the envelope as if it might bite her. "We were waiting for everyone to be together."

"And now we are." Nico rubbed his chin. "Do you think the worst has happened?"

"There aren't any Torchbearers left," Emma said. "What could be worse than that?" Rabbit-quick, she grabbed the envelope and tore it open, removing a single sheet of paper from within. "I'll read it out loud—" Emma paused, noticing the others' stunned expressions. "What?"

"You ripped open the mystery envelope." Tyler groaned and covered his face. "I thought you watched scary movies. That *never* ends well."

Emma rolled her eyes. "*Please*. Like we weren't going to open it." She lifted the page and waved it lightly. "Do you want me to read this or not? It looks like it was written on a typewriter."

Logan leaned forward and cracked his knuckles. "Do it."

Opal and Nico both nodded.

"Okay." Emma cleared her throat. "*To the brave soul who opened this letter: If you are reading these words, all Torchbearers are gone, and an unspeakable danger has been left unattended. The end of the world may result.*" Emma stopped and licked her lips. "Maybe we shouldn't have opened it after all."

"Too late for that!" Tyler spat.

"So there *was* more than one Torchbearer at a time," Opal said.

Emma face lit up. "Like us!"

"That explains the secret office in town," Nico said. "It was their boardroom."

"Can we get back to the 'end of the world' part?" Logan said tensely.

"Wait a *second* . . ." Tyler gasped loudly. "Guys! Hold up! We *already* handled the problem. This letter must be talking about the Darkdeep!"

Nico's eyes widened. "Could be." Logan nodded rapidly.

Opal threw up her hands. "How about Emma reads the rest of the message, and we'll know?"

"Right." Emma returned to the letter. "*The seal on the Rift*—that word is capitalized—*must be maintained at all costs. Those worthy of the Torchbearer mantle will do what is necessary to prevent catastrophe.*"

"You see?" Tyler said. "This Rift it mentions. That's gotta be the Darkdeep, right?"

"No," Opal said suddenly, a sick feeling forming in her gut as she recalled earlier words inscribed on slug-covered pages. "In the *Index*—after the list of Torchbearers—they call the Darkdeep by a different name. You read it too, Ty. Remember? That book called it *The Deepness.*" Opal swallowed. "The Rift must be something else."

Tyler's grin died. "Oh, crap. You're right."

Emma snapped her fingers impatiently and began again. "*By reading this letter, the responsibility now falls to you. Seek the platform. Tend the seal. Secure the Traveler and maintain the balance! Do not rest until the portal is still. Good luck.*" Emma looked up. "*Do not fail* is printed in capital letters across the bottom." She flipped the page, but the other side was blank. "That's it. That's all there is."

"What? You can't be serious!" Logan slammed a fist on the table. "That doesn't help at all! Man, we *never* catch a break."

"Are there, like, instructions?" Opal asked hopefully. "Any hint about what we're supposed to do?"

Emma shook her head. "Maybe there was another page that got lost."

"What's the Traveler?" Nico muttered. Everyone shrugged.

Tyler scrunched his shoulders. "Sounds bad, like everything else that ever happens to us." Then he moaned in frustration. "This letter assumes we already know how to fix the problem, but we don't even know what the Rift is. *Or what the problem is.*"

Nico reached for the wrinkled page. "If the Darkdeep isn't the Rift, maybe it's the portal the letter mentions? Does that make sense?"

"Maybe we didn't really fix it," Tyler said glumly. "The well might just *look* calm."

Opal barely heard. Her heart was pounding. She remembered the seascape picture in the Torchbearers' secret office. The feeling she'd experienced. Words in her mind that had echoed down to her bones.

Seek the platform, the letter said.

The oil platform in the painting?

Go there, a voice had instructed.

Was it Thing?

The platform. How were they supposed to find it? And when? Right now?

Sure. Steal a boat and head out into a raging electrical storm. Great idea, Opal.

She closed her eyes. If she tried to communicate, could Thing hear her thoughts? Would it answer?

Concentrating, Opal sent out a question. *Platform?* She waited several breathless heartbeats, but felt nothing in response. No voice in her head *now*, when she'd desperately welcome one.

She pictured Thing, floating in its jar.

What did it know? What could it see?

What *was* it?

"So let me get this straight," Logan said, pulling her back to the conversation. He started ticking off fingers. "Sulfuric gas bubbled up through the pond somehow, then a huge algae bloom appeared outside Still Cove, and now there's more algae by the beach, but it's a different color. Meanwhile, the sky has gone bananas in like three different ways." A second finger rose. "At the same time, Opal found a medal that made her think of Fort Bulloch, so we went there and found a plaque with a funky torch next to the name Charles Dixon. That led us to the graveyard and Dixon's crypt. Inside, Opal found a compass, which fit onto the dock railing, which led to the Custom House, which had a secret Torchbearer office underneath it. That's where we found this letter."

A pause.

"Right," Nico said.

"Don't forget we've got figments on the loose," Tyler

added. "Stupid gremlins running around Razor Point. And, *oh by the way*, the Beast is real, it tried to eat us for a late-night snack, and there's a buffoon with cameras in town trying to upload it all to YouTube."

"This is a mess." Logan grimaced. "Real talk: I have no idea what we're supposed to do about any of it."

"Same," Emma said miserably. Tyler nodded.

Even Nico looked defeated. "The *Freakshow* crew are taking a boat to Still Cove in the morning," he said anxiously. "They're determined to uncover the Beast's magical lair."

Logan popped from his seat. "We can't let them. Think about what they might find!"

"That's a problem for tomorrow."

Opal had spoken quietly, but they all turned to look at her. "Tonight," she continued, "we're stealing Bridger's rental and heading somewhere else."

Tyler dropped his chin to his chest. "Do what now?"

"You heard me." Opal locked eyes with each of the others in turn. "I know it sounds crazy, but Thing told me where we need to go. This letter confirmed it. Something terrible is happening, and as Torchbearers *we* have to step up."

Silence. Then Nico leaned back and spread his hands. "I'm listening. Please explain."

Opal paused. Would they believe her? *I have to try.* "There's a painting in the Torchbearers' office, with an oil platform

143

hidden inside the seascape. When I noticed it, Thing spoke in my head as clear as day. It told me to go there." She closed her eyes briefly, opened them. "So. Do you trust me or not?"

Emma popped to her feet, pulled her jacket down from its peg, and tugged on her ski hat. Then she spun to face the table, arms crossed.

The boys sat in stunned silence. Finally, Tyler's shoulders sagged. "You want us to commit grand theft boat," he said in a resigned voice. "With the sheriff already on our backs."

"Opal," Logan tried, his voice pleading. "Boating in the ocean at night is *super* dangerous. And that storm! No one's crazy enough to go out in this weather."

"It's not as dangerous as the end of the world. You read the letter. Can't you *feel* it? We're running out of time!" Opal took a deep breath. "The Darkdeep is only a small part of this, I'm dead certain. There's more we have to do." Her eyes found Nico's. "I need you to believe me."

Nico was quiet a long moment. Then he spoke in a rough voice. "Okay, Opal. I'll go with you."

Opal nearly collapsed in relief. She turned and spoke quickly to Tyler and Logan. "You guys don't have to come with us. Tyler, your dad's the freaking harbormaster. He'll skin you alive if you get caught stealing a boat from his pier. And Logan, you're already in hot water with the sheriff. I don't want you getting into more trouble. The three of us can handle this one."

"No way." Flushing slightly, Logan pulled his Torch-bearer necklace out from under his shirt. "We stick together. Right, Ty?"

Tyler nodded, exhaling through his nose. "*We watch the Darkdeep, and watch out for each other.* Those weren't just words. That was an oath. I'm in."

Opal felt a rush of gratitude. "We can do this, guys. I can get us there."

Nods. Some were hesitant, but they all backed her plan. They *trusted* her. That's what mattered.

Everyone rose and pulled on their cold weather gear. Opal led the group out into the blustery night, trying to project confidence.

This is going to work.

Thing helped us before. It will again.

This was the right choice. The *only* choice a real Torch-bearer could make.

The wind kicked up a notch, swinging her long black braid. Darkness swallowed them as they headed for the docks.

Please please please let that be true.

15
NICO

The boat to steal was obvious.

"I'm guessing . . . *that* one," Emma whispered, stifling a giggle as she pointed.

Nico shook his head. "Does this guy do *anything* that isn't over the top?"

Salt-crusted floodlights cast dim pools along the waterfront. Nico was examining an electric-blue eyesore parked in a slip off the main pier, in the tiny marina reserved for private vessels. A flagpole attached to the rear had a giant *FREAK-SHOW* banner hanging from its apex.

"I can see Bridger posing in the bow like George Washington," Tyler cracked, flipping up the collar of his windbreaker as an icy breeze swept the docks. "Telling Emma to film his good side."

Opal glanced around like a secret agent before hopping into the boat. "This is one of Sammie's Speeders." She reached under the captain's seat, smiled, and pulled out a pair of keys dangling from a purple rabbit's foot. "I love small towns."

"Man, if my dad ever finds out about this . . ." Shaking his head, Tyler leaped down beside Opal. "Taking a joyride on a speedboat docked in *his* harbor? Mercy."

Emma climbed in after him and patted his shoulder. "We'll get you a new passport and a slush fund." She glanced up at a line of low, bulbous clouds marching in from the west, oddly lit from within by the full moon lurking somewhere above them. "At least it's not raining right now."

Tyler shuddered. "Maybe a fake beard, too."

"Think anyone will notice the boat is missing?" Nico whispered, eyes roving the darkness as he and Logan untied the lines. They both jumped aboard, and the boat drifted away from the dock.

"No one should," Emma said. "The *Freakshow* crew is done for the night, Ty's dad is gone, and Sammie lives on the other side of town. We'll be back before anyone has a clue."

Tyler jabbed a finger at the others. "You know if we get caught, we'll legit be arrested. This isn't like toilet-papering somebody's house. Stealing a boat is the same as stealing a car, and none of us have licenses, either."

"Who needs one?" Logan shot back. "I've been driving my dad's powerboats since I was eight years old."

Nico felt the same—like most coastal towns, every kid in Timbers over the age of twelve knew how to pilot a boat—but he understood Tyler's point. This was a *crime*. A serious one. "They're gonna notice the missing gas," he muttered. "But there's nothing we can do about that."

No one had taken the captain's seat. Nico felt the keys hit him in the chest and caught them as they dropped. He looked up to see Opal's wide smile. She nodded hopefully.

Nico snorted and sat behind the wheel. "Here goes nothing." He inserted the key and pressed the starter. The motor coughed to life, making everyone cringe. Tyler gave him a pained look as he flipped on the running lights, and Nico shrugged apologetically. "Sorry, no way to avoid it. We don't want to hit the rocks."

They slid away from the marina and into Timbers' tiny harbor. Within minutes the speedboat cleared the breakwater and they were out in open ocean. "Okay," Nico said, throttling up to gain speed. "You're sure about the location, Opal?"

Opal was eyeing the sonar, monitoring for hidden sandbars. "According to the satellite map, the platform is just over four miles due west of town, where the ocean shallows up along an underwater ridge."

Tyler gave Opal a speculative look. "Due west, huh?"

"Yeah, why?"

"When we set the compass into the railing, it lined up exactly with old Timbers buildings in three directions, plus the torch engraving and the Custom House. But due *west* aimed at nothing but ocean." He shrugged. "That's the way we're headed now. Maybe this oil rig is landmark number five."

Nico's eyes widened. "You could be right! Maybe the Torchbearers *were* keying on it."

Opal grinned fiercely. "Let's find out."

"What do we know about this place?" Logan shouted over the rising wind.

Opal answered him. "According to Wiki, prospectors built the platform in the late 1920s. It's called Broken Shoals. One day after a bad storm, oil just started gushing up from this fractured little island, and the water surrounding it was shallow enough to run a pipe all the way to shore. Even though it seems way out at sea, the ocean's no more than six feet deep in that area. We'll need to be careful with the boat as we get closer."

Nico nodded. "I do *not* want to run aground." He shivered. "I can't even imagine making that distress call."

"This was one of the first offshore rigs in history," Tyler chimed in, staring at his own phone as the speedboat sliced through choppy surf. "Drilling only lasted ten years though, and nobody made an effort to preserve the site. Some company bought it decades ago but never did anything with it."

The lights of town disappeared behind them. Overhead, the thick cloud wall broke, the moon shimmering in a thin, misty veil that diffused its light and glazed the sea with an otherworldly feel. Rain spattered down in haphazard bursts, but didn't evolve into a full-blown downpour. The sky rippled with an odd purple-black glow that was visible even in the darkness.

Nico had never seen anything like it—almost a dark, twisted version of the northern lights. He felt a tension in the air around him, as if the sky was holding its breath. Everything felt off. Wrong. Out of balance. The ocean seemed calm, but would it last? *If another lightning explosion happens while we're out here . . .*

The trip proved uneventful. Opal had plugged coordinates into the navigation system, and Nico simply followed a blinking line. Powerful spotlights affixed to the speedboat's gunwales lit the way forward like twin laser beams.

"Look," Emma said suddenly, her finger darting out. "I see it!"

The rig's jagged outline emerged from the darkness like a haunted castle, a hulking steel square girded by splintered wooden hoardings. Its outer walls dropped all the way down into the water, completely covering the islet on which it stood. A manmade line of rocks stretched from one end of the structure out into the ocean.

"It's getting shallow around here," Nico said, watching the sonar display. "I'm not sure how to get close enough."

"There!" Opal pointed to a break in the rocks, where an old buoy bounced in the waves. "We can moor to that line and climb onto the jetty."

Tyler was furiously rubbing the side of his neck. He

glanced at the heavens. "Whoever's up there, please, protect me from the insanity of my friends."

Nico eased the speedboat into the gap, alongside the buoy, and killed the engine. As Logan and Emma tied off lines, he flashed a shaky smile. "Piece of cake," he mumbled, wiping sweat from his brow despite the chill. "Really difficult, awful, terrifying cake."

The group scrambled onto the breakwater and carefully worked their way down to the square building. Once safely there, Logan aimed one of the boat's detachable spotlights at a corroded iron staircase ascending halfway up the rig's outer wall. "You trust those steps?" he asked. "They look . . . neglected."

Nico didn't answer. A low humming sound filled his ears. "You guys hear that?"

The others nodded. "Sounds like a washing machine," Tyler said. "On full spin."

"It's coming from up there." Emma pointed to the door. Then her nose crinkled. "Oh no. Not *that* smell again."

Nico started. The rotten stench of sulfur was leaking from the building. "Just like our pond," he whispered.

"Well, we didn't steal a boat and risk our necks to chicken out now." Opal rolled her shoulders, then stepped onto the first riser. "Wait for me to reach the door."

Opal began to climb, tentatively at first, but with growing confidence as the stairs held firm. At the top she waved for the others to join her. When Nico drew level, he noticed the noise was much louder. There was something atonal and jarring about the sound that crawled up his spine. It was definitely coming from inside the building.

They all stared at the door. The smell had grown much worse.

"What's supposed to be in there, exactly?" Tyler asked, plugging his nose.

"Just a big drilling room that's open to the water," Opal said. "This rig is a really primitive structure. The outer wall was only built as a weather shell to protect the equipment."

"So now we . . . go inside," Emma said, making no move toward the door.

The noise thrummed.

Logan remained similarly motionless. "Yup."

"I could try the handle," Nico offered. But his feet seemed rooted in place.

Opal made a noise of frustration. Straightening to her full height, she tugged on the knob.

It didn't move.

Tyler's hands were shaking. "I'm not even mad. Let's take it as a sign, okay?"

Opal looked at Nico. He nodded, steeling his nerve. Together they stepped forward and pulled. The door opened an inch with an angry groan. The rumble inside grew louder. Nico wrapped his fingers around the edge and yanked, pulling the door wide. After a round of deep breaths, they all crept through the opening, onto a metal catwalk that ran around the interior walls and provided a clear view of the chamber's open center.

A nightmare greeted them.

The catwalk looked down on a vast vortex, rust red and swirling like a tornado. A thick metal wall formed a cylinder around it, at least thirty feet across, separating the seething whirlpool from the gray-green ocean water lapping against the barrier's opposite side. Light flashed deep within the cyclone. Sparks hissed and spat on its surface. The air in the room was hot, humid, and foul, reeking of musty grime and sour rotten eggs. Nico's mouth went dry. *Sulfur.*

No one moved.

No one spoke.

Nico's heart nearly stopped.

Prowling within the whirlpool were darkly familiar shapes with smooth faces like Halloween masks. They pushed against the water, as if seeking to escape.

Nico's terrified gaze shot to Opal. She was staring back at him.

"I think we found the Rift," Opal breathed. It took everything Nico had just to nod.

Those faces. Nico and Opal had seen one up close. Inside the Darkdeep, when they'd confronted a creature that had been using the well to create their darkest fears.

Yet here were . . . dozens.

"Oh man," Logan whimpered. "We are *so* screwed."

"What do we do?!" Tyler grabbed his head. "*Look* at all those things!"

Every cell in Nico's body had frozen in horror. He didn't know what to think. How to react. They weren't prepared for something like this. Then a voice thundered inside his skull, driving away everything else.

REPAIR THE SEAL.

"What was *that*?!" Emma shrieked, pressing hands over her ears.

Logan spun wildly, glancing in every direction. Tyler looked like he might pass out.

Nico stepped back and shuddered uncontrollably.

Opal clamped a hand on his forearm. "You heard it, too?" For some reason she seemed elated.

Nico nodded, feeling haunted. He'd *definitely* heard. And the image of a little green blob had blinked into his mind for a split second. Its eyes had been open.

Nico stumbled and grabbed the rail. Below his feet, the creatures inside the vortex continued probing its edges.

"Repair the seal?!" Logan shouted. "How do we do that?!"

Nico's stomach lurched. He nearly puked over the side. Shutting his eyes, he thought a message as hard as he could.

We don't know what that means!

16
OPAL

Opal watched Nico stammer something with his eyes closed.

He heard. They all did!

Thing had finally spoken to everyone.

Below them, the vortex raged like a liquid firestorm, electricity streaking through it. Ghostly figures slithered within its walls, like dogs straining at leashes. The red-orange maelstrom seemed on the verge of spinning over the metal tank containing it. What would happen if that torrent spilled into the ocean?

We need to fix this right now!

"Help us, Thing!" Opal yelled, hoping her connection held. "We don't know what to do!"

STORAGE LOCKER.

"A locker!" Emma shouted, her chest heaving. "You guys hear that?"

"Yes!" Opal said. She saw Tyler swallow and nod. Logan was already scanning the catwalks.

"Where's the locker?" Opal asked the mystery voice, as calmly as she could. *Thing. It's Thing talking to us somehow.*

OTHER SIDE.

HURRY.

Nico's eyes popped open. Opal watched him take off down a catwalk crossing the center of the drilling chamber. The others dashed after him. The room reeked of sulfur, yellowish steam rising up around them. Opal's clanging footsteps mixed with the roar of churning water.

HURRY.

"I *am* hurrying!" Tyler snapped, skidding to a halt behind Nico on a platform spanning the opposite side of the building. He squeezed the bridge of his nose. "Uh, my bad, ghost voice. I'm kinda freaked right now."

Logan was staring at the Rift in awe. "It's like the Darkdeep on steroids."

"There!" Opal pointed to a large metal cube pushed against the wall. "A storage pod!"

Nico's jaw firmed into a hard line. "That must be it!"

The pod looked newer than the rusty platform it occupied. Opal ran over and tried to raise its garage-style sliding door.

"Can Thing, like, hear *everything* we say?" Emma was breathing so hard Opal worried she might hyperventilate.

"Does it know what we think? I'm getting really creeped out!"

"I don't know," Opal said honestly. "It's never responded to me before. But it's real!"

No doubting that now. Not for any of them.

"It only answered you." Logan gave a shaky laugh. "You must be the little blob's favorite."

The Rift thundered. The horrible faces faded into the waves for a moment, then returned. Were the creatures caught up in the current, like logs in a flood? Or were they *creating* the turbulence? Opal shivered. They looked exactly like what she and Nico had battled in the Darkdeep's void. What if they'd done something wrong then? *What if we attracted more of them?*

"Will the door open?" Nico yelled, trying to be heard over the crashing whirlpool.

Opal glanced down, realized there was a catch. She flipped it sideways and yanked again. The door slid up easily. "Unlocked!"

Logan snorted. "I guess there aren't a lot of burglars out here."

HURRY.

FASTER.

Opal spoke through gritted teeth. "*What* do we do faster, Thing?"

SEAL THE RIFT.

"Okay already!" Nico glanced helplessly at the others. "Look around for . . . sealant?"

A boom echoed from deep within the vortex. The water level rose. Eyes peered up at them from beneath the roiling surface.

"Come on, let's get out of here!" Tyler wailed through chattering teeth. "Straight home on the boat, then we call the Coast Guard or something. We're not up to this!"

HURRY HURRY HURRY.

Opal gripped Tyler's arm. "Whatever we need to do, it's *here* somewhere. Just look around!"

He exhaled a moan. "*Fine.* But please let's hurry! This whirlpool seems really, *really* mad."

The squeal of the cyclone reverberated off its metal boundary. Opal rushed inside the storage pod, spotted wooden crates, lanterns, hand tools, a life raft, and a dozen oversized industrial-plastic sacks. One had ripped at the corner and was seeping a stream of silver-gray dust.

"Be careful with this stuff," Nico cautioned, tapping a red-and-yellow label on the bag. "We don't know what's inside." The warning was written in a language Opal couldn't even guess.

THE RIFT.

POUR IT ALL.

"Dump the bags into the Rift?" Tyler squeezed his head. "That's it? That's the answer?"

Logan tried to lift one. "*Oof.* These are heavy." His forehead creased as he glanced up at the ceiling. "You sure about this, stupid-blob-guy?"

"Don't insult Thing!" Opal hissed. "It's helping us!"

Logan gave her a flat look. "We don't even know what's happening, Opal."

"The Thing in a Jar is *speaking to us*," Opal scolded, smacking a fist into her open palm. "It's our only chance, so do what it says!"

"Okay, okay." Logan hauled one of the hefty sacks onto his shoulder. "Sorry, squishy-liquid-dude! Just making sure!"

ALL.

HURRY.

"Great." Nico gritted his teeth as he looked at the enormous mound of bags in front of them. "Juuuuust perfect. Let's get moving!"

HURRYHURRYHURRYHURRYHURRYHURRY.

Opal's heart fluttered. She, Logan, and Nico began lugging sacks out onto the catwalk, where Emma ripped them open and Tyler dumped their contents into the vortex. The Rift hissed as silvery particles rained down, disappearing into its swirling throat. Bubbles exploded like medicine tablets dissolving in water.

The churning slowed. The sparking ceased.

The vortex lowered back into the tank.

The water turned lilac, then a deep violet. The whole chamber seemed to exhale.

Emma grinned at Opal. "Thing seems to know its stuff."

Opal smiled wearily. "That's what friends are for. Look— the Rift's already calming down."

Emma tilted her head curiously. "You guys are friends already?"

Opal shrugged. She couldn't explain it, but she felt like she knew Thing. At least a little. On some level, they'd had a weird connection for weeks. Was Thing the reason why she'd walked along the dock that afternoon? Did Thing *make* her notice the cutout in the railing, or nudge her to investigate the Custom House? Opal didn't know anything for sure . . . but she suspected.

"Final bag!" Logan called out, dumping it over the side. As the last granules dissolved into the Rift, the whirlpool's surface began to vibrate.

Nico frowned, stepping closer to the edge. "The water's getting . . . strange again."

As they watched, a thick plume shot up from the Rift's center, then dropped back down like a fountain.

The pool went silent.

"We did it!" Emma cheered. "Score one for the Thing in our heads!"

TOO LATE.

Opal flinched. "Too late? But the roaring stopped." She glanced over the railing. The faces were gone. The Rift was rotating serenely, though eye-melting colors kept flashing in its depths. "No, it worked. It's okay! We weren't too late!"

Thing was silent.

Below the catwalk, the Rift stopped moving. All sound vanished.

Opal peered into the water, which had turned a livid purple-red, like a rotting plum. An ear-splitting hum rumbled in its depths. The Rift sank into itself, the way sick people's faces sometimes did.

"Is it . . . draining?" Emma asked.

Nico gripped the railing tightly, his knuckles bone-white. "I have a bad feeling ab—"

The Rift exploded.

A column of water shot straight up into the air, slamming against the rig's ceiling and raining down around them. Every drop was hard and cold, and stung like dry ice. Opal shielded her face. Emma screamed.

TOO LATE TOO LATE TOO LATE TOO LATE.

Faces appeared near the surface, empty eye sockets staring. Cavernous mouths gaped in hunger or—surprise?

GO.

"Run!" Opal shoved Tyler ahead of her and sprinted back across the catwalk, the others a step behind. More icy, stinging spray cannoned out of the Rift. *Don't touch me!* Opal thought wildly, slapping at her arms. She remembered how the Darkdeep's flow had pulled them into it. Could the Rift do the same?

The group crashed through the outer door, stumbled down the steps, and raced across the breakwater toward the speedboat. The ocean teemed with dark waves as a simmering ball of electricity formed directly above the oil rig. Opal's braid nearly stood on end as a dangerous charge filled the air.

The lightning, she thought in horror. *This is where it struck earlier!* With a shiver of terror, she glanced back at the building. Blinding light was leaking from its gaps and corners.

GO.

NOW.

They thudded down into the boat, arms and legs tangling in the mad rush to get aboard. Emma and Tyler released the lines while Logan reattached the spotlights. Nico started the engine. Opal fired up the navigation and they pushed off from the buoy with as much force as they could muster. The boat drifted clear of the breakwater, and Nico spun it in a tight circle, slamming the throttle.

BREACH.

The word thundered inside Opal's skull. Her friends' faces were grim and drawn.

"*Come on come on come on*," Nico whispered, urging the speedboat through the surf. They raced at breakneck speed for a quarter mile, bouncing over the waves like bobbleheads, before he finally slowed to a saner pace.

"Everyone okay?" Opal asked, glancing around. Emma and Logan nodded in stunned silence.

"I think I'm going to be sick," Tyler groaned, then he leaned over the side and suited action to words.

Behind them, there was a deep coughing sound, like the ocean backfiring. Opal clambered into the stern to see.

Glowing purple-red water was thundering skyward in a giant column, completely obscuring the rig. The colossal geyser shimmered in the starlight, showering luminescent droplets around the islet. Opal heard an enormous splash out at sea, and realized it was the platform's roof. Then the water fell back and everything went silent.

Opal didn't need anyone—or any Thing—to tell her what that meant.

We failed.

PART THREE

THING

17

NICO

Nico tiptoed into the houseboat's showroom.

Opal and Emma were a few steps behind him, with Logan standing near the tattered velvet curtain. Tyler refused to come even that close—he was pacing the foyer, unable to face the floating creature in its glass jar.

The one that spoke inside my head.

Nico shivered.

He approached the pedestal as quietly as possible. It was early, no more than an hour after dawn. *Halloween morning. How's that for creepy?* Nico had spent the night at Tyler's house—his dad had agreed to a sleepover without much fuss, despite Nico texting to ask permission much later than usual. Logan had crashed there as well. They'd spent the whole time locked in Tyler's room, endlessly debating what had gone wrong at the Rift. Emma had stayed over at Opal's so they could all meet up at first light and pedal out to Still Cove.

They needed to see. To know.

And here they were. Nico had no idea why he was sneaking across the room like a cat burglar—no idea *what* he was doing, honestly—but he was a ball of frazzled nerves, and extreme caution seemed appropriate. Drawing level with the jar, he swallowed and peered inside.

Thing drooped in the viscous liquid, its body as placid as ever.

No movement. No sign of life.

Nico straightened. Frowned. He began to feel very, very stupid.

Logan, Opal, and Emma piled up behind him and peered over his shoulder. "Nothing," Nico huffed, unsure whether he was relieved or disappointed. "Same as always in Jar Town."

Thing opened its eyes.

Hello.

"Whaaaa!" Nico slammed back into Logan and Opal, knocking all three of them to the ground.

Only Emma was left standing. She gaped at Thing, who watched her calmly, wearing a small smile. Then it waved a skinny arm.

"Cool," Emma whispered. She inched closer.

"Emma, get away from there!" Tyler called out, his head barely poking through the curtain.

"Why?" Emma's gaze never left the pedestal. "Thing lives in a jar, Ty. What's it going to do?"

"Don't ask questions like that!" Tyler hissed. "That's when the alien *shows you* what it can do. Like melt your face off!"

"It spoke in my mind," Nico whispered, scrambling to his feet. "That's by far the scariest thing a figment's ever done." Opal and Logan rose too, though Logan remained in a crouch, ready for fight or flight.

"Figment?" Opal tore her eyes from the pedestal to regard Nico curiously. "Why do you say that?"

Nico shrugged. "What else could it be?"

I'm not a figment, a voice echoed inside Nico's skull.

He froze. "Anyone else hear that?"

"Yes," Logan rasped, tugging at his shirt collar.

"I heard," Opal said, a note of exhilaration in her voice.

The little green creature dipped its head. *Yes, I expect you all did. I will speak to everyone at once, to make things easier. And please excuse me if I sound tired. I haven't done this in years, and I've expended a tremendous amount of energy this week already.*

Nico stared. Thing was hovering in the center of the jar, black eyes shining. The blob was suddenly, totally alive, as if it hadn't spent every day since they'd found the houseboat suspended in a lifeless stupor.

I suppose you're wondering why I haven't spoken to you all before.

"You read my mind," Logan joked. Then his face paled.

Tyler whimpered over by the curtain.

Nico swallowed. *Oh man, did Thing actually read Logan's mind?*

To answer your question, Nico: No, I did not just read Logan's mind.

Nico stiffened.

Thing's smile became coy. *Nor did I read yours just now. Some concerns are easy to guess.*

"You spoke to *me* before," Opal cut in, eyes burning with a wild intensity. "And you . . . you made me see things. You wanted me to find that medal."

Thing nodded inside the green liquid, an odd sight.

I did, Opal. Our connection was the quickest to form. I first made contact during your delightful radish cere-mony, but it fatigued me more than I'd expected. I had to rest again, and was only able to send images and impressions as the Rift grew more and more unstable. Tell me: Are there no more Torchbearers left to tend it?

"Just us," Nico said, jutting his chin. "We're the Torch-bearers now."

Thing nodded graciously. *A noble sentiment, though not particularly useful in our current predicament. Since you don't seem to know what's happened, or how to correct it.*

"What are you even doing here?" Tyler had sidled over to join the group in a loose semicircle around the pedestal. Thing bobbed in the center, holding every eye in the room.

I live here, Tyler.

Tyler shook his head in irritation. "No, I mean . . . why are you on this houseboat, stuck inside a glass jar?"

That's a long story. I wonder if now is the best time to tell it?

"Oh, it's a good time." Logan turned and strode to a bench in the far corner. He lifted it and lugged it back across the room, and they all sat facing the jar. Everyone except Tyler, who stood behind the others with his arms crossed.

Logan jabbed a finger at Thing. "Speak. Please."

Very well, but it's a complicated tale, so for now I'll stick to the most salient points. To begin most simply: I'm not of this plane of existence.

"Whoa." Emma blinked rapidly, her blue eyes rapt. "Where are you from?"

It's easiest to explain it as another dimension. I'm from the same realm as the frightful being Nico and Opal confronted within the Deepness weeks ago—you saw quite a few more of them last night at the Rift. In our realm, they're known as Takers.

"You're one of *those*?" Nico tried not to shudder. The creature he'd faced inside the Darkdeep had nearly scared him to death.

No, I'm not a Taker. You would describe me as . . . an explorer. I became marooned here very soon after the Rift came into existence. I found an identical opening in my world, and decided to see what was waiting on the other side. To my horror, I discovered that I could not endure your atmosphere. I was nearly dead when someone found me and placed me inside a liquid suspension suitable for my survival. I've been here ever since.

"Wait a minute," Tyler said, eyes narrowing. "How'd they know what to do with a dying alien?"

Thing gave a thin smile. Nico felt something like a snort inside his head. *They didn't. It was a primitive embalming solution intended to preserve my corpse for further study, but it kept me alive instead. We spent years afterward tweaking the mixture, eventually arriving at the formaldehyde cocktail I currently inhabit.*

Logan wrinkled his nose. "Mr. Kress keeps the dissection frogs in that stuff."

"You got lucky," Emma said, ignoring Logan. "Who saved you?"

The first Torchbearer. Her name was Yvette Dumont. She and I struck a deal. The Rift was unstable and raging out of control, threatening everything around it. Indeed, it had pulled the ship she was traveling on far off course, causing the vessel to founder and sink. Dozens of lives were lost. Even worse, dangerous beings on my side of the breach—such as Takers— had sensed the opening and wanted to pass through into your world. Yvette and I discovered how to seal the Rift by manipulating the chemical composition of the ocean water around

172

it, *creating a tenuous barrier that prevents anything from crossing over in either direction. Then she brought me here. I've lived among the collection ever since, helping in whatever ways I can.*

Nico stared at the little green creature. "So you're a Torchbearer, too."

Thing blinked. *Thank you, Nico. That's a very kind observation.*

"What about the Darkdeep?" Opal asked suddenly. "Is it the same thing as the Rift?"

Thing shook its head. *Not the same, but the Deepness is connected. It's difficult to explain.*

"Why didn't you tell us this stuff when we first showed up?" Tyler's glare remained hard and suspicious. "We nearly ruined everything by jumping into the Darkdeep like fools. You knew *that* was a bad idea, right?"

I wasn't awake, Tyler. My liquid hasn't been changed in nearly a decade. When Roman stopped coming by, I was forced to make a choice. I decided to enter a dormant state, hoping another Torchbearer would arrive and revive me. It was only the sudden activation of the Deepness that jostled me from my slumber.

Nico ran a hand across his face. "When we got here . . . There wasn't . . . You were just a floating blob of goo!"

My dormant state is extremely disassociated. It took me a week to reformulate, and by then you'd already handled the problem. The Deepness had been freed from the Takers' influence.

Opal tapped a finger into her palm. "You sent me clues, nudging me every step of the way to that oil platform. Why?"

The Rift must be tended. If a Torchbearer doesn't perform certain functions, the seal can be torn open, creating a possible pathway between our realms. Dire creatures will seek to pour through, and unlike me, some are capable of surviving anywhere. Thing's pinched face grew solemn. *There are worse than Takers on my side of the Rift.*

Tyler's breath caught. "The Beast!" he blurted. "That's where it came from! And why it lives around here."

Thing's glittering eyes focused on him. *Correct, Tyler. The leviathan is from my dimension. It was the first creature to cross into this realm, before even me. It survives by spending most of its time in the waters surrounding the Rift.*

The Traveler! Nico thought. *From the Torchbearers' warning letter.* But Tyler spoke again before he could voice the connection.

Tyler was squeezing his ears. "Oh man. This is too much. You're telling me the Beast is a freaking demon?"

Thing seemed to mull the word for a moment. *As good a term as any.*

Emma leaned close, her nose mere inches from the jar. "The Rift went crazy last night. We did what you instructed, but the whirlpool overloaded in a way that can't be good. What happened?"

Thing frowned. *I had you add iron powder to the vortex in an attempt to correct the chemical balance, but the Rift was already out of control. The seal cracked. A path between our dimensions may soon form.*

Nico groaned. "So we really are too late?"

Thing pursed its lips. *Not . . . completely.*

Opal sat forward. "What do you mean?"

There's a way to seal the Rift again, but it's dangerous. Tell me, have apparitions manifested on the island recently?

"You mean figments?" Nico nodded firmly. "We've caught three over the last few weeks, and dispelled them, but a pack of gremlins is still roaming somewhere right now." His shoulders slumped. "One more problem to deal with."

I suspected as much. The Deepness—or the Darkdeep, if you prefer—is connected to the Rift. Even I don't fully understand, but it seems to function as a release valve. If the Rift grows unstable, the Darkdeep grows erratic as well.

"The Darkdeep is connected how?" Logan said.

"How do we fix the seal?" Opal asked at the same time.

Thing grimaced. *I grow weary. For now, just know we must neutralize the Darkdeep in order to reseal the Rift.* Its black, marble-like eyes traveled the group. *You will have to be brave.*

Tyler glowered at the jar. "You better not mean jumping into that freaky well again. Because I'm all done with that."

We will talk again soon. For now, keep a sharp watch out for figments. With the seal ruptured, more will come. They cannot be allowed to disrupt our task.

Nico rose to his feet. "When will they show up? What should we do about the Rift now?"

But no answers came.

Thing had closed its eyes, resuming a motionless, lolling float.

18

OPAL

Opal frowned at the TV reporter.

"Halloween is finally here, and Timbers has gone *viral*," the man said into a camera, his capped teeth gleaming. "As questions without answers pile up, and tensions escalate, it's clear that for one tiny Pacific Northwest town, there's no cure for Beastmania in sight."

"Dude, that's terrible," Tyler grumbled. "Did he make that garbage up on the spot?"

Everyone in town seemed to have gathered by the waterfront on the blustery Saturday morning. Having biked straight there from the houseboat, Opal and her friends were now attempting to blend in with the bundled-up crowd, anxious to see whether anyone noticed that the *Freakshow* boat had been "borrowed." The sun rose in a shockingly clear sky behind them, but it did nothing to chase away the chill.

"We never made any plans for tonight," Emma said

peevishly. "Halloween is *today*, and I have no idea whether I'll get to enjoy it or not. I never even got a costume together. This stupid Rift has a lot to answer for."

"I've got a Snickers in my backpack," Opal said. "That help?"

"Not even close." Emma sighed through her sulky frown. "Oh well. Time to go to work." She started over to where the film crew were stomping boots and blowing into their hands for warmth. "I'll report back when I can!" she called.

Logan slipped off to find his dad, explaining, "He's got my new shirts." Nico and Tyler melted toward the edge of the throng. Opal was following them when she spotted Evan Martinez and some of his soccer buddies. They were already in costume, dressed as Teen Titans.

He noticed her and nodded, his expression serious. "Check it out, Opal. We're famous now."

Opal folded her arms. "Famous?"

"You haven't watched yet?" Evan popped an eyebrow, which only accentuated his sleek Robin costume. "You might be the only one left in town who hasn't."

"Watched what?"

"The first three episodes of *Freakshow: The Beast* were posted last night. They've gotten nonstop hits ever since."

Opal's heart sank. "How bad is it?"

Evan scowled. "Incredibly bad. Although if I wasn't from Timbers, I'd probably love the stupid show."

Before Opal could ask what he meant, people made shushing noises around them. Opal rose to her tiptoes, trying to see what was going on closer to the pier. She spotted Colton Bridger being interviewed by yet another reporter.

Kate O'Conner of Channel 5 news was using her superserious voice. "I'm here with Colton Bridger, host of the smash YouTube hit *Freakshow*, whose boat was attacked last night in a *highly* suspicious manner."

"Oh crap." Opal ducked away from Evan and beelined over to Tyler and Nico. When she got close, Tyler whispered into her ear. "This is *not* good. What'd we do to the boat?"

"Nothing!" she whispered. It was true. Nico had docked the boat in the same slip where they'd found it. They'd used up a lot of gas, sure, but that couldn't be considered an "attack." They hadn't put a scratch on the thing.

"Our flagship," Bridger said, his voice carrying to the expectant crowd, "was ready for the next dangerous task—a thorough investigation of the mysterious wilderness where the Beast is rumored to live." He paused, weighting his words. "Still Cove."

"*Shut up shut up shut up*," Tyler muttered, eyeing the rapt faces around him. "Nothing to see here. Move along."

Two large LCD screens came to life behind Bridger, displaying images of the speedboat's fiberglass hull. The garish blue paint was scratched and dented. One of the side railings looked . . . gnawed.

Opal was so shocked that it took her a moment to wonder why the screens were there. They loomed behind Bridger like he was headlining a rock concert. She saw the *Freakshow* cameraman circle around the reporter's film crew, and realized he was recording, too.

"This whole thing is a setup," Nico growled. "Bridger trashed his own boat to make it look like a Beast attack."

Logan barreled up to them lugging his giant duffel bag, as the screens changed to a shot of the crowd.

"Wow," Tyler said. "This is getting meta."

"Look how many people here are wearing my shirts," Logan said gleefully. "You can't buy this kind of advertising!"

"Focus," Opal hissed. "Bridger is stirring people up to get better footage. But is he still going to Still Cove or not?"

"That wasn't even his boat!" Tyler fumed. "It's Sammie's. He better pay for the damage!"

Logan tugged on his earlobe. "Trashing a rental is a crime, right? Would Bridger go that far for ratings?"

Opal blew out a breath. "Of course he would."

O'Conner had adopted her "concerned" face. "There's been a lot of strange phenomena in the area recently," she said to Bridger. "A red tide appeared offshore, followed by yesterday's bizarre electrical storm, and a stream of blue-green algae littering the beaches. Now a local eyewitness is claiming that a column of purple lightning erupted over Skagit Sound last night." She paused, drawing out the moment. "In your *extensive* world travels, have you ever come across these kinds of occurrences before?"

Bridger looked directly into her camera, then over at his. "In all my career, I've never seen *anything* like what is happening here in Timbers."

O'Conner shoved her mike closer. "Tell us what you mean."

"Sorry." Bridger winked roguishly. "I have to save those discoveries for the next episode of *Freakshow: The Beast*."

The crowd *aww*-ed in disappointment.

"Oh, for the love of . . ." Opal shook her head sharply. "I can't watch this anymore."

"Breakfast?" Logan suggested. "We can eavesdrop in the cafe. I want to hear what everyone is saying."

"Fine by me," Nico said. "But it's gonna be crowded. The Halloween carnival just started on the square."

"We can watch the *Freakshow* episodes while we wait," Tyler said. When Nico shot him a dark look, he shrugged. "We need to know what Colton's saying, Nico. And I need *something* to think about besides an exploding fissure in space-time lurking four miles away. Or the alien that spoke inside my head before powering down for a nap."

Opal thought of those horrifying Takers. Who knew what might be preparing to pass through the Rift at this very moment.

Thing, she thought. *Wake up.*

Nothing.

Bridger, his interview concluded, crossed the wharf and flashed a thumbs-up at his cameraman. He whispered something and they both laughed.

Opal frowned, turning on her heels. "Let's get out of here."

Timbers Cafe was packed with both regulars and tourists, many of whom sported costumes, face paint, or Logan's Beast gear. Nico put his name in for a table and sat with the others on a bench by the door. Tyler pulled out his phone. With great reluctance, Opal scooched close to him. Together the group watched all three episodes in a row.

When finished, Tyler slumped back and covered his eyes. "I can't even."

"Awful," Logan mumbled. "We look like a town of idiots."

Opal couldn't speak. The show felt like a running joke, and Timbers was the punch line.

"Nico Holland? Table's ready!"

They rose and trudged to a booth in the back of the crowded restaurant. "Where'd all these people come from?" Tyler mumbled, sliding onto the red vinyl seat. "I thought everyone was down by the docks, but there are more tourists than locals around these days."

Opal opened a menu and noticed the Beastburger was no longer listed inside. She glanced up as Melanie, the part-owner, came over with a tray of waters. She'd worked there longer than Opal had been alive.

"No more Beastburgers?" Opal asked.

"Honey, I am *over* that." Melanie tapped her order pad with a stubby pencil. "Out-of-towners coming in here laughing at Timbers. Thinking we're a bunch of *fools*. All they care about is the Beast, even though this town has so many other things to love. Consider me *out* on this nonsense."

"Isn't it good for business?" Logan asked, looking surprised. Opal wondered how much he'd made on shirts.

"I had enough business before all this, thank-you-very-much," Melanie snipped. "And I don't need more if it means putting up with tourists jabbering their stupid monster theories and stealing all my napkins. Now what'll you kids have?" She took their orders—pancakes, pancakes, pancakes, french toast—then said with a frown, "That ridiculous webcast pushed me over the edge. Never seen such a pack of lies."

"No argument here," Nico muttered.

Melanie left with a harrumph, and a promise from Nico to tell his dad she said hello.

"What are we going to do about Bridger?" Logan asked when they were alone again. "I don't think he'll give up on Still Cove—not now that his show's a hit. He'll definitely follow through."

"I didn't expect the show to be so good," Opal said quietly.

Tyler squinted. "Good? *Excuse* me?"

Nico looked incredulous. "Opal, it was a disaster. Bridger made Timbers look like a doofus convention."

Opal fluttered a hand, trying to gather her thoughts. "Evan Martinez told me that if he didn't live in Timbers, he'd have loved it. I get what he's saying. People are *absolutely* going to binge that show. The episodes are creepy, and they stayed interesting the whole time. The camera work is solid, and Bridger seems likable if you've never met in him real life." She took a deep breath. "We're in trouble, guys. I think *Freakshow* is going to explode."

Logan nodded unhappily. "I hate that you're right, but I get it. People love this kind of stuff."

Their food arrived, and everyone fell silent. Nico picked up a fork and stabbed his french toast. "The rest of the world will think Timbers is how Bridger frames it—a hick town in the middle of nowhere with a silly monster obsession. And it's just . . . it's not like that at all."

"That's not our biggest problem," Tyler said. "Still Cove, remember?"

Logan grunted. Shoved a whole pancake into his mouth.

"Emma can help," Opal said. "Maybe she can sabotage their trip somehow."

Nico looked at Opal. "Emma's with Bridger right now, helping him film more of this trash."

Opal sighed. Watching the episodes, it was clear Emma

was more involved with the production than she'd let on. She even appeared on camera, as plucky local helper "Elizabeth." In one scene "Elizabeth" told Bridger a completely made-up Beast story while they sat around a campfire, making freaking s'mores. Opal had no idea when they'd filmed it.

The most upsetting part was Emma personally introducing Bridger to Sammie during the third episode, to negotiate the boat rental. Had the Beast-damage hoax been planned ahead of time? *Did she know and not tell us?*

"Emma's just playing a part," Tyler said defensively. "Misdirecting them, like we asked her to. That's all."

Opal knew Tyler always thought the best of Emma. And she knew Emma would never intentionally cause problems. She just couldn't resist the pull of a real TV show. And she was *good* at it—cheery and interesting and smart, hitting all her marks perfectly.

"So what do we do now?" Nico said. "We've got so many problems, I don't know where to start."

Before anyone could answer, the door bells jangled loudly. Opal and Tyler glanced up as it slammed open.

"*Oh no,*" Tyler said in a strangled voice.

A gremlin walked inside.

19

NICO

Nico's head nearly exploded.

No no no no no no!

The hostess stumbled backward with a yelp as the gremlin slowly surveyed the crowded cafe. He was short and squat, with scaly, forest-green skin and a yellow slash running across his forehead. Nico remembered him as the leader during the cemetery fight, before the Beast appeared.

The creature grinned. "*Yum, yum, yum,*" he growled.

Nico couldn't breathe. A figment was standing right there in broad daylight, inside a packed Timbers Cafe, in the middle of downtown for everyone to see. *We're finished. The cat's out of the bag now. Everyone is going to freak.*

Slash leaped onto the bench by the door. Baring pointy teeth, the gremlin unleashed a high-pitched, chittering cackle, then started dancing in place.

Wide-eyed, Tyler grabbed his head in both hands. "Stop it. He's *flossing*."

The room had frozen in shocked silence. Slash reached out a clawed hand and casually knocked a candy dispenser to the floor. Then he capered along the bench and did a backflip over a terrified old lady. Incredibly, some of the patrons started to laugh.

Opal gripped Nico's shoulder hard enough to bruise. "They think it's a Halloween costume!" she hissed. "Or a trick!"

Logan's face was sheet-white. "We have to do something. Fast."

"Out! Out of my cafe!" Shoving her order pad into an apron pocket, Melanie stormed toward the front door. "None of that Halloween nonsense in here. The Beast looks nothing like that, anyway. Now *get*!"

Nico lurched to his feet, nearly cracking both knees on the underside of the booth. He stumbled into the aisle and shouted, "Jack, stop that right now! You're supposed to be at the carnival!"

Heads turned, their owners frowning in consternation. Slash stopped capering. Hands on his hips, the gremlin gave Nico a dark look. "*Torchbearer.*" Then he spun and bolted back through the door. Nico heard a startled scream outside, followed by a string of curses.

"Dumb joke, kid!" someone yelled.

"Sorry, folks," Nico said quickly, arrowing for the front door. Opal and Tyler were right behind him as Logan ran to the register, shouldering his bag as he waved the bill in a frantic rush to pay.

"That's, uh . . . that's my cousin. Jack. He's . . . he's *very* excited for trick-or-treating." Nico gritted his teeth, praying hard that people would accept his version of reality.

"I don't know this cousin of yours, Nicolas Holland," Melanie snapped, crossing her beefy arms. "But my cafe is *not* a playground. Tell that boy not to pull another stunt in here again, you hear?" She shook her head. "Beast fever's got this whole town acting loopier than a hula hoop." But as she turned back to the counter, Nico heard her mutter, "Nice costume, though. They get more real-looking every year."

Nico yanked open the door. "Yes, ma'am! Sorry!" He ran outside, scanning the busy street.

"There!" Tyler pointed to town square, where a trio of green shapes clung to the branches of a sprawling oak tree and were firing acorns at people on the sidewalk.

"All three of them," Opal said miserably. "I can't decide if that's good or bad."

"Come on." Nico charged over into the park, dodging acorns as he came within range. "Knock it off!" he shouted up at the green monsters.

The gremlins laughed. The tallest made a rude gesture with his finger.

"Oh, *real nice*." Nico barely resisted a return salute. "These are the most annoying figments ever."

People on the sidewalk were watching the commotion, scowling and shaking their heads. One kid wore an Iron Man costume and carried a plastic jack-o'-lantern full of candy. The baker, Mr. Ellis, spotted Nico and the others under the tree and called out to them.

"Tyler Watson, is that you?" Mr. Ellis stepped closer, his bushy white eyebrows tilting sternly. He nearly took an acorn to the forehead for his trouble. "Tyler, if you know the children in that tree, tell them to quit misbehaving right now. I've half a mind to call Sheriff Ritchie. Cursed Halloween foolishness."

"Yessir, sorry! Those totally normal kids up there just really love pranks!" Tyler spun back to the group. "Okay, *panic time*. How do we handle these fools without blowing our cover? We can't dispel them here. Creatures popping out of existence in front of Town Hall might be a little hard to explain, you know?"

Logan's foot was tapping out of control as he glared at the restless gremlins, who'd run out of acorns to throw and were now chewing the tree bark. He slapped his thigh in frustration. "We have to chase them away somehow."

Nico bit the inside of his cheek, thinking furiously. A bigger crowd was forming, a few people staring at the gremlins in horror. He wasn't sure how much longer the truth would stay hidden. Whatever they were going to do, they had to act now.

"Food," Opal said suddenly. "Gremlins are greedy, right? Maybe we can lure them down."

"I have snacks!" Logan unzipped his bag, pulling out a box of maple syrup rock candy. "I've been rewrapping these as Beast energy supplements. They might do the trick."

Tyler shook his head. "Is there anything you won't do to make a buck?"

Logan shrugged. "I'm a businessman. Gotta strike while the iron's hot." His gaze slid to the crowd. Out-of-towners were dropping food wrappers on the ground, laughing as they side-eyed Mr. Ellis. "Although I'm starting to lose my taste for Beastmania."

"Gimme those." Nico snagged two packages and waved them over his head. "Hey, Slash! I've got something you might like."

Slash froze, then crept to a lower branch, sniffing curiously. Drool began leaking from his mouth. "*Yum, yum.*" All three gremlins began slinking down the tree trunk, eyes intent on the treats in Nico's hands.

"Uh . . . guys?" Tyler said, retreating a few steps. "Maybe we didn't think this through."

"That's it," Nico coaxed, backing farther onto the common. "Come get your special candy." Opal and the others clustered around him as he cautiously withdrew across the grass. The Halloween carnival was in full swing—town square was full of booths, festival games, and spooky kiosks, even a haunted pumpkin patch. Parents and kids gaped as the Torchbearers and figments crept past, Nico and the others slowly backpedaling, the gremlins advancing in lockstep, their reptilian eyes glued to the snacks Nico carried. Three little girls in *Fortnite* costumes stopped playing ring toss to stare.

Nico heard a slurred voice carry from the sidewalk.

"I *love* that they hired entertainment. This goofy town's all right."

Someone snorted derisively. "Next time they should spend more on costumes. These monsters are so fake-looking, it's not even funny."

The gremlins stalked the Torchbearers toward a jungle gym at the north end of the square. Beyond it, a dense wooded area stretched up into the hills. "Get ready to bolt for those trees," Nico whispered to his friends.

The others nodded. Slash drew closer, his clawed hands gouging furrows through the grass. They'd nearly reached the edge of the park. A smattering of applause rose from onlookers who thought the show was ending. They had no idea.

Nico counted down in his head.

Three . . . Two . . . One . . .

"Go!"

Like a flock of birds, they banked and darted for the tree line.

"*Mine!*" Slash screeched.

Angry growls sounded in pursuit.

Nico raced under the jungle gym, through a parking lot, and into the woods. He sprinted up a steep hill to a clearing out of sight from the park below, then hit the brakes. Panting, the others gathered around him. Logan threw down his bag with a gasp.

"No more running," he said grimly, slipping his Torch-bearer dagger from a jacket pocket.

Logan did the same.

"You carry one everywhere now?" Tyler asked, surprised.

Nico kept his eyes on their back-trail. "Ever since the Charmeleon."

Logan dug inside his duffel. "I have a few more." He tossed a dagger to both Tyler and Opal. "I was thinking about making toy plastic ones to sell," he admitted sheepishly. "I know, bad idea."

"Logan!" Opal scolded, glaring at the tall boy. "This isn't a game. Torchbearer stuff is way off-limits!"

Ears burning, Logan nodded. "Sorry. You're right."

The gremlins appeared, bounding over tree roots and bushes, getting in each other's way. Slash skidded to a halt ten feet from the group.

"*Candy,*" he rasped, then cocked his head. "*No more run?*"

"You don't belong here." Nico stepped forward, gripping his dagger tightly. "It's time to go."

Slash spotted the blade. His gaze snapped to Logan as he moved to stand beside Nico. Opal and Tyler flanked out wide, circling the figments.

Slash's eyes narrowed. "*Torchbearer scum.*" He charged at Nico, clawing for his face.

Nico was ready. He ducked under the attack, slamming his dagger into the gremlin's side with a snarl of triumph. But the blade passed straight through the figment's body without resistance. Nico stumbled and fell flat on his chest. *What?* He rolled to his feet, eyes wide with shock.

Slash was still there.

The dagger didn't work!

Slash jumped back with a howl. Hissing like a cat, he spun and grabbed his two companions by their necks, dragging them to the edge of the clearing. There he paused to glare at the stunned group. "*Soon, no more Torchbearers.*"

Before anyone could react, the gremlins vanished in a cloud of swirling leaves.

20
OPAL

Opal hurried along the scenic walkway.

A voice erupted to her left. "Hey, kid, what are you doing? We're filming!"

Opal cringed but didn't slow, moving past the *Freakshow* van. "I'm looking for someone."

The overlook trail in Orca Park provided gorgeous views of the ocean, which was probably why Bridger had moved his team there. Opal had been relieved to find them shooting only a block from her house. She'd worried they might already be motoring toward Still Cove.

She needed to speak with Emma. They had a huge mess to sort out.

"Dude, I'm serious!" A red-faced guy in an Oregon Ducks sweatshirt jogged around the van to catch up with her. His stringy brown hair was pulled back into a man-bun atop his head. "You have to wait, okay? We're working here."

Opal halted and crossed her arms. "This is public property."

Mist and fog were creeping in from the sea, the sky darkening from clear to dreary as afternoon approached. At the head of the trail, Opal could see Bridger gesticulating wildly, with Emma and the other two crew members gathered around to listen. Picnic tables had been hauled aside to create space for their equipment.

"Listen, kid—"

Opal pointed at Emma. "My friend's mother wants to speak with her right away."

Man-Bun seemed unimpressed. Opal changed strategies.

"Does the mayor know you have minors working on your show for free?"

His face became stony. "No children are employed by *Freakshow*," he snapped.

Opal rolled her eyes. "Emma is literally right there."

"Huh?" He scratched his head. "You mean Elizabeth?"

Opal huffed. She was so done with this conversation. "I'm going now. Goodbye."

"Wait!" he said doggedly. "Jake's about to start shooting again. Can't you just grab her when they're done? I promise it won't take long." His eyes brightened, and he snapped his fingers. "I've got an idea! Do you want to watch the scene live? I bet you've never seen a real-deal mobile film production before."

Opal's temper boiled. *I've looked the Beast dead in the eye, fought a bus-sized cockroach, and chased off a creature from another dimension. Your van does not impress me.*

Out loud, she said, "Fine."

Man-Bun led her around the vehicle, to where a pair of monitors sat on a battered metal cart. Tangled wires snaked inside the van's open rear doors. Opal stood next to a worn and stained camping chair, not wanting to touch it. Glancing at the left-hand screen, she realized a camera was already rolling. Emma was saying something to Bridger.

"Here." Man-Bun handed her a set of bulky headphones. "You can hear their mikes through these. I'm Derek, by the way."

Opal pulled the headset on. Emma's lilting voice filled her ears. It sounded like she was delivering scripted lines, and Opal felt anxious all over again. When had Emma planned to tell them she was a cast member on *Freakshow*?

"So, Elizabeth, I have to ask." Bridger was using his warm, you-can-totally-confide-in-me hosting voice. "Do *you* believe in the Beast? Does it really prowl these waters?"

Emma nodded, pointing toward the Sound. "Of course," she said. "At the edge of our world. It's out there."

"It's out there," Colton Bridger repeated, gazing dramatically into the lens. Opal recognized the tagline from the episodes they'd watched in the cafe. He always said it near the end of a show.

"And, cut!" Bridger yelled.

Emma shared a thrilled smile with Jacqueline, the lighting expert, but Bridger stomped away from the camera. The cordless mikes were still live.

"This ending won't work," he snapped. "There's no *oomph* to it. No sizzle. I wanted footage of Still Cove, but *no*—that horrible woman took her boat back. Without a refund *or* returning my deposit!" He kicked a rock over the cliff. "How did the stupid thing run out of gas?"

Opal shook her head. She was watching a child have a temper tantrum.

"It's a mystery," Emma mumbled. "Sorry you couldn't explore this morning. But the boat got torn up anyway, right?"

Bridger flinched. "It wasn't *my* fault it got damaged, and now we won't have any decent closing visuals. *Gaah.* I'd trade both my arms for a Beast-sized cave, or a giant footprint. *Anything.*"

"Can't we make tracks?" the bearded cameraman said. "I could carve dino-feet into the mud somewhere."

Jacqueline straightened with a frown. Opal watched as Bridger made a throat-cutting gesture behind Emma's back. Out at sea, a thunderhead was building, its massive gray body rising from the waves in a billowing column.

"We don't *invent* stuff, Jake." Bridger's tone was icy. His gaze darted to Emma, then away. "That kind of deception is not what *Freakshow* is about."

"We examine reality in new ways, with totally open minds!" Emma chimed, sounding delighted as she spat out one of the show's marketing slogans.

"Exactly right," Jacqueline said approvingly. "Ignore Jake. He just shoots the footage."

"If there *were* any strange prints, we'd certainly have to record them." Bridger said, eyeing his cameraman. "The Beast must come ashore sometime, right?"

Emma's expression grew pensive. Opal watched Jacqueline fidget, then busy herself with the lights. A frigid gust tore through the makeshift set, rattling the array and pushing Bridger a step sideways. Shoulders tensing, he shoved his hands into his pockets.

"What about the boat?" Jake said, packing his case. "We have the body damage to close with."

Bridger glanced at Emma. "We found it like that this morning," he said quickly. "Looks like a ferocious animal attack for sure." Then he shook his head angrily. "But it's not enough to finish the series. The first episodes are a smash hit, and I promised the audience a truly spectacular finale. We need something huge and shocking to bring everything to a crescendo."

"The ending *is* the most important part of a series," Emma said slowly. "We have to finish on a high note."

"We?" Bridger covered his smirk. "No, you're right. *Freakshow* has put Timbers on the map. But without a satisfying conclusion, the whole production falls apart. Viewers will turn on us. I'll never win another Clicky Award, and the series will be a failure. *Freakshow: The Beast* will go from hit to flop like *that*." He smacked his hands together.

Opal could tell that prospect offended every particle of Emma's soul.

"We *can't* let that happen," Emma swore. "What do you need to save the show?"

"A Beast appearance would be nice," Bridger snarked, drawing a laugh from Jake. "Without something extraordinary and tangible, we'll be just another flash-in-the-pan web program that started with a bang but fizzled out."

The look on Emma's face was starting to make Opal uneasy. "What would help *exactly*?" Emma asked. "You said a cave?"

"Well, sure." Bridger leaned back against a split-rail fence and folded his arms in annoyance. "Or something genuinely unexpected. An eerie setting, or an inexplicable piece of evidence. Anything to make the audience believe the Beast is real."

"*Be careful, Emma*," Opal whispered, watching the monitor intently.

The wind roared across the overlook again. Behind Opal, Derek began hastily packing things up around the van.

Emma was staring at the ground, her nose scrunched in concentration. Then her head popped up, her face aglow with excitement. "There are these weird sea caves near the mouth of Still Cove! On clear days you can see them from the island. Some are *super* creepy."

Emma, no!

The moment the words were out, Emma's eyes popped. She clapped a hand over her mouth.

"Island?" Bridger said, his eyebrows forming a V. "What island?"

Opal tore off the headphones and bolted up the trail. Emma saw her coming, and her cheeks turned scarlet.

"Emma!" Opal shouted. "We have to go. *Right now.*"

"A dark, mysterious . . . *deadly* island." Bridger was nodding to himself, growing excited. "Hidden at the heart of the Beast's lair . . . We can shoot from above *and* below all that fog. *Yes*, Elizabeth. That could be exactly what we need!"

Emma turned to Opal, fighting back tears. Opal could read her friend's thoughts as if she'd shouted them.

What have I done?

21

NICO

Nico sped down the narrow path.

The heart-stopping drop to his left—from the cliffs above Still Cove down to its icy water—was *not* one he wanted to repeat, but Nico was so panicked, he risked more than he should.

What was Emma THINKING?

Nico knew she felt horrible. Emma had barely been able to speak when she and Opal had found them packing up Logan's Beast shop at the hardware store. Emma had covered her face while Opal explained that Bridger was refocused on Still Cove. This time, he and his team planned to climb down into the rocky bay.

If they find the island . . .

Nico didn't want to think about it.

And why didn't my dagger work?! He couldn't figure it

out. Slash had barely noticed when Nico swung his blade straight through the figment's abdomen. *What is going on?*

He reached the cave and bolted into the hidden passage, jogging down the switchbacks that descended below the cove itself. Mind racing, Nico scarcely paused as he passed the Torchbearers' secret ritual chamber inside the tunnel. Maybe Bridger wouldn't see the trailhead, or would chicken out at the cave mouth. The odds seemed low that he'd actually find a way onto the island.

Don't panic. This could still blow over.

But Nico had a sinking feeling it wouldn't.

In a shaky voice, Opal had explained how driven Bridger was to find the perfect ending to his series. He'd promised viewers something amazing, and now had to deliver. Bridger was clever and capable, Nico grudgingly conceded. If he looked hard enough for a way down from the cliffs, Nico thought he'd eventually find one.

That's why Nico had left the rowboat tied up below the ledge at the mouth of the cave. He didn't want the film crew poking around inside—the Torchbearer tunnel was too obviously built by human hands. Film of that alone would be enough to boost ratings. People would flock to the cove to figure out why a secret passage was there.

But if Bridger and his team paddled out in the rowboat, they might get turned around in the heavy fog and miss the island completely. And even if they didn't, they would have to come ashore on the beach. Maybe they wouldn't climb over the ridge to where the houseboat was hidden.

That's a lot of maybes.

Gritting his teeth, Nico climbed the opposite side of the tunnel and emerged into open air. He scrambled up the ridge without pausing. Dense mists covered the island, blocking all view of the houseboat from the heights. Nico nearly sobbed in relief. *We can do this. We can still protect the Darkdeep.* He started down toward the stepping-stones across the pond.

The others would be right behind him. Opal, Logan, and Tyler were spying on the van, hoping Bridger wouldn't follow through on his plan. Emma had gone to rejoin the film crew. It had taken hugs and reassurances to pull her back together, but she was the most important member of their squad right now. She could embed with the *Freakshow* team as they searched. Maybe steer them away.

Nico raced up the front steps of the houseboat and charged through the foyer. Inside the showroom, he made sure the panel concealing the stairs down to the Darkdeep was still blocked by a bookcase. He doubted anyone who didn't already know where the door was could find it, but if Bridger got footage of the houseboat, it was only a matter of time until others showed up. Someone would discover the secret entrance. And the Darkdeep.

Nope nope nope. Not gonna let that happen.

Nico took a step back and spun, straining to think of anything he could do to protect the collection.

Is something wrong? a voice sounded in his head.

Nico nearly jumped out of his skin. Thing was staring at him from the pedestal, a concerned look on its face.

"You're . . . you're back."

Nico swallowed. He didn't like being alone with Thing. Not when the creature could touch his mind.

I never left, Nico. I needed to rest. It was difficult reconstituting into a state recognizable by humans. But I'm feeling much better now. Thing paused, the skin above its left eye arching. *You seem distressed. Can I assist you in some way?*

Nico stared for a moment, then barked a laugh. "There's a film crew headed to Still Cove, searching for this island. You see the problem, right?"

Thing frowned. *I do indeed. Would you like me to help?*

Nico ran a hand over his face. He still had a hard time exchanging telepathic pleasantries with an alien blob floating inside a glass jar. "Help how?"

Before Thing could answer, the curtain swished aside. Opal ran in with Tyler and Logan. "They found our rowboat!"

Nico's heart sank into his shoes. "Are they in the cove?"

Opal nodded grimly. "We hid on the path behind them, above the fog. But we heard them climb down to the water

204

and row out. They could be anywhere right now." Opal cleared her throat. "Emma's with them."

"Don't you mean Elizabeth?" Logan snarked, but no one laughed. Outside, the wind howled like a pack of wolves. The weather had deteriorated swiftly as the massive thunderstorm moved in from the Pacific.

"It's good she's there," Tyler said. "She can keep them away from the island."

Nico's eyes met Opal's. *Will she, though?* Could Emma bring herself to trick the crew, when working with them was all she'd ever dreamed of?

They're here.

Everyone jumped. Logan took a step away from Thing.

"Here?" Nico's eyes shot to the curtain. "On the houseboat?"

No. The island. They arrived on the beach and are staring into the forest. Emma has told them there are rabid bats in the trees. The bearded man is setting up a tripod.

Tyler made a strangled sound in his throat. "We're sunk. They're going to find the houseboat and ruin everything."

Opal moved face-to-face with the jar. "Thing, can you read their minds?"

Thing squirmed in its lime-green bath. *Not read them. But I can track their communications. I can hear—for lack of a better word—anyone who sets foot on this island.*

Right now the brown-haired man is speaking directly to a camera about . . . Oh my. Why does he think the leviathan lives here?

"Long story." Nico scraped both hands over his scalp. "Maybe that's all they need? Bridger on the beach, talking about the Beast?" He knew his words sounded more wishful than anything.

Thing dashed those hopes immediately. *They've decided to climb the ridge. Emma is telling them it's full of snakes, but they're ignoring her. Why does this Bridger fellow call her Elizabeth?*

Opal was peeking between her fingers. "The noose is tightening, guys. I'm out of ideas."

Would you like me to misdirect them?

"Can you do that?" Nico blurted, eyeing the jar nervously. Tyler started the pacing the room.

I can send images into their minds and try to lead them astray. I was able to communicate with Opal in this way when I nudged her toward the cemetery. Shall I try?

"Yes, Blob Man!" Logan shouted. "Please don't let them find us here, mind-melding with you and hiding an inter-dimensional waterslide in the basement!"

Thing closed its eyes. Silence swept over the room like a weighted blanket. For long seconds, no one moved a muscle. Then Thing reopened its eyes with a frown.

This Bridger is a stubborn man. He has an idea fixed in

his brain that I can't seem to dislodge. He thinks something incredible must be on the other side of the ridge.

Nico could barely ask the question. "What does that mean, Thing?"

It means they're coming, Nico. There's nothing I can do to stop them.

22

OPAL

Opal ducked to avoid a shooting rainbow.

"Where did *these* stupid figments come from?" she snapped, leaping behind a flowering shrub halfway up the slope overlooking the pond. The air outside was bitingly cold— the temperature had dropped several degrees since they'd left the houseboat in a rush to intercept the *Freakshow* team.

The boys were up ahead, herding a group of pastel-colored teddy bears off the ridge. As Opal watched, the green one turned and snarled at Logan, paws on its hips as it fired a shamrock-shaped laser beam from the design on its stomach. Logan yelped and hit the dirt as the burst sizzled past him.

"Care Bears are supposed to be nice!" Tyler squawked, stomping toward a bright yellow one with a shining sun on its chest. Growling, the figment tried to bite his leg, but Tyler kicked out and it scurried into the bushes.

"Keep them on the pond side of the ridge!" Nico yelled,

as he chased after an orange teddy emblazoned with flowers. "If Bridger sees one of these things, we're cooked."

The creature spun suddenly and extended its claws, nearly gouging Nico's eyes. Nico shoved the vicious little cub with both hands and it tumbled downhill.

There were five Care Bears in all. Thwarted on the hilltop, they had gathered inside a circle of broken rocks just below the summit and were glaring up at their pursuers. Opal worried they might try a group stare, shooting more lasers from their emblems. She didn't want to find out what those colored beams could do if they struck a target.

"How do we get rid of them?" Opal grumbled. "I've never wanted to knife a teddy bear before, but if that's what it takes . . ."

Are you asking me? Thing said in Opal's mind. *I thought I was supposed to track Bridger.*

"Yes, keep doing that," Opal said aloud. "We need to know where he is at all times." A thick fog was seeping through the trees, reducing visibility to only a few feet in every direction.

"Talking to the alien glop ball again?" Tyler shook his head. "Remember when the weirdest thing we did was play dinosaur charades?"

"We have to get these little jerks out of here." Opal stretched her arms wide and flapped them at the Care Bears. They responded by gnashing short, pointy teeth. The brown one with a heart on its stomach seemed ready to chomp Opal's arm off. She paused to wipe sweat from her forehead. "Okay, I'm getting creeped out."

Opal glanced down at the pond. The mist was weakening—she could see the houseboat's roof poking through a rolling eddy of fog. *If Bridger and his crew make it this far, they'll notice it for sure.* And how would Opal explain being on the island in the first place?

Logan growled suddenly, deep and convincing, making himself big as he stomped toward the figments like the Frankenstein monster. The Care Bears recoiled as one, then fled into the lower woods, bouncing and tumbling as they scampered down from the ridge. Their yowls of outrage floated on the spanking breeze.

"Not bad," Nico said, hands on his knees as he tried to catch his breath.

"No problem," Logan said. "I'm the natural enemy of stuffed toys. I destroyed every one I had when I was little."

Opal listened intently to make certain the unruly bears were truly gone. "What if they circle around us to the beach? There's zero way to play those guys off as a Halloween prank."

"Emma has a dagger," Logan said. "She knows what to do."

"That won't help her, remember?" Tyler shivered in the icy wind. "I got one of the Care Bears with mine just now, but the blade passed right through it, like I was fighting a ghost. The little punk stuck its tongue out at me and ran."

Opal winced. Just like the gremlin in the forest. She met Nico's eyes, and saw her concern mirrored there. *If our daggers really have stopped working . . .*

"But we handled that Charmeleon same as always," Nico muttered. "It doesn't add up."

"Later." Opal brushed loose hairs behind her ears. "We have to focus on Bridger. It's game-over for our secrets if Emma has to fight a band of laser-shooting teddy bears in front of his camera crew."

Nico slapped a hand against his side. "Fine. Let's just hope we catch a break."

Opal snorted. *Right. Lots of those so far.*

Logan grunted sourly. "We wouldn't *be* in this mess if it weren't for Emma."

Opal wheeled on him, eyes blazing. "She didn't mean for this to happen, Logan."

Logan crossed his arms. "I know that, Opal. But does it matter? Emma screwed up big-time, and now everything we've worked to protect is at risk."

Opal didn't respond. How could she? Logan was right. She hugged herself in the chilly air.

Thing's voice sounded. *The strangers are not deterred. They are headed your way.*

"Crap." Nico wiped damp palms on his jeans. "We're going to have to confront them."

"And say what?" Tyler peered into the gloom-soaked

forest surrounding them. "Hey, guys, no worries, we checked for the Beast already and it's not here?"

Opal shook her head. "Bridger is obsessed with finding a game changer for his show. The only thing that might lure him away is—"

"The Beast itself!" Nico blurted, inspiration dancing in his eyes. "Opal, are you thinking what I'm thinking?"

Opal laughed nervously. "I don't know. What do you think I'm thinking?"

"That Thing could summon the Beast for us."

Opal blinked. "You think Thing can do that?"

Nico rubbed the back of his neck. "I dunno. The little guy seems . . . fairly . . . capable."

Tyler slapped his hands together loudly. "Guys! Hold up. You're talking about *intentionally* attracting the Beast here? To this island? How does that *help* us, exactly?"

"Bridger wants authentic Beast footage more than anything," Opal replied. "So if the monster were to appear somewhere else, like out in the cove maybe . . . He might chase after it?"

"Or the Beast might decide to come ashore and eat everybody," Tyler squawked. "This is a terrible plan!"

Logan shrugged. "At least it's *something*. They're going to be here any minute."

Thing, where is Bridger right now? Opal asked silently.

For a moment there was no answer. Was Thing there? Could it still respond?

He's just below the other side of the ridge.

Opal looked at the others. "Did you hear?"

"Yes." The boys muttered in unison.

Opal exhaled. "Okay, here's the plan. Thing, you're going to call the Beast into Still Cove and make it swim around. When the film crew sees it, send the Beast away again. Can you handle that?"

Yes. But the intruders are very close. You must stop them now.

Opal didn't ask if the others had heard. She sprinted to the top of the ridge and down the other side, nearly slamming into Bridger. "Turn around!" Opal shouted, causing him to flinch back in alarm. Tyler grabbed Emma and began whispering furiously in her ear.

Their sudden appearance had rendered Bridger speechless. He blinked at Opal like a startled bird.

Opal grabbed his sleeve. "Hurry! It's this way!"

Nico and the others ran past them, bolting down toward the beach. Jake lowered his camera and met eyes with Jacqueline and Derek. They all three looked to Bridger, who was staring at Opal with his mouth hanging open.

"What are you doing here?" he finally spluttered.

"Now's your chance, Bridger!" Opal pointed after Nico.

"You're about to get the footage of a lifetime!" She released him and sprinted downhill without looking back.

That was enough for Colton Bridger. "Let's go!" he shouted, pounding down the trail after her. His crew struggled to keep up as they all raced back the way they'd come. On the beach, Emma and the boys were at the water's edge, pointing into the fog and jumping up and down. The film crew arrived and began hastily preparing equipment. Bridger was trying to look everywhere at once.

Okay, Thing, Opal sent. *That's your cue!*

"The monster is here?!" Bridger shouted, then dropped his voice. "It's *real*? There *is* a Beast in Still Cove?"

Opal tried to sound shaken. "I guess so. Maybe. I don't know! Something followed us in from the Sound."

"Where's your boat?" Jacqueline asked suspiciously. "I don't see one anywhere."

Before Opal could answer, something dark and heavy rippled the cove's glasslike surface. Everyone fell silent as a crest of water swept around the island. Opal raced over to stand with her friends.

"Ho boy," Tyler breathed. "We really stepped in it now."

"There it is!" Bridger shouted, then he impaled his cameraman with a wide-eyed glare. "Tell me you got that."

"I wasn't ready!" Jake whined, fumbling with a detachable battery. "This thing isn't an iPhone, you know!"

Bridger howled in frustration. "*Get in the boat.* We can't miss it again. *Use* a freaking iPhone if you have to!"

The *Freakshow* team began piling into the rowboat, though Jacqueline tossed a skeptical glance at Opal and the others as they huddled on the sand. "You better not be pranking us," she warned, but at a shout from Bridger, she helped push off into the water.

A rumble echoed from the walls of the cove. Everyone froze. Another line of wake slid past, this time arrowing in the direction of the open ocean.

"*Are you getting this!?*" Bridger shouted as they oared away from the island.

"Hey!" Emma called out. "What about me?"

Bridger flapped an annoyed hand as the rowboat slid into the fog. "Sorry, Elizabeth, but it's not safe for you to come with us now. Your friends can give you a ride home!"

The water was still once more. Where was the Beast headed? Toward Timbers? To the Rift? It dawned on Opal that Bridger and his crew were now chasing a very real sea monster from another dimension in a rickety dinghy. "I wouldn't go out there if I were you!"

"Are you kidding?" Bridger laughed maniacally. "I live for these moments!" His face was alight with excitement as the *Freakshow* team vanished into the mist. Their voices carried even after they'd disappeared.

"I saw it too, boss," Derek babbled excitedly. "What could make a wave like that?"

"I saw . . . something," Jacqueline agreed. "But I don't know what it was."

"Thanks again for the tip, Elizabeth!" Bridger shouted. Then they were gone.

Opal turned to look at the others, releasing a long-held breath. She was already exhausted, and Halloween had barely begun. She should be eating candy and watching scary movies with her friends. Instead, she was living one.

"Thing," she said quietly, "did you send the Beast away?"

Yes. But there's a slight problem.

Opal covered her eyes. "And what is that?"

It's not listening to me anymore. And it's coming back.

23

NICO

Nico slumped onto the sand.

The sun was sinking below the surrounding cliffs, bathing the cove in a spectral half-light.

"What'd you say, Thing?" He was too tired to process another threat. The rowboat was out of sight—the Beast had lured Bridger away from the island like a well-trained dog. Thing had made it happen. But now . . .

"So . . ." Tyler was standing beside him. He rubbed his eyes. "A telepathic goo-man inside a glass jar . . . just used a legendary sea monster as an accomplice . . . to protect the interdimensional vortex hidden on our secret houseboat." He paused. "I have that all right?"

Nico ran both hands across his face. "That about covers it. Only now the sea monster is off its chain, apparently."

"Nico, this is getting too crazy."

"Which part?"

Logan cackled darkly. "Did you see the wake that nightmare threw off? It was going *fast*."

"It's coming back, you know," Tyler said dully. "You heard the green goblin. And we're just chilling here on the beach, chatting away."

But Nico was still too overwhelmed to move. Opal made as if to flop down next to him, then reconsidered, as if even sitting might be too much work. They'd been up since the crack of dawn, and everyone was exhausted. This Halloween was already one for the record books, and it hadn't even really started.

Emma trudged over to join the group. Her shoulders rose, then fell. "This was all my fault, you guys. I'm so sorry. I never should've breathed a *word* about Still Cove. I . . . I just wanted . . ." Her voice broke.

Nico stood up and put an arm around her. "We know, Emma. Making a TV show has been everything to you. We understand how you got carried away."

Emma cleared her throat. "No more, though. I'm done with *Freakshow*." Her expression soured. "They left me here. Ditched us all on a deserted island with a sea monster swimming around. Bridger just . . . took off!"

Something rustled in the woods behind them.

Opal glanced over her shoulder, then rolled her eyes. "Oh, great. Look who's back."

Nico was almost too weary to care. But he turned, spotted

a squat green shape in the branches of the closest pine tree. Two more shadows joined the first, and all three began cackling madly.

"These guys again?" Tyler pinched the bridge of his nose. "Wonderful. *Fan-tastic.*"

Nico stared dispiritedly as Slash spun and shook his butt at them. "I really hate gremlins."

Emma frowned at the trio. "They've lasted for at least two full days. What gives?"

Could I have everyone's attention?

Nico clenched his teeth. No matter how often it happened, he'd never get used to Thing invading his thoughts.

We have a . . . situation on our hands.

Opal sighed. "What's the matter, Thing? Is the Beast back inside the cove?"

Not just that. The Darkdeep has become active. I can feel it churning beneath me. I . . . I think . . . Be very careful out there.

Nico shook his head to clear it. *No time to be tired.* He glared up at the gremlins, but they'd stopped moving, their long green ears cocked as if listening. The last glints of daylight were fading.

Logan went still as a sudden silence swept the island. "What's goi—"

"*Shhh.*" Nico's danger sense began tingling madly. "You guys hear that?"

A loud crack. Another.

The island began to vibrate. Softly at first, but then the sand beneath their feet began to shift and dance.

"Is that a tremor?" Tyler blurted, his gaze darting to where the mouth of Still Cove hid behind a curtain of mist. "Guys, this is a *horrible* place to be if an earthquake's happening. We're in Tsunami City down here!"

The shaking ceased abruptly.

No one moved.

"I don't think . . . ," Nico began to whisper, but he didn't finish, staring into the forest.

"It felt more like—" Logan cut off as Tyler's fingers dug into his arm. "What the heck, Ty?"

Tyler's hand shook as he pointed into the cove.

A sinuous curve was slicing through the slate-gray water, moving faster than it had sped away. The wave was headed directly for them.

Torchbearers. I seem to have lost contact with the leviathan.

Nico swallowed. "We found it, Thing."

"It found us," Emma warbled.

Oh dear. In that case, I suggest vacating the beach immediately.

"You don't have to mind-message me twice!" Tyler turned to bolt into the trees, but it was Nico's turn to grab ahold of someone.

"Not an earthquake," Nico croaked, staring into the misty woods.

Up in the branches of the tallest tree, the three gremlins began to sing.

A gigantic form was lumbering through the forest.

The creature towered over the canopy, its head at least fifty feet off the ground. The figment's skin was a deep, liquid red. Steam rose from its body as the monster wrapped thick fingers around an alder tree. The trunk burst into flames.

The gremlins stopped crooning, their voices morphing to howling cheers.

Opal's jaw dropped open. "What is *that*?!"

Nico couldn't answer. The flame giant glared down at them, as if noticing their puny existence for the first time.

Logan's head whipped from the now-smoking forest to the approaching wake. "The Beast is almost here! But, uh, this fire monster doesn't look like much fun, either."

Emma removed her dagger and clutched it in a white-knuckled grip. A dry, baking wind radiated from the forest, blasting the gang as they cowered on the sand.

"How do we dispel something like that?" Emma moaned. "We can't even get close!"

A giant wave crashed onto the beach, rolling over their sneakers and soaking their legs. The Beast's sinuous head emerged from the shallows, its huge jaws parting with a thunderous roar. The sea monster stomped ashore on thickly muscled legs. Logan and Emma flattened on the sand as its massive tail whipped over their heads. Tyler had frozen like a statue.

Opal was cowering beside Nico. Their eyes met. They were trapped between fire and water, with no place to hide.

Nico had a sudden thought. Unsure how to communicate it, he shouted into the gathering wind. "Thing, the Beast hates fire! Make it see the figment in the woods!"

Opal gave Nico a dazed look. "How can he miss it, Nico?"

Quick thinking, Nico. I'll make the leviathan understand.

The fire monster raked a hand through the treetops. Sparks erupted from its fingers. The gremlins' laughter turned to terrified shrieks as their perch began to burn. They scrambled down and ran off under the eaves, shaking their fists at the red giant.

The Beast reared back, glinting black eyes locked on to the creature in the forest. Baring razor-sharp teeth, it made a low, growling sound deep in its throat. The sea monster backed into the shallows and ducked under the surface.

Nico was stunned. *It's running away?*

But the Beast exploded back up and spat a stream of salt water at the fire creature.

Steam billowed where liquid struck the figment's flaming skin. The creature darkened to scarlet, bellowing in rage as it ripped a tree from the ground. It squeezed until the wood caught fire, then hurled the blazing missile at the Beast, which sprang sideways to avoid it, screaming in fury. The fire monster growled and crouched lower, as if intending to charge.

"This is a bad place to be!" Nico shouted. He grabbed Tyler's arm and dragged him down the beach. "Opal! Logan! Emma! Let's go!"

The leviathan is out of my control. It hates fire but will fight to protect its territory.

"Its what?" Nico shouted, backpedaling across the sand. "It really lives here?! How have we not seen it?!"

No time. Get away while the creatures are focused on each other.

Nico spun and led the others away. The Beast hunkered in the water, hissing and snapping its jaws. The fire figment towered on the beach, its feet melting sand into glass where it stood. A tense standoff ensued—one creature howling and shooting water from its mouth while the other tossed flaming brands like hatchets.

Nico didn't know what to do. Fires were spreading in the forest. He shut his eyes and thought hard.

Thing, we need help. The flame creature will burn down the whole island if we don't stop it somehow.

Understood, Nico. I will try to motivate the leviathan, but the threat of fire has made it difficult.

A moment later, the Beast coiled in on itself and shot a huge stream of water at the red creature. Then it darted forward while the figment was distracted, sinking its teeth into the fire monster's leg. Steam exploded between the Beast's jaws as it heaved backward with a shriek of pain, yanking the blazing giant off-balance. Before the figment could recover, the Beast dragged its prey into the fire-quenching water.

The ocean boiled. The flame creature screamed, then went black as ash. A beat later it faded from existence.

"Okay," Tyler breathed. "That was intense."

The sea monster was still thrashing in the water, jaws scorched and bleeding. It whirled to regard Nico and the others as they huddled in the darkness.

"Uh-oh," Emma wheezed. "It might be hungry after such a big brawl."

The Beast began stalking toward them, red lines dribbling from its mouth. As Nico watched in horror, it spat out a pair of charred, blackened teeth.

Tyler's eyes rounded with concern. "I think it's really hurt."

"Not enough!" Logan wailed. "It's *maaaaad*, and we're the only ones left."

But the Beast stumbled, then halted, snuffling a burn mark on its foreleg. The monster howled in what seemed like frustration. It threw a last glare at where they huddled, quaking in fear, before jerking around and lumbering back into the sea. Moments later the cove was still and silent.

"Ha," Emma said in a shaky voice. "Just like we planned it."

"Great job, Thing Guy!" Logan shouted, a relieved smile spreading across his face. "That was amazing!"

The little green creature didn't respond. Nico glanced at Opal, who frowned.

Thunder cracked overhead. A weird light was seeping through the mist, painting everything in a sickly yellow cast. Drizzle began to fall, quickly strengthening to a downpour. Tyler pressed his fists against his temples. "Man, can this day get any worse?"

"No!" Emma said, clapping in delight. "This is good! The rain will put the fires out."

She was right. Nico saw the remaining flames wither and die under the strengthening shower.

"I'm going after the gremlins," he swore, scraping wet sand from his hair. "I have had *enough* of those guys."

As if summoned by Nico's words, Slash appeared under the dripping boughs of the forest. He grinned, pointing a long, clawed finger at the group. "*Yum, yum, yum.*"

Nico removed his dagger from his jacket. "Oh *bring* it, you stupid lizard. I'll brain you with the handle of this knife if I have to."

Something is wrong. Return to the houseboat immediately.

The command was so intense, Nico actually staggered. He felt the blood drain from his face.

Something in Thing's sending . . . It had felt like . . . anger?

Movement behind the gremlins caught Nico's eye. A *lot* of movement.

"Nico," Opal said quietly, as if afraid to voice what she was seeing. "There are more than just gremlins on this beach."

Emma gasped.

Tyler and Logan covered their mouths.

Behind Slash, scattered among the rain-slicked trunks, snarling figures appeared.

Hundreds of them.

Nico spun to face the others, saw his fear reflected in their eyes.

He shouted the only word he could force from his throat.

"*Run.*"

24
OPAL

Opal slammed the front door shut behind her.

"Did you see that mob?!" Tyler moaned, backing through the houseboat's foyer. "How many figments are out there?"

Emma's chest was pumping like a bellows. "*Hundreds* of them."

"We should've gone for the tunnel," Logan fumed, throwing his hands in the air. "Now they have us trapped!"

Nico raced into the showroom. Everyone else followed. "They'll be here any minute," he said, seizing another dagger from a battered coffin filled with weapons. "Grab something to fight with. Now!"

Not a good idea.

Opal stumbled. It was the second time Thing had spoken like that—in a tone that pierced straight through her brain. She whirled to face the jar. Thing stared back at her, suspended in liquid, its eyes open and watching.

"What do you mean?" Opal said. "There's an army of figments outside. We have to protect—"

No.

Opal staggered against the weight of the word, the way it slashed into her mind. The others all grabbed their heads.

"Thing, stop," Opal said, a shiver of unease running down her spine. "You don't need to . . . to yell. Or whatever it is you're doing. We hear you."

Another sound filled her head. Low and echoing.

A chuckle.

The hair on Opal's arms stood up.

Thing was *laughing*. At what? At them?

Sorry. Thing's mouth twitched into a satisfied grin. *There will be no more fighting today.*

"Why? Are they gone?" Logan strode to the window and peered out into the darkness. Then he stiffened, a sickly look creeping over his face. "They're everywhere. Even on the stepping-stones. But they . . . they aren't moving." He spun, eyes scared and confused. "They're all just standing in place, watching the houseboat. Like . . . like they're waiting for something."

Opal felt her stomach knot. She met Nico's eyes. As one, they rushed back into the foyer. With a shaking hand, Opal swung open the front door. Outside, nightmare creatures ringed the pond in a mass of gleaming eyes and teeth. Some bobbed in the water. Others crowded the field, or lined the surrounding ridges. Slash and his companions crouched on the closest entry stone, teeth bared.

Adrenaline flooded Opal's body. She yanked the door closed and tried to lock it.

Return to the showroom, please.

"Come on," Nico whispered. "Something's not right." They passed back through the curtain, joining Emma and Tyler in front of the pedestal. The group stood a full step farther away than before.

Logan kept his position by the window. "We need a lookout."

Unnecessary. I am holding the figments at bay.

Thing's expression hardened into something less than friendly.

Don't make me change my mind.

There was a wild hammering on the front door. Monstrous faces suddenly pressed against the bay window, driving Logan back with a yelp. Footsteps thumped on the roof as spindly bodies crowded the skylights. Opal's skin crawled at so many deadly creatures being so close.

Logan was breathing fast, his whole body rigid. Tyler and Emma stood with their shoulders pressed together. Nico's face grew pale. His gaze flicked to the wall panel hiding the Darkdeep. Opal felt trapped between the horrors outside and the little green creature who no longer seemed like a friend.

And what was that other sound?

Like waves smashing against jagged rocks. A roiling hum that reminded her of the Rift.

Oh no.

Thing's voice rang inside Opal's head.

The Darkdeep is rising, my friends. Isn't that wonderful?

Logan shot forward and clamped Thing's jar in between his hands. "What's going on?" he demanded.

Thing smiled without humor, or the slightest hint of warmth. Its beady black eyes drilled into Logan. *An injustice that has existed for centuries is being righted, human. Now, step back before you get hurt.*

"I'm not scared of you!" Logan shouted, though his voice cracked. "Quit whatever you're doing or I'll . . . I'll make you wish you had. You're just a stupid . . . *Thing* . . . in a freaking *jar!*" His knuckles whitened against the glass.

Thing sneered, an expression so hostile Opal shuddered.

Logan's hands flashed red and he reeled backward with a screech.

"Not good," Tyler breathed, edging away from the pedestal. "In fact, this is really bad."

You didn't think you could hurt me, did you, Logan? Thing's gaze shifted. *Tyler, stop moving. Or you won't like what happens next.*

Tyler froze. Nico stepped in front of his terrified friend.

"Thing, what's going on?" Nico said quietly. "What injustice are you talking about?"

Emma's eyes sparkled in the light reflecting off the jar. "I . . . I thought you were an original Torchbearer?"

Thing pressed tiny hands against the glass. Fury seeped into its voice. *No. I was their prisoner.*

"Prisoner?" Tyler repeated, his brow furrowing. "Come again?"

"Let's smash the jar," Logan hissed. "If Thing is controlling the figments outside, that might make them go away."

Thing's lips curled into a snarl. *Try nothing, human. My patience is nearly spent.*

"We've been helping you!" Emma snapped, stomping a foot. "Doing whatever you said to seal off the Rift. How can you turn on us now?"

Again, the horrible chuckle. Opal covered her ears, but that only made it worse. The sound was *inside* her head.

Thing eyed Emma calmly. *Turn on you? No. You have it wrong.*

Emma shivered. Opal reached out and took her hand.

The cabinet blocking the wall panel toppled over on its own. The hidden door to the Darkdeep swung wide. A churning sound echoed up the staircase, reverberating to the rafters. Opal heard the ping of liquid lapping against metal.

I can't betray those I was never working with in the first place.

Opal's breath died in her chest. She watched Nico sag. Tyler blocked his eyes.

I don't belong here. I've been caged in this world far too long. It's time for me to go home.

"Fine!" Logan spat. "*Go!* Why'd you even come here in the first place?"

I was curious. Wouldn't you have been? I wanted to see what was on the other side, but then I couldn't return.

Sadness washed through Opal. A painful childhood memory came roaring back—being lost in a crowded amusement park. Being scared and all alone. She hadn't thought of it in years.

Yes. Alone.

But an undercurrent of rage tinged Thing's next sending.

Because of the Torchbearers.

"The Torchbearers are good!" Nico shot back, eyes blazing. "Without them guarding the Darkdeep—and the Rift too, I guess—this world would be in constant danger. We've seen it ourselves!"

The Torchbearers are not who you think they are.

Yvette Dumont found me and placed me in this jar, which I admit saved my life, however inadvertently. We worked together to preserve this realm from destruction, but then she made me her captive. I've been trapped here ever since . . .

A pause. "How long?" Opal whispered.

Centuries. Yvette refused my repeated pleas to return home, as did those that followed in the Torchbearer order,

decade after decade. All claimed it was for the greater good,
but at what cost to me?

Opal felt Thing's immense sorrow again, but anger crack-led through it twice as strong. Anger that had been bottled up and held in, held *close*, because there was no place for it to go.

The Torchbearers needed my unique skills to control the Darkdeep and keep the Rift sealed. The Rift is a terrible wound between our dimensions—a broken way to pass back and forth. The Taker you and Nico battled inside the Darkdeep—there are thousands more like it, waiting on the other side. They want to come through. They want this world.

And I'm done saving it for you.

"Wait," Opal said, curious despite her fear. Down the staircase, the rushing sound was getting stronger. "You tried to help us seal the Rift. We went to the platform like you said. We threw the iron mixture in. We did everything—"

Thing laughed in their minds.

You didn't help me restore the seal, child. You helped me tear it open. The amount of iron you added to the water anni-hilated the delicate chemical balance on which the barrier relies.

Tyler winced, squeezing his eyes shut. "Ah, crap. We did the legwork for you."

Yes. Thanks to you, little Torchbearers, everything is ready. The seal is irreparably broken. A way through the Rift has been cleared. All it needs now is a push from our side.

The pounding on the door, window, and roof grew louder.

This group of figments is mine. I pulled them from the Darkdeep myself.

"Even the Beast?" Tyler sputtered.

Thing shook its tiny head. *I didn't lie. The leviathan is not a stray thought. He's a being of my world. He's lost, too.*

Opal heard hungry shrieks outside. Every bit of her wanted to cower and hide, but Thing's icy stare kept her rooted to the floorboards.

Opal. You were the first to listen. Hear me now. I don't want to hurt anyone, but I will if you get in my way. I am going home.

"You said the Rift is a . . . wound." Opal pressed a hand to her temple. "That the Torchbearers imprisoned you here to keep it contained. Why did they need you?"

That is no longer relevant. Just know that my presence kept the Rift neutralized, though a few things did slip through from time to time. But none of that matters now.

Logan grunted. "So if you go back, what happens?"

My passage will rip open the gateway. You won't be able to close it again.

"But then those creatures from your world will enter ours!" Nico shouted. "We won't be able to control them without you. You're dooming us!"

That's not my problem anymore. And you cannot stop me from leaving.

Opal heard the front door crash open. The curtain flew apart as a mob of figments sauntered into the showroom. Gnomes, horned devils, a dragon with smoke curling around its neck. Slash cackled as he rode atop the shoulders of an enormous troll with insect eyes.

Into the basement, please. You will remain there until I cross over. After that . . . good luck.

The figment mob pressed closer. Suddenly, Emma's hand whipped out, a Torchbearer dagger flying from her fingers. The blade passed straight through the insect-troll's head, thudding against the far wall and dropping to the floor.

Thing scowled. *That won't work against the army I've created. And now my patience is gone.*

The creatures moved forward again. Opal and the others fled into the stairwell. The Darkdeep was down there, but at least Thing's figments wouldn't be. Nico closed the wall panel and bolted it from the inside. Figments started beating on the wood, howling and laughing. Some of the laughter was Thing's.

A ball of rage sparked in Opal's gut. They were trapped. Below them, at the base of the steps, the Darkdeep's swirling water filled the chamber. Opal looked at the others, huddled on the slowly flooding risers.

She knew the awful truth, even before Thing spoke it inside her head.

You're my prisoners now.

PART FOUR
THE RIFT

25

NICO

Inky black water was creeping up the staircase.

"We have to get out of here!" Nico shouted, switching on the electric lantern they kept tucked in a wall niche by the entry panel. Beyond it, he could hear figments laughing and snarling, mixed with occasional ripping and smashing sounds. The houseboat was filled with deadly creatures, and they seemed to be having a party.

"Is that the Darkdeep?" Tyler yelled, eyes wide as he stared at the flood, which bubbled and fizzed like a shook-up soda can. "Or is the houseboat sinking? Or is the houseboat *sinking into the Darkdeep?*"

Logan swallowed. "Oh man, I never thought of that."

Opal chewed her bottom lip, her eyebrows forming a worried V.

They couldn't go back through the showroom—not with dozens of monsters waiting to rip their heads off, and Thing sitting in its jar like a king on a throne. But what was in the surging liquid below? Could they still pass through the Darkdeep and reach the pond? Even if they did, what was waiting for them out on the island?

The water level had risen to the middle of the steps. "Should I touch it?" Emma said.

"No!" Tyler shouted, waving his arms back and forth.

"There must be a way to escape," Opal said urgently, flexing and squeezing her fingers. "We can't let Thing get away with whatever it's planning. We have to stop the Rift from breaking open before it's too late."

"Did you *see* outside?" Logan said. "It's already too late! Even if no more figments appear, how can we possibly stop the ones here? And they don't even respond to our daggers!" Logan gnashed his teeth, seemingly on the verge of a total meltdown. "They'll find a way off the island eventually, and then Timbers is doomed. Some of these creatures can swim!" He paused, visibly trying to get ahold of himself. "It's Halloween. Kids will be out trick-or-treating, and these monsters are real!"

Opal paled. Like Nico, she seemed to have no answers. How were they supposed to stop an army they couldn't fight?

Tyler snapped his fingers. "The figments! They belong to Thing!"

Nico blinked at his friend. "Thing said it created them, but what difference does that make?"

Tyler shrugged, eyes wide. "No idea, but we've seen how

the Torchbearer daggers don't work anymore. Maybe Thing made, like, a different *type* of figment. Since its an alien or whatever."

Opal clamped a hand onto Tyler's forearm. "Yes! These figments don't come from human imaginations, so they don't act like the ones we created before. That makes sense! We just have to figure out how to dispel them."

"Great." Logan threw his hands up in frustration. "How do we do that?"

Emma's eyes suddenly bugged in the dim light. "Wow, tonight is a *really* bad time for a figment breakout. Bridger is planning something. If we don't—"

The water below them geysered in the center. A dark wave swept around the room, forcing them up a few steps. The simmering ceased and the flood went still, dropping the chamber into an uneasy silence. The breaking sounds beyond the door had disappeared as well.

"Something just happened," Tyler whispered.

Logan cautiously unbolted the wall panel, but found the way firmly blocked. "The door's jammed. I can't open it."

The water gurgled, then settled smooth like obsidian. The flood had stopped rising but they were trapped.

Nico balled his hands. He had to make a decision. There was only one choice to make.

"I'll go first," he said, moving past the others to the edge of the water.

Are you the Darkdeep, escaped from your well? Am I going into the void again?

"Uh-uh," Tyler snapped, reluctantly joining Nico on the last dry step. "No one goes anywhere by themselves." He inhaled deeply, then spoke in a thin voice. "Even in . . . in that. I'm with you, Nicolas. We'll do this side by side. The two of us."

"You can quit it with that macho stuff," Opal said curtly, crowding onto the riser behind them. "If you're going, I'm going. That's not up for debate."

Nico glanced at her, ready to argue, but Emma spoke before he could. "Same here. Torchbearers stick together."

"Like when they bottled Thing in a glass prison for hundreds of years?" Logan said sarcastically, but he wilted under Emma's stony glare. "Fine. Sure. We all go." He grimaced at the murky flood below Tyler's feet. "I'm certainly not staying here by myself."

Nico was touched, but in this instance, his friends were wrong. He had to make them understand.

"Guys, I'm going first, and I'm going alone." He held up a hand before anyone could disagree. "We don't know what this water is, or whether the Darkdeep still works at all. We don't know if this way even leads out to the pond. There's no point in five people getting tangled up underwater." *Or everyone getting sucked into whatever horror might be waiting down there.* But he didn't say the last part out loud.

"Why should you take the risk?" Opal said immediately. "I'm a great swimmer. I can do it."

"You're a better swimmer than all of us, but I need you ready to launch a rescue mission. In case I pop out of the pond to a giant figment barbecue on the field, and they make me its main course." He tried to smile, but knew it was forced. "If I'm not back in five minutes, don't come after me. Break through the wall somehow and try your luck against Thing."

Nico could feel the others hesitating, though Logan seemed relieved and was trying to hide it. The water had stilled to a glossy mirror that stretched wall to wall across the basement.

"Let me do this," Nico said softly. "It's my turn to lead."

Opal's face wobbled, but she nodded. "Okay, Nico. Show us the way." Her next words spilled out in a rush. "But I'll be right behind you if you don't come back fast so you'd better hurry and get the job done."

Nico snapped a nod. He felt Tyler squeeze his arm, even as Emma crushed him in a hug from behind. Logan tapped a fist on his shoulder. Nico shrugged out of his jacket, and, after a moment's reflection, took off his jeans as well to avoid any extra drag. His ears burned as both Emma and Opal whirled to face the wall. The room's chill hit him like a physical blow.

No point drawing this out.

Taking three deep breaths, and holding the last one, Nico dove into the black pool.

The icy water nearly paralyzed him. Nico immediately coughed out all the air in his lungs, struggling to see through the lightless flood. He swam downward, aiming for where he thought the hole in the floor should be. Where the Darkdeep had been contained before it overflowed.

His limbs began to lighten. The cold faded from his bones. Was he going numb? Succumbing to hypothermia? Nico kicked harder, stretching down into the darkness.

Colors flashed in his mind. Sparks of violet and red, mixed with yellow streaks. He knew this wasn't normal water. His fingers brushed the floorboards, and he swept his hands in a circle. Caught the lip of the well. Lungs burning, he pulled himself into its mouth.

The colors intensified. Odd tones echoed around him.

Braver than I thought, a voice said, sounding close and far away at the same time. *But you shouldn't fully enter the Darkdeep right now. Things are getting . . . electric. Plus, my figment army has found something new to divert them that might interest you. The citizens of Timbers are in for quite a night.*

Ignoring the voice, Nico swam through the hole in the floor. Was he underneath the houseboat? Inside the Darkdeep's limitless void? Where did this world end and the other begin?

He was out of air. Light filled Nico's eyes. He gasped and drank in salt water, his mind reeling in panic.

Nico began to sink, screaming soundlessly in the depths.

No.

He was being pulled . . .

Some force gripped Nico around the waist. It was cold and powerful, and filled with menace. He tried to squirm away, but was dragged farther down, his oxygen gone, his strength slipping. The acrid taste of sulfur enveloped him.

Nico was sucked closer to a freezing . . . *presence* below. His head spun. The was different from when he'd entered the Darkdeep's void with Opal. This was stronger. Older. His body thrummed at its withering touch. Gathering the last of his strength, Nico kicked and slithered, fighting to break free.

The ruthless drag released him.

He floated up, without the will to resist.

Nico felt a blast of heat.

His brain blanked and consciousness slipped away.

Nico awoke on the edge of the pond.

He rolled and puked a gallon of dirty water onto the grass, hacking and spitting. His teeth chattered uncontrollably, Still Cove's frigid air prickling his skin. *I need to get my jeans back on.* But he was alive. He'd exited the well into the pond, like so many times before. But what had he encountered down there in the black? What had pulled at him?

Not now. Help your friends.

The rain had stopped. Full dark settled in. Nico stumbled to his feet and glanced around.

Nothing. No figments anywhere.

How long had he been out? He thought of Opal diving into that dark pool behind him and nearly got sick again.

Nico spotted the houseboat's lights and sprinted for the entry stones. He crossed and snuck up to the front door, but it hung open, with no noise carrying from within. The houseboat seemed empty. Steeling his nerve, Nico bombed through the door and foyer, charging into the showroom, ready to knock Thing's jar from its perch and smash it to pieces.

But he stopped short, staring at a stained circle of wood on an empty pedestal.

Thing was gone. The figments were all gone, too.

No time to think about it. Nico ran to the hidden door, but found it blocked by a massive bureau the figments had maneuvered into place. Using all his strength, Nico tried to shove it aside, but the hulking piece of furniture refused to budge. He pounded on the wall panel.

"Opal! Tyler! Can you guys hear me?"

"Yes!" came Logan's muffled reply. "Nico, hurry! The water. It's . . . it's glowing!"

Nico spun around, spotted an old spear in the weapons coffin. He ran over and snatched the weapon, then bolted back to the door. "Logan, the panel is blocked by a huge dresser. I can't move it by myself. I'm gonna try to lever it out of the way, but I'll need help. When I count to three, push from your side, okay?"

Logan shouted an assent. Nico wedged the butt of the spear behind the dresser.

"One . . . Two . . . *Three*."

Nico put a foot against the wall and pulled hard, straining with every muscle. He heard a grunt from the other side of the door. For a few painful seconds, nothing happened, but then the bureau slid backward an inch. The panel opened a crack, and Logan's eyes appeared.

"It's working!" Nico said. "Keep it up!"

"Hurry, Nico! The water's rising again!"

Another heave. Another inch gained. Nico took a deep breath, then put both feet up against the wall and yanked with everything he had. The dresser tipped over and crashed to the floor. Nico dropped onto his back with a thud, the air exploding from his chest.

Emma slithered through the opening with something clutched in her hands. "You okay? Um, here are your pants."

"Wonderful," Nico wheezed, face scarlet as he staggered to his feet and yanked his jeans on. "Never better. Help me push."

Working together, Nico and Emma shoved the toppled bureau back another foot. Nico sagged, wiping his brow, then came face-to-face with Tyler as his friend nearly trampled him exiting the stairwell.

"It's almost to the top!" Tyler shouted, his eyes rolling like a spooked horse. "The Darkdeep's coming for us!"

Opal squeezed out next, followed by Logan, who sucked in his chest and forced his body through the gap. He quickly shut the panel behind him. "I hope this is a watertight seal," he panted, eyes skeptical.

"You had one more minute," Opal said, smiling a little too wildly as she handed Nico his jacket and sneakers. "Then we were going in, too."

Nico slumped onto the bench and put his hands on his knees. "Easy peasy," he mumbled. Then he wriggled his shoes on and wrapped the warm jacket over his freezing skin.

Logan's eyes darted around the empty showroom. "Where'd all the figments go?"

Nico's head shot back up. "Thing said they found something else to target that might interest me. Anyone have a guess?"

Emma went white as a ghost. "I do."

They all glanced at her. She had both hands in her hair. "Like I said earlier, it's a *bad* night for a figment breakout."

"What do you mean?" Tyler asked. "When's a good night?"

"You don't understand," Emma squeaked. "When I was with the crew earlier, Bridger was discussing his big new plan. They're gonna shoot a reenactment scene down on the beach, to simulate the Beast attacking shore or something."

"Oh no." Opal covered her mouth. "They'll be filming outside with all those figments on the loose."

"It gets worse." Emma swallowed. "Bridger said he'd already told the mayor and some other locals, so by now the whole town knows. Lots of people will probably hike down to watch the production. I think Colton wants a crowd. He's been playing up that it's Halloween night, and anything could happen."

Nico stared at Emma in horror. "Where are they planning to shoot?"

Emma squeezed her eyes shut. "Just off Razor Point."

Logan sucked in a ragged breath. "That's less than a mile from here. Everyone will be right by the water. In the dark."

Nico nodded, barely able to speak the words.

"They'll be sitting ducks."

26

OPAL

Opal peered from the top of the bluff.

"There!" Her finger shot out. "Lights on the beach. That must be where they're filming."

Emma shivered, the electric lantern bouncing in her hands. "We have to stop this somehow."

Opal nodded, gathering herself for another sprint. They'd run all the way through the tunnel under Still Cove. Then, hearts pounding from fear and exhaustion, they'd hurried up the narrow trail and jogged to Razor Point, skirting Fort Bulloch to its right. Below them, a wide, hard-packed beach ran from the lighthouse to another set of jutting sea cliffs a mile short of Timbers itself.

There were only two trails leading down to this section of beach—one where they stood, and another at the far end closer to town. Opal spotted movement on the sand below. A small crowd stood at the edge of the floodlights, murmuring like a herd of cattle.

Nico swore under his breath. "Half the town must be here. Is no one trick-or-treating?"

Logan slapped a hand to his forehead. "Oh, jeez. I think I see my dad. I wonder if the sheriff's here, too? I'm not looking to get arrested tonight."

"I was hoping Bridger might cancel this and chase the Beast instead," Nico muttered glumly. "Our luck stays bad."

Opal saw Bridger step into the glaring lights—arms flailing as he barked instructions at his crew—but she was too far away to hear what he was saying. "Come on. Colton looks worked up. Who knows what he'll do now that he thinks he's seen a real sea monster."

"He did, though," Tyler said. "That's the crazy part."

Opal led the others down the trail. They reached the back of the crowd and began worming through it. She saw lots of familiar faces—Mayor Hayt, Megan Cook, her mom, and even Mrs. Johnson, the ancient town librarian. Carson and Parker were hovering near a camera tripod, barely resisting the urge to mess with it.

Plus a *ton* of teenagers. Evan Martinez was standing with a girl in a Wonder Woman costume, who whispered something in his ear and giggled. *Ugh.* Then Logan spotted Sheriff Ritchie and steered the group in the opposite direction.

The assembled throng watched the film crew set up with varying degrees of enthusiasm. Some seemed enamored by the lights and undeniable feeling of excitement. Others frowned at the van parked on a protected beach, where it wasn't supposed to be. Bridger was racing around, framing his shots and ignoring all scrutiny. For better or worse, this was a Halloween night that no one in Timbers would ever forget.

"Make way, please!" Emma called out. "Film team grip, coming through!"

A reluctant gap appeared, and the gang shimmied to the front. They stepped beyond a pair of orange traffic cones and approached the cameras.

Jake's eyebrows rose. "You're back."

"No thanks to you," Emma snapped. "We paddled all the way here. Turns out that island isn't very secret—some lame summer camp uses the other side for archery practice. I told you Still Cove was boring."

Jake shrugged, then nodded to where Bridger was berating Derek about the placement of a boom mike. "I wouldn't bug him if I were you. Ever since . . . *whatever* it was got away from us, it's like he's hooked up to a car battery." Jake shivered, no doubt remembering the line of wake they'd chased into Skagit Sound. "We clipped a rock leaving the cove and that rowboat almost sank. Bridger was furious. When we got to the beach, he decided to shoot the reenactment anyway, or we wouldn't have anything for a finale. So now I'm stuck here working on Halloween."

Emma and Opal walked over to where Bridger was clipping a mike to his collar. He looked up at them and flinched, nearly losing his balance, with one arm stuck inside his shirt. His gaze narrowed on Emma.

"So glad you could join us, Elizabeth. I was wondering if you'd quit."

Emma stared, openmouthed. "You *ditched* me!"

"*Pshhh.*" Bridger flapped a dismissive hand. "I knew you'd figure something out." Then, eyes gleaming, he leaned forward and spoke in a low, urgent voice. "I nearly caught the monster on film. It was *tremendous*. Did you see it?"

"I saw a wave," Nico said, forced-casual as he sidled up next to Emma. "Those happen in the ocean. Or maybe an orca got lost in the cove?"

Bridger frowned deeply. "Nonsense. That must've been the Beast. It's . . . it's *real*." He said the last word to himself, as if he could hardly believe it. "We're going full steam ahead. I'm calling this production Beast-O-Ween! A thrilling reenactment of last week's eyewitness sighting. We have props and everything."

Opal noticed a length of molded purple plastic pushed against the van. Beside it was a second manufactured piece, with tentacles dangling from its top. Derek, having stripped down to a wetsuit, was strapping the first section to his body with a scowl.

"*That's* your Beast?" Logan scoffed.

"It'll look fine once we edit in post," Bridger snapped. "Now, off my set please. I've got magic to make." He stomped away, hollering for quiet.

Opal darted after him. "Colton, please! You have to cancel this shoot. It's not safe for people to—"

Bridger whirled like a top. "Cancel? What are you talking about?" He pinched his thumb and index finger together. "I'm *this* close to making history. A real, live, *actual* sea monster! After I shoot this scene as a precaution, I'm going to find the creature, and record footage that will change . . . *everything.* Nothing can stop me."

Opal stared. Bridger was nearly foaming at the mouth. She wondered if coming so close to seeing the real Beast had snapped something inside him. Backing away, he cupped his hands to his mouth and yelled, "Quiet on the beach!"

Nico tapped Opal's shoulder. "We tried. We just have to hope noth—"

A sound echoed, from somewhere far out at sea. A wet, sibilant hiss.

Opal felt a shiver roll through her body. "Oh no."

A rogue wave crashed onshore, its glittering foam surging underneath the lighting array. The film crew danced back in alarm.

"We're too late," Nico whispered.

Eyes appeared in the darkness. Hulking shapes.

Bridger squinted in confusion. "What's going on? I never said action. Why is Derek already in the water?" Then he saw Derek standing beside the van, scratching his head. Bridger turned back to the ocean, all color draining from his face.

Shadowy forms slowly crept from the surf. Opal felt blood rush to her head.

"*Guys.*" Logan's voice cracked. "I think it's time to get the heck out of here."

"Past time," Tyler agreed, edging away. He bumped into Emma, who'd frozen in place.

Opal couldn't stop staring into the darkness. The worst was about to happen, and there was nothing they could do to stop it.

Thing's figments had arrived.

It was like watching the end of the world.

The army stormed from the water, land-bound figments leaping off the backs of those that could swim.

Screams erupted all around as the beach exploded into pandemonium. In the floodlights' harsh glow, people shrieked and ran. Then the entire array toppled, its spotlights dropping haphazardly to cast lurid shadows. Figments darted everywhere, spreading panic as townspeople fled toward the bluffs.

Opal felt close to hysteria. *They're everywhere! We'll never cover this up!*

Slash appeared, still riding the enormous insect-troll. Cackling wildly, the insufferable gremlin started chasing Old Lady Johnson across the dunes. Jacqueline, Derek, and Jake took off down the beach, abandoning the cameras and everything else.

"Where's Bridger?" Opal shouted.

Nico shook his head, then dove to the side as a giant spider skittered across the sand. A sky-blue Care Bear was perched on its back and firing trophy-shaped lasers from its chest. Tyler and Logan had frozen into statues, gaping at the chaos.

Not Emma. She raced for the *Freakshow* van like she'd been shot from a cannon.

Opal couldn't believe it. She'd never seen Emma run from anything, but her friend yanked open the rear door and launched herself inside, slamming it shut behind her.

Tyler shook himself. "Emma! *Wait!* What are you doing?" He sprinted to the vehicle and pounded on the back. It opened a crack. Tyler yelled something, then his eyes popped. He clambered inside.

Tyler shut the door. They were gone.

Emma and Tyler had bailed.

Opal, Nico, and Logan exchanged disbelieving glances as figments yowled around them. The paths off the beach were clogged with panicked townspeople. Dangerous creatures stalked toward the bluffs.

Opal grabbed Nico's arm. "We have to do something!"

Before he could respond, Opal spotted movement in the van's front seat. Its wheels began to spin, tossing sand but going nowhere. Someone inside was punching the gas, yet the vehicle was stuck, its tires gouging deep trenches into the beach.

Opal took a step toward the van. *Is Emma trying to drive?*

A two-headed pegasus stomped out of the waves in front of her, shedding water as flames exploded from its jaws. Its savage glow illuminated the van's windshield. Opal spotted Colton Bridger hunched in the driver's seat, frantically working the gearshift.

He was abandoning the beach.

He was ditching his own crew.

A cry sounded behind her and Opal spun. Carson Brandt tripped and fell in the sand, curling into a ball as a snarling, red-eyed sphinx loomed over him. The figment reached down with claws extended, fanged jaws spreading wide.

Logan shoulder-slammed into the creature, knocking it sideways. He hauled Carson up, and they both backed away as the enraged figment struggled to regain its balance. Smoke poured from the sphinx's nostrils as it flapped its wings, preparing to attack.

A stone rocketed into the side of its head. The sphinx snorted angrily, but took another direct hit to the temple.

Seconds later a third missile struck its broad nose. The figment howled in pain and pranced backward, then whirled and slunk away.

Opal shot a glance to her left. Hands shaking, Nico fumbled to find another rock on the beach.

"What was *that*?!" Carson wailed. He shot a wild-eyed look at Logan, then took off before anyone could speak.

Logan wheeled to face Opal, a vein pumping in his neck. "We have to stop this soon, or it could turn into a bloodbath!"

Fear made Opal's voice bitter. "How? *We* didn't create these figments, Thing did."

Logan shrugged helplessly.

A shadow moved in the corner of Opal's vision, but when she turned to look, it slipped away. Then she spotted a knot of scaly, eel-like creatures skittering across the sand. Opal removed her dagger from her jacket but knew it wouldn't do any good.

"Stick close together," Nico said, licking his lips as he removed his own blade. "We'll take them down one at a time if we have to."

Logan slammed a fist to his thigh. "The daggers *don't work*, Nico! We have no way to fight back!"

Nico sighed in despair. "What else can we do?"

Slash reappeared, chasing the *Freakshow* crew back up the beach. He was laughing so hard he nearly fell from the insect-troll's shoulders.

The wheels on the van squealed once again. Opal smelled burning rubber. She spotted Bridger twisting around in the front seat, trying to escape in reverse. Opal raced over and pounded on the window. "Get out and help!"

Shoulders hunched, Bridger shook his head furiously. Then his eyes widened as he gaped over her shoulder.

Opal whirled.

The sphinx was right behind her.

27

NICO

Nico charged, waving his arms at the sphinx.

Opal cringed back against the van and swung her dagger wildly. The blade passed straight through the creature's body without leaving a mark. The figment hissed and sprang away, leaving deep gouges in the sand.

Why won't the daggers work?!

"Get away from her!" Nico shouted, raising his own blade in what felt like a useless gesture. But then a high-pitched voice boomed over the chaos, freezing everything in place.

"HEY THERE! Great show, everyone!"

The sphinx paused, glaring up at something. Nico glanced at the van and gasped.

Emma was standing on its roof, a microphone in one hand and a sweatshirt-wrapped bundle tucked under her other arm. The mike's wire ran to the rear door, which was open again. Tyler's face poked out as he fumbled with a ball of cables.

"What is she doing?" Logan breathed, standing at Nico's side. Nico just shook his head.

"HEY!" Emma boomed again, as more speakers amplified her voice. Tyler was now hunched over a soundboard inside the van, adjusting dials and muttering nervously.

Figments stared in confusion. The panicked crowd cowered in shocked silence as a weird stasis swept over both groups.

"Everyone is doing *fantastic*!" Emma said cheerfully, though Nico heard a quaver in her voice. "You're really nailing this scene. But you have to listen for your next instructions."

Clamping the mike with her chin, Emma uncovered the bundle in her arms and held up a glowing jar. "Look what *I* have," she announced in a singsong voice. In a flash, Nico realized she was now talking to the figments. "Do you think I should drop it?"

Nico stared.

Emma had Thing? How?!

She raised the jar overhead. It was still partially obscured, but the figments had locked in on the gleaming glass. The sphinx cocked its head, released a hair-raising whine. Nico could hear townspeople babbling in terrified confusion farther up the beach. Ignoring them, the mass of figments began creeping back toward the van.

Nico saw Opal slip to the rear door and jump inside beside Tyler. In the front, Bridger's hand darted out and locked the doors, then he slid way down in the driver's seat, attempting to hide.

Emma made as if to drop the jar. The figments froze. Did they care about Thing? Did they know who'd created them?

"Residents of Timbers, tonight's shoot is officially over!" Emma spoke into the mike awkwardly, since it was still wedged on her shoulder. "Thanks for taking part in this exclusive *Freakshow* re-creation. Colton Bridger wanted to make sure you were authentically scared during filming, for, um . . . authenticity. Sorry for any confusion!"

The figments began to fidget, watching the glowing jar as they moved closer. Nico spun to check the exit trails. Most townspeople had taken advantage of Emma's distraction to hightail it up the bluffs. Some were frowning darkly, casting angry looks back at the van.

Sweat appeared at Emma's temples as the circle of figments tightened around her. "Timbers, we can't wait to show you this amazing footage later!" she persisted gamely. "For now, please head on home. As fast as you can. And, um, maybe forget trick-or-treating and lock all your doors. Enjoy the rest of your evening!"

Nico laughed nervously. Would anyone believe Emma? People had been hurt. They'd come face-to-face with a rampaging monster horde. But convinced or not, within moments no one was left on the beach—not even the *Freakshow* crew—except the five Torchbearers, Bridger, and the van.

And a seething mass of extremely riled-up nightmare creatures.

"Guys?" Tyler whispered from the back door. "I think maybe you should get inside here now."

Nico nodded. He and Logan began edging toward the vehicle. The figment mob continued to stare hungrily up at Emma. Slash glared from atop his terrible steed, his good mood apparently vaporized. Nico lost his nerve and ran the last few steps, jumping into the van. Logan piled in nearly on top of him and Tyler slammed the door.

Nico watched as Emma let go of the mike, swung the jar in a tight circle like a hammer throw, and released it with both hands. She dropped down through the sunroof as the jar flew out into the night, crashing somewhere on the dark beach. "Colton, time to go!" she yelled.

"I'm *trying* to go!" Bridger shouted through the sliding window to the front. "We're stuck!"

Roars outside. The van began to shake as creatures rocked its sides.

"This is really, finally it," Tyler moaned. "We're completely doomed, no take-backs."

But the rattling stopped. Nico waited, breathing hard.

"Maybe they're checking on Thing," Opal whispered. "Was it really inside?"

"No," Emma croaked, sounding near the end of her nerve. "That was glowing algae. I collected some of the blue-green stuff in soda bottles this morning, and stowed it here. I thought it might make a cool effect." She unleashed a wild giggle. "Guess it did, huh? The color was close enough to work."

As Nico's eyes adjusted, he spotted more gleaming bottles in a corner of the van.

"Genius." Opal squeezed Emma's arm. "Do you know how to get vans unstuck from sand?"

"Sorry." Emma sounded genuinely contrite. "Didn't anticipate that part."

Nico broke into a shaky laugh. "Well, points for effort."

"*Hey!*" Bridger hissed from the front seat. "I think . . . the *monsters* . . . are . . . are . . . they're leaving."

"Really?" Tyler scrambled to the sliding window and peered through the windshield. "Are they taking the jar with them?"

"No," Bridger whispered. "They're just . . . going." His hushed tone became elated. "They're marching up the trails off the beach. All of them!"

Emma stepped onto a crate and poked her head out the sunroof.

"Emma!" Opal grabbed her pant leg and tugged, trying to get her back down.

"They *are* leaving," Emma reported, sounding confused. "I hope everyone already cleared off the bluffs. If not, they'll have company soon."

"I wonder why they took off?" Tyler slid back to rejoin the

others. "And where *is* Thing, if not with its army? Do you think it went—" He glanced at the front of the van, where Bridger's head was slowly emerging from hiding, and lowered his voice. "You think Thing went to that *other* place we found?"

Nico frowned. The Rift? He felt a twinge of anxiety. *But where else could Thing be?*

"Worry about that later." Logan moved toward the rear doors. "Let's get out of here. This van's dug in. It's not going anywhere."

"Wait," Emma whispered, still peeking out the sunroof.

Bridger suddenly whimpered. "What is *that*?"

"What's what?" Nico joined Emma on the crate and stuck his head through next to hers. She was staring at the surf. For a moment, he couldn't tell what she was looking at.

Then he saw.

Two oil-black circles, glimmering in the moonlight.

Eyes.

The Beast.

Nico didn't realize he'd said it out loud until he heard Tyler gasp.

"Are you sure?" Opal asked from below.

Emma and Nico both dropped back inside. They heard Bridger's panicked breathing from the front.

"Torches!" Logan said. "We have to make some, remember?" He yanked off his Beast hoodie. "We can tear this into strips. There's driftwood outside. We just need an accelerant."

He aimed a glare at the driver's seat. "Bridger! Do you have a spare fuel canister in here? Acetone? Anything flammable at all? Or we could siphon the gas tank."

"You know how to siphon a gas tank?" Tyler hissed.

Logan shook his head. "I was hoping you did."

There was no answer from the front. Bridger had frozen behind the wheel, like a deer caught driving on the beach.

"Maybe we can just sneak away?" Opal whispered. "Use the van as cover."

Nico nodded. "Try the back."

Emma slowly opened the door. Opal slipped to the sand. Nico eased down beside her, followed by Logan.

"Tyler," Emma whispered. "Come on, Ty!"

Nico turned. Tyler wasn't moving. He sat perfectly still in the corner by the glowing bottles. Their hazy aqua light cast an eerie radiance on his face.

"Ty." Emma scurried over and put a hand on his arm. "You okay?"

"It's coming for me!" Bridger shrieked. Before anyone could react, he fumbled for the door handle and jumped out of the van.

A growl sounded that fluttered Nico's stomach. He snuck to the corner of the vehicle and peeked around its bumper.

The Beast loomed a dozen yards away, illuminated by the van's headlights. The monster was staring at a quivering Colton Bridger, who stood frozen in front of it. The Beast blinked its black eyes, then leaned forward—jaws dripping, massive teeth glistening. The monster roared.

Bridger wet himself.

Someone jostled Nico from behind. "What the—"

Tyler raced past him, a glowing bottle in his hands. He ripped the sweatshirt from Logan as he rounded the van, skidding to a stop directly in front of Bridger. Legs shaking, Tyler reached down and snatched a piece of driftwood off the beach.

The Beast stared at him.

"Tyler! What are you—" Nico began, but before he could finish, Tyler had wrapped the hoodie around the branch and was dumping the soda bottle onto it. Oily, bioluminescent algae oozed over the fabric.

The Beast dug a foot into the sand, like an enraged bull preparing to charge. Nico could hear its tail whipping.

Incredibly, Tyler took a step *toward* the sea monster.

Nico's jaw dropped.

"*TYLER!*" Emma lunged after him, but Nico and Logan caught her by the shoulders.

Opal shifted indecisively, her mouth working but no sound coming out.

"Let me go!" Emma screeched.

"He's terrified of the Beast, but went out there anyway," Nico whispered urgently. "We have to trust him!"

"Stay back!" Tyler shouted, his eyes never leaving the creature before him. His voice had a ring of authority.

Emma stopped struggling, began chewing on her fist.

"Hey," Tyler said to the Beast. "I'm *really* afraid of you, FYI." Arm quivering, he held up the glowing green hoodie stick, but not as a weapon. More like he wanted the Beast to see it. "My name is Tyler. I'm a Torchbearer, okay?"

The Beast yowled, but didn't charge. Instead, it waited, eyes following the glowing brand. Bridger stood rigidly behind Tyler, not moving a muscle.

"Should we attack?" Logan whispered. "Tyler has it distracted. Maybe we could—"

"No." Emma blinked, licking her lips. "You were right, Nico. He's figured something out."

Glowing algae dripped from the weird blue-green torch Tyler had made. Nico thought his friend looked taller somehow. Steadier than he'd ever seen him.

The Beast dipped its head level with Tyler's. Sniffed once, then snorted. In the soft glow of the bioluminescence, they looked each other in the eye.

Then the Beast turned and vanished back into the sea.

28

OPAL

Opal took her first full breath in minutes.

She rushed to Tyler, who'd collapsed as soon as the Beast retreated. "Dude, you're a hero!"

They surrounded him on the sand. Bridger sat down heavily a few yards away and covered his face.

Tyler's whole body was shaking. "It worked," he said quietly, almost to himself.

"Yeah it did!" Logan pulled Tyler up and wrapped him in a bear hug. Then he stepped back, eyeing the smaller boy in astonishment. "What, um, did you . . . do, though?"

"The torch," Tyler said simply. They all looked at it lying next to him, emitting an aquamarine glow. "Thanks, algae."

"Man, the Beast is scared of everything, huh?" Logan joked.

"It wasn't scared," Opal said, remembering how Tyler and

the Beast had met eyes. *Something happened there.* "Tyler, you used algae, not fire. Why?"

"I've been researching," Tyler said, as Bridger slowly staggered to his feet. "Know your enemy, and all that." He ran a hand over his scalp. "After the cemetery, while you guys were checking into the name Charles Dixon, I doubled-down on learning everything I could about the Beast. To be ready."

"What are you talking about?" Bridger's voice was tinged with hysteria. He stared at Tyler in horror. "What's going on here? How did you *know* that monster?"

Opal glanced at Nico, who shook his head firmly. He had no interest in bringing Colton Bridger into their confidences, and neither did she.

Emma caught the exchange. "It's been quite a night, Colton." She stepped forward and took his arm. "Let's get this van unstuck so you can go home, huh?"

Bridger gaped at her, but he allowed himself to be led away. He seemed to be having trouble thinking clearly. Logan snagged his other arm and started explaining how to position boards behind the tires.

Opal wondered where Bridger's crew had gone. *What's happening in town right now?*

Her breath quickened as reality crashed in. There was no way to cover up what had just happened. This night changed everything. *The worst Halloween ever. And it's not over yet.*

"So what's the algae thing?" Nico asked in a lowered voice, so that only he, Opal, and Tyler could hear.

"I searched the houseboat's library for any info about the Beast," Tyler explained, warming to the topic. "If all the rumors are true, that means Torchbearers and the Beast have occupied Still Cove at the same time for decades, right? And neither side killed the other. So I started to wonder if maybe they had some kind of truce."

"You actually found something about the Beast?" Opal couldn't remember seeing anything in the books she'd read, but she hadn't spent nearly as much time with the collection as Tyler. "And you didn't tell us?!"

Tyler gave a guilty nod. "Sorry. There's been a lot going on lately."

Nico snorted. "That's an understatement."

Tyler avoided Opal's eye. "One of the books I took home had some interesting things in the last chapter. I meant to tell you guys, but so much crazy stuff started happening at once that it slipped my mind until now."

Opal frowned but motioned for Tyler to continue.

"The Torchbearers call the Beast a different name," he said. "The *Lotan*. It means the same as leviathan, like Thing calls it. Once I figured that out, I made progress. The book mentioned a signal that Torchbearers use to show the Lotan they mean no harm. The paragraph described it as 'the pale light of the sea.'" Tyler shrugged. "I took a shot."

"You could have told us *that* much," Nico scolded.

"I didn't figure it out until the answer was staring me in the face. I looked at those glowing bottles in the van, and suddenly it all came together. That algae emits a bioluminescent light, which is kinda watery and washed out." Tyler barked a laugh. "I'm *really* glad I guessed right."

"Me too," Opal said. "That gamble took serious guts."

"Something Thing said helped me." He looked over at Logan and Emma, who were trying to back the van out of its hole while Bridger stood there uselessly, staring at nothing. "It said the Beast wasn't a stray thought, like a figment, but instead it was a creature from the other world."

Opal and Nico both nodded.

Tyler looked out at the dark, rolling sea. "If the Beast is stuck here too, I figured the Torchbearers might monitor it like they do the Darkdeep. As part of their oath."

A realization struck Opal. "You guys, I haven't heard Thing in my head for a while. Could it be gone already?"

"Good riddance," Nico said. "That lime goo-ball locked us in a flooding basement."

"It can't be that easy." Tyler glanced at the van, which was finally easing out of the ruts.

"Do you think Thing recalled its figments?" Opal asked. "Maybe had a change of heart?"

"Maybe the Beast scared them off," Tyler said. "They scattered right before it appeared."

Opal peered up at the bluffs. "Where do you think they all went?" She closed her eyes, suddenly drained, then opened them to look at her friends. "Guys, how are we going to explain all this? Dozens of people saw a figment horde attack the beach. Most of them aren't going to buy what Emma was selling."

Tyler was still staring at the ocean. "When the last Torchbearer died, the Beast was all alone. That's sad."

"Until we showed up on the island." Opal breathed, connecting the dots. "Do you think it wondered about us? Or even thought we were intruders? That might be why it started coming out of the water more!"

"We waved *fire* at it in the cemetery," Nico said, cringing. "That couldn't have made a good impression."

Logan walked back over to join them, carrying another algae bottle. After they filled him in, he bounced the container in his hands. "Will people think it's weird if I carry one of these around 24/7?"

Opal and Tyler laughed, but Nico seemed preoccupied. Opal reached out and tugged his sleeve. "What is it?"

"We should go to the Darkdeep," he said. "I . . . I have an idea."

"Back to the island?" Tyler groaned. "We just *left* there. Plus, the houseboat might've sunk while we were gone."

Opal exhaled. "I'm not really looking to trudge through that creepy tunnel again tonight, Nico."

"Maybe the Beast will give us a ride," Logan quipped.

Tyler *tsk*-ed loudly. "It's a wild animal from another dimension. Not some pet."

"Could've fooled me." Logan glanced down at his phone. "Crap. My parents are lighting me up. I was supposed to help give out candy."

"Same." Emma waved her cell as she joined them. After a quick update on the conversation, she sighed. "What do we do with Captain Clueless over there? Bridger's basically shell-shocked right now, but he saw *a lot*." Her brow knitted, worry lines digging across her forehead. "He's going to be a problem, you guys."

Opal had been ignoring the buzzing in her pocket, except to send a single text to her parents.

At a Halloween party! Talk later, phone dying.

She knew she was going to be grounded for ignoring the frantic messages that came back in reply.

Or the world might end instead. Who knew at this point?

She looked at Nico. "If you say we need to visit the Darkdeep, I'll go with you." He'd followed her to the oil rig despite his doubts about Thing. It was time to return his trust.

A cold wind swept the beach. Clouds in the sky were shifting and flowing as if stirred by giant hands. Static electricity prickled her neck. *What a night.*

Tires screaming, the van finally lurched free of its trench. Rigidly avoiding eye contact, Bridger sped down the empty beach, leaving them stranded once again. Opal shook her head as the vehicle tore away. "There's literally nothing that creep can do anymore to surprise me."

Emma glared after the receding taillights. "Total coward. To think I used to work for him."

Out across the waves, purple lightning began hammering a distant point in the ocean. The electrical storm strobed for several seconds before stopping. Then it came again, with double the ferocity. Opal watched in mounting horror as the jagged bolts rained down. She could guess where they were striking.

Pale blue-green light leaked from the jar in Logan's hand. Nico turned to face the others, his jaw set. "I know things might be bad in Timbers right now, but we still have to stop Thing. This isn't over yet."

"What can we do, though?" Tyler asked. "We don't even know where Thing is."

"Yeah we do." Nico spoke with such certainty that Opal blinked. "Thing's at the Rift. That's been its goal all along. We have to stop it."

Nico looked back at Still Cove.

"And I think I know how to get there."

29

NICO

Nico stared at the flooded stairwell.

Black water sloshed to the top step, but was no longer rising. Or pouring into the showroom and swamping the houseboat, dragging it down to the bottom of the pond and destroying their clubhouse forever.

Why? What's stopping it? What started the overflow in the first place?

Nico knew he'd guessed right. This wasn't a normal flood. He was looking at the Darkdeep itself, which had slipped its cage and come prowling up toward the sky, only to stop short at the very last moment.

As if it waited for something.

"You want us to go into that?" Opal said quietly. "For real?"

Tyler was unable to repress a shiver. "I'm extremely not sure about this, Nico. It seems . . . not smart."

"It's *insane*," Logan huffed, standing beside Emma. The five of them had trekked back to the island from the beach, ignoring the increasingly frantic calls and texts from their parents. Based on the unanswered messages, things weren't going well in Timbers. Reports of monsters prowling the streets had everyone spooked, though many blamed tourist pranks, the *Freakshow* crew, and Halloween shenanigans.

Nico knew better. Figments were rampaging unchecked. It was a disaster. Their secret was out, and it was only a matter of time before someone called in the National Guard. Yet all that was secondary, Nico felt sure. The real danger was lurking out in the ocean. Thing had gone to tear the Rift open once and for all.

Which meant the Torchbearers had to stop it.

They had to reach the oil platform somehow, and Nico thought he knew the quickest way.

He turned to face the others, ignoring the empty pedestal where Thing's jar had always sat. "I swam through this to escape the basement earlier," he began, choosing his words with care. "It worked, but something happened as I sank to the bottom. I felt the Darkdeep pulling me. Trying to drag me in another direction. It's still connected to this houseboat, or the pond. Or the island. Whatever. The point is, if we give in to that pull, I think we can enter the void at the heart of the Darkdeep, like Opal and I did before." Nico took a deep breath. "And from *there*, I think we can reach the Rift."

"How?" Logan asked incredulously. "Are we supposed to swim the whole way?"

Nico shook his head. "Thing said the Darkdeep is a part of the Rift, like some kind of release valve. I think that's where the sulfur in the pond came from—the gas was expelled from the Rift. You guys remember how bad the oil rig reeked of rotten eggs? We've only encountered that smell in two places, and both were guarded by Torchbearers. They *have* to be connected."

Nico felt Opal inspecting him. "You think the Darkdeep can take us directly to the Rift. No boat. No ocean crossing. We jump in here and wind up there?"

"It took us over thirty minutes to reach the platform by speedboat." Logan glanced around like he couldn't believe what he was hearing. "Even if the Darkdeep does suck us out toward the Rift, we'll drown along the way!"

"No," Opal said suddenly. "The void is different. When Nico and I went into the Darkdeep together—and battled that . . . that Taker—we weren't holding our breath or anything. We entered an in-between space that was separate from the water. We didn't have to worry about oxygen." She shuddered. "That empty place is, like, *beyond* physical needs."

Nico nodded, but he sensed the anxiety level in the room skyrocketing. "I can go first. Alone. I'll take my phone wrapped in a plastic bag and text back when I arrive. If you guys don't receive anything . . ." He swallowed. "You'll know."

"Texts stopped working ten minutes ago." Emma held up her phone. "Service is down. Either those figments got to the tower or the system overloaded, but we can't send or receive messages right now. We wouldn't know what happened to you."

Nico grunted in frustration. "Then I'll do this by myself. You guys go back and deal with the figment army. You can save Timbers while I . . . I face Thing."

"No way." Opal shook her head so firmly that her braid whipped Tyler in the face. "No one is going anywhere alone." She took a deep breath. "I'll go too. Me and you together, like before. We made it work once. We can do it again."

"I'm in!" Emma piped up. Then she glanced around as if uncertain. "Is this when we say that? Because I'm definitely not letting you guys go alone. Plus, I never got to see this next level of the Darkdeep. No way I'm missing out a second time."

"Missing out?" Logan blinked at her. "Emma, sometimes you're a lunatic."

She smiled brightly. "Thank you!"

"*Fine.*" Tyler swung both fists down to his sides and growled through clenched teeth. "In. We'll all dive into that black toilet like a team of dummies."

Logan peered from face to face, a helpless terror growing in his eyes.

Nico spoke quickly. "Logan, there's something else we need. Can you handle it?"

Logan licked his lips. "Handle what?"

Nico put a hand on his shoulder. Felt the tension coiled there. Logan hadn't been a part of those first days of diving into the Darkdeep—when all the figments were amazing, and everything had still been fun. The idea of entering the pool now had him near full-blown panic.

"Whatever happens," Nico said, "we're going to need a ride off that oil rig when it's all over. It's gonna be rough out there, and I doubt we'll be able to use the Darkdeep to get away. Can you find a boat and meet us?"

"A boat." Some of the color returned to Logan's cheeks. "Yeah, sure. I can do that. My dad has three."

"Perfect." Nico stepped back. "Go snag one now and meet us out there as soon as you can."

"Got it." Logan took a step toward the door, then hesitated, half turning back. "Are you . . . you sure you don't—"

"Logan," Opal said, capturing his gaze. She smiled. "We're counting on you. You're our getaway driver. Hurry, okay?"

"Right." Logan spun and jogged for the exit. "I'll be there!" He swished through the curtain and was gone.

Emma bumped her shoulder into Nico's. "That was nice of you."

"Why can't I steal the boat?" Tyler grumbled, but he waved Nico off before his friend could reply. "Joke. Let's just get this over with." As one, they faced the dark water filling the bottom of the houseboat.

Opal cleared her throat. "No point drawing this out, right?"

Nico snapped a nod. "Time your dives five seconds apart. Swim straight for the well opening. You should feel a tug pretty quickly. Once you do, lean into the sensation. Let it have you, I guess. That should lead to the Darkdeep, and *that* should lead to the Rift. Okay?"

"Got it," Emma said, her voice wavering slightly. "See you guys on the other side."

"Should we—" Opal's face went red. "Should we take off any clothing? To swim, I mean!"

Nico's cheeks burned to match hers. "Let's skip that part this time." Tyler and Emma nodded emphatically.

"This is crazy," Tyler mumbled. "But *our* kind of crazy. Remember when we just played tag?"

Everyone laughed nervously before falling silent. Nico stepped to the edge of the metal riser. Stared at the black water.

I'm right about this. I know I am.

With a last deep breath, he shut out his nagging, terrifying doubts and dove headfirst into the inky flood.

Nico splashed to the surface, a purple glow surrounding him like a fresh bruise.

Catwalks crisscrossed the chamber above his head. The water churned and spun, carrying him around the room like a leaf in a tornado. The acrid stench of sulfur was everywhere, bombarding his nostrils and seeping into Nico's mouth.

He'd made it.

He was inside the Rift.

Nico tossed out a hand and managed to snag the top of the cylindrical barrier around the vortex. Hanging on for dear life, he pulled himself up and out of the spin cycle and sat heavily on the lip of the containment wall. Metal rungs beside him stretched up to the catwalks overhead. On the outside of the barricade, ocean water lapped gently against the welded metal plates.

Nico stood quickly. He wanted away from that terrible, raging whirlpool, and the creatures trapped inside it. With the seal compromised, what was keeping them back? And how long would it hold?

Balancing precariously atop the yard-wide barrier, he scanned the drilling room for figments. Strange sounds echoed from deep within the purple cyclone. Bits of iron still swirled on its surface.

Just like Thing wanted. We were such fools.

Nico tensed as his mission came screaming back. Thing was here somewhere. But where were his friends?

A second later, Opal's head broke the surface and did a circuit of the giant tank. Nico dropped onto his stomach and held out a hand. "Opal, grab hold!"

She twisted around just in time to see him and reached out. Nico caught Opal's arm firmly and haul-dragged her out of the water. She slumped down next to him, wide-eyed and puffing hard, purplish water dripping down her cheeks.

"It worked!" Opal was shivering from more than just cold. "The Darkdeep brought us straight here! All I had to do was think about it. But did you feel those creatures in there, Nico? They're super close to breaking through, I could sense it. We're almost out of time!"

Before Nico could answer, Emma's blond head appeared, followed seconds later by Tyler's—he clearly hadn't waited before jumping in after her. Nico and Opal fished them both out, and soon they were all straddling the rim of the thick metal wall.

Tyler wheezed like he'd just run a marathon. "I'm . . . not . . . doing . . . that . . . *ever* . . . again."

Emma leaned against his shoulder. "I swear something tried to bite me at the end. Like, a mini-Beast."

"Let's never talk about it," Tyler insisted, slashing a hand through the air in front of him. "Like, not ever." Then he pressed his palms together and glanced at the sky, visible through the giant hole where the ceiling used to be. "Please, Logan Nantes, show up with a boat."

You shouldn't have come here. There's nothing you can do. Leave now!

Nico grabbed the lowest rung and started hauling himself up the ladder. "Thing! Come on!"

"And do *what*, though?" Opal hissed, though she was right behind him. "We still don't know!"

Nico glanced down at her. "Find Thing, and *make* it tell us how to fix this mess. That's all I've got."

"Works for me." Emma pushed Tyler before her and bought up the rear. They reached the catwalk level. Nico crouched warily, peering down the grated walkways. He spotted Thing's jar perched on a railing of the main catwalk, the one spanning the room's center and passing directly over the Rift, which seethed below like a hurricane.

Nico cupped his hands to his lips. "Thing!"

The creature whirled in its glass prison, a deep frown creasing its tiny face.

Enough. You're too late. The seal has failed completely. Nothing can fix it now.

Thing spun again. Nico felt words in a language he couldn't fathom arrow through his brain.

Slash and the two other gremlins ran onto the other side of the central catwalk. While his chittering companions halted halfway, Slash stalked past Thing toward the Torchbearers, scraping his claws along the railing. A terrible screech filled the chamber.

"*Yum, yum.*" Slash drooled onto the catwalk. "*Dinner party.*"

Opal seized Nico by the arm. "They're opening Thing's jar!"

Nico flinched. It was true. As Slash stomped closer, the other gremlins had snatched the jar off the railing and were unscrewing its lid.

In a flash, Nico understood. They intended to dump Thing into the Rift.

Thing would escape. All would be lost.

Nico's body thrummed with anger. His Torchbearer dagger was useless against these figments. He didn't know what to do. Punching his side in frustration, he felt a lump in his pocket. Confused, he dug into his jeans, his fingers closing around a smooth, egg-sized stone he must've picked up off the beach. Without a better plan, he reached back and fired the rock at Thing's jar.

The stone clanged against the glass, creating a hairline crack. Thing wobbled in the oily liquid, holding its head, its eyes glazing momentarily.

A ripple of light ran through all three gremlins, though none of them seemed to notice.

"What the . . . ," Tyler mumbled, squinting at their sneering adversaries. "Did you guys see—"

Emma reacted first. She snapped both arms to her sides, palms up, fingers open and flexing. Two daggers slid out of her shirtsleeves and into her waiting hands. Emma raised them and strode forward, like some kind of tiny blond Terminator, stopping a few yards short of Slash. She flicked her wrists. The daggers flew past Slash on either side and pierced the two gremlins holding Thing's jar.

The knives traveled straight through their squat bodies and clanged down to the catwalk. Both gremlins grunted and disappeared. Thing's jar crashed to the metal grating, the lid wobbling off and some of the fluid sluicing out.

"Whoa," Opal whispered, staring at Emma.

Tyler whistled. "*Dang.* Remind me never to make you mad."

Nico felt a jolt of adrenaline. "Emma, what'd you do?! Your daggers worked!"

"Hurry!" Emma urged, pointing at Thing, who was holding its head in tiny lime-green hands. "Thing created these figments and must have some kind of special hold over them. But when you rattled its cage, the gremlins flickered. I think Thing lost control!"

Slash shot a glance over his shoulder at Thing, then faced Emma squarely, baring his teeth.

"*Torchbearer scum.*"

Opal darted forward with her own dagger. "Not this time, Slash."

Slash roared, lunging at Opal's throat. She dropped to the catwalk and swept the blade up. It passed cleanly through the gremlin's midsection.

Slash's eyes popped as he landed short. Then he vanished with a yowl.

Opal whooped in victory. Emma pulled her into a hug. Nico and Tyler raced down the walkway, hands up for high fives, but then Nico noticed movement beyond them.

Thing.

The creature was out of the jar, dragging itself toward the edge of the catwalk.

Nico sped down the walkway and scooped Thing up off the grating. Its skin was soft and oozy, and stank of chemicals, but Nico didn't let go. Ignoring Thing's struggles, he dropped the furious alien back into the viscous fluid. Emma tossed him the lid, and Nico resealed the jar.

Noooooo! Release me!

"Not so fast." Nico tapped the glass, drawing an enraged telepathic hiss. "We like our world, and you're going to tell us how to keep it safe. Or else, in you stay."

Opal pumped a fist, while Emma clapped her hands in relief. Tyler danced in place.

Thing pounded on the wall of its prison with a tiny fist.

You're just like the others. Users and tyrants. I want to go home!

The creature sagged. Impossibly, the little green blob began to weep.

Nico felt a hand on his wrist. Opal stepped close and took

the jar from him. She set it down on the catwalk and knelt before it. "Please, Thing. Just tell us how to fix the Rift. Then we can . . . we can make some kind of deal."

Thing sobbed. It wiped its eyes, even though it was suspended in liquid.

The Rift is doomed. And so am I. I'll be stuck here until I dissolve into a murky cloud.

Nico watched Thing wilt. He felt horrible. Opal glanced at him, eyes shining, and Nico understood. He nodded.

Emma tapped his shoulder and gave a thumbs-up. Tyler nodded as well.

Opal rose and lifted the jar. Thing glared at her, startled. *What are you doing?*

She spun the lid and removed it. "You've done a terrible thing, Thing. But we don't believe in cages."

Sighing, Opal tipped the jar and poured its contents into the vortex below. Thing dropped with an audible gasp, striking the purple water with a tiny splash. Thing's head bobbed up once, a smile breaking out on its pinched features, then the little green creature sank into the raging torrent and was gone.

Opal dropped the jar to the catwalk with a resigned grunt. "Now what?"

A voice boomed inside Nico's head, stronger than ever before.

Torchbearers. You shock me. You've shown true mercy. Perhaps you're not all evil.

Nico met Opal's eye. They shared a smile. If nothing else, they'd gotten this part right.

The voice began to dwindle, but Nico still heard Thing's next words clearly. *The seal fails, but the Rift will not fully open until I pass through it. Adding too much iron upset the physical equilibrium, but that was only part of what held the way closed. Restore balance and perhaps you can seal the Rift again. Good luck.*

Nico felt Thing's presence fade, falter, disappear. It was gone.

At the same moment, the center of the Rift exploded.

Nico stared down in horror as stretched faces reappeared.

Except this time, the Takers began climbing out of the water.

30
OPAL

Opal kicked over the empty jar.

Thing was gone, back to its own world.

And now that world was coming for them.

Takers swarmed out of the Rift, climbing up the rusty metal ladders. Opal spun to her friends. They had their daggers out, but no one moved.

She and Nico had battled a Taker before. It had required both of them working together to defeat the ghoulish monster. Opal frantically tried to remember what they'd done—how they'd severed its unnatural tie to the Darkdeep, banishing the invader from this plane of existence.

But we're not inside the Darkdeep now. This is happening right here.

Takers boiled up from the depths. Opal glanced at the jar, now cracked and toppled on its side. How had Thing kept the Rift closed?

Directly below her, the gash between dimensions frothed and convulsed. How could they stop something so powerful? *Where's Logan?* Had he stolen his dad's boat yet? Maybe they could escape back to town and hide. Stay safe.

Right.

Safe.

Their home was already being overrun by figments, and the leering nightmares creeping out of the vortex wouldn't stay on this platform. *They'll find Timbers, and who knows what will happen.* These were creatures from another world.

And Thing had warned of other horrors that might pass through the Rift.

Opal teetered on the brink of panic. "How do we close this?! Tell us, Thing!"

"Thing's gone!" Tyler yelled, eyes wild. "We dumped our only chance into the Rift!"

"It was the right thing to do!" Nico shot back. "We can fix this ourselves. Thing said so."

"Guys!" Emma had retrieved her daggers and was eyeing the advancing Taker mob. "Arguing won't help. Thing told us to restore the balance!" The ghastly creatures had nearly reached the catwalk level. One noticed them and mewled horribly.

"And how do we do that?!" Tyler shouted. "We don't even know what to balance!"

The Takers filled the outer walkways and began circling to the ends of the central span. The Rift sizzled and sparked below. Tyler and Emma moved back-to-back with Opal and Nico, forming a tight square.

Nico lifted his dagger. "These worked for Opal and me against a Taker in the void. Trust the Torchbearers."

Opal cringed. *But we imagined those weapons into existence. This isn't the same.*

Emma's voice shook as she raised both blades. "Okay. So . . . where do we stab?"

"There was a tether," Opal said quickly. She could feel Tyler's shoulders quaking against hers. "Some kind of cord snaking out of the Taker's back. We severed it."

"I don't see anything!" Emma shouted. "What's it supposed to connect with?"

"No idea," Opal admitted. "Maybe their world?"

Nico winced. "It linked to the Darkdeep. But these Takers are completely free of the Rift."

"We need a new strategy, then." Emma quailed as the lead Taker stepped onto the main catwalk. "Like, *right now.*"

Without warning, the whole rig shuddered violently, the walkway tilting under Opal's feet. Shrieking, she grabbed the railing with both hands, her dagger ricocheting off the grating and dropping into the Rift. Before she could catch her breath, a geyser erupted from where her knife had disappeared. The whirlpool swelled.

A huge shape blasted out of the ocean water beside the Rift.

The room darkened. A roar thundered across the chamber, so loud Opal had to cover her ears.

The Beast shook water from its neck like a wet dog, latching its claws onto the rim of the containment wall, then launching up to snare a catwalk. The metal groaned beneath its massive weight as the sea monster pulled itself onto the grating.

The blood left Nico's face as he scrambled up from his knees. "Is that . . . *our* Beast?"

"Does it matter?" Opal said, swallowing bile. "We're toast either way."

The Beast dropped on all fours and sniffed the air. It glared at a Taker reaching for Emma with long, spindly fingers.

Tyler dug into his jacket and pulled out a plastic bottle filled with blue-green algae. He waved it overhead. The Beast tensed. Then it roared again, but this note was different. The call had a tenor of recognition.

Several Takers moved toward the sea monster, lifting their arms in what looked like a calming gesture.

The Beast bared its teeth and sprang. Opal heard something crunch as a giant paw smacked the closest Taker over the railing. Then the Beast's tail whipped out, sending three more flying off the catwalk. Before Opal could react, the Beast stormed onto the central span where they cowered. The walkway buckled but held.

The Beast went berserk, pummeling and crushing Takers

left and right. Opal and the others dropped into terrified balls as the massive creature bounded over them to attack the Takers on the opposite side.

The Taker beside Emma tried to back away, but the Beast's head darted forward, jaws snapping. Gleaming teeth sank into its chest. The Beast lifted the creature like a kitten and hurled it into the Rift. The remaining Takers shrank back, slinking down off the catwalks as they searched for an escape.

The Beast dove into the whirlpool after them.

"It's . . . it's *helping* us," Nico said, his mouth hanging open as he watched the Beast crunch another fleeing invader. "The Beast is wrecking shop!"

"It sure seems to hate those creatures," Emma said. "We'd better act fast while they're getting housed."

"Aren't you forgetting something?" Tyler squealed. "We still don't know what to do!"

Opal tried not to panic. She took a deep breath, thinking hard. In addition to the chemical seal, Thing had done something else to secure the Rift. But what was it? How had Thing kept the gateway shut?

Below them, the Beast was laying waste. Most of the Takers had disappeared into the vortex, but a handful had slipped back up to the catwalks and were closing in again.

Opal popped to her feet. The Beast was bashing the rig's outer walls to pieces as it chased the remaining Takers below.

The sea monster was winning the battle, but the whole building threatened to collapse.

"I dropped my dagger," Nico said, his shoulders rigid as the Takers slunk toward them. They were coming down both sides of the catwalk again.

"So did I." Opal looked at Emma, whose hands were empty as well. A heavy, wordless despair engulfed her. "There has to be *something* we can do."

A Taker drew close, its awful face exactly as Opal remembered from inside the Darkdeep. Was it the same one? She didn't understand these creatures. Why come across to another world if all you wanted to do was destroy it?

I just wanted to see.

Opal flinched. *Thing!*

Did the others hear, too? The voice was tiny and far away. Opal worried she was imagining it. *I might be losing my mind for real this time.*

No, you're not. I came back a little way into the gap between our worlds. To thank you again. To . . . to help.

"We're out of time!" Nico blurted, glancing into the vortex. He clearly hadn't heard Thing speak. "We should jump. We'll swim down into the Darkdeep. Go back to the houseboat and get help. This is too big to handle alone."

"Are you crazy?!" Tyler shouted. "It's not a slip-and-slide down there, Nico! Plus, that's where the other Takers went!"

"How will we find the Darkdeep?" Emma worried. "What if we miss and go . . . somewhere else?"

No, Nico is right. You must enter the vortex.

"What? Why?" Opal was yelling out loud, staring at nothing. The others shot worried glances at her.

When I first came, I wanted to stay in your world. Yvette and I experimented, and we learned that a certain amount of iron dissolved in salt water created a seal over the Rift. Too much or too little, and the barrier could rupture. At first, I was glad to help, and interested in all we learned, but I could never leave my jar. Eventually, I wished to return home. Yvette wouldn't let me. She feared my passage back through the Rift would upset the equilibrium that had formed between our two dimensions.

"But how did you keep the way shut?" Opal asked, speaking so the others could hear. "Please, we need help!"

Balance.

I was in your world. Something of your world was in mine.

Opal's eyes popped.

Balance.

Thing had left, and the equilibrium was off.

They had to restore it.

Suddenly, she knew what to do.

Opal grabbed Nico by the sleeve. Yelled into his ear.

"You were right! Over the side, now!"

He gave a thumbs-up. "We'll find the Darkdeep down there somehow!"

Opal shook her head furiously.

"Not the Darkdeep! The other way! We have to enter the Rift!"

31

NICO

Nico stared at Opal in shock.

"Actually, I'm starting to agree with Tyler," Nico said. "Maybe jumping into a rip in space-time is a bad call."

"You *think*?" Tyler yelled over his shoulder, as three Takers crept toward him. Below them, the Beast slithered out of the writhing whirlpool and vanished into the gray-green ocean, hunting any creatures trying to escape that way. The Takers on the catwalk level sensed an opening and were closing fast.

"No, I figured it out!" Opal swung a leg over the railing. "There's no time to explain, but we have to jump now!"

Nico blinked at Opal. Made no move. Above them, scarlet lightning lit up the night sky as rain began to pour through the shattered roof. Ocean waves crashed against the outside of the Rift's containment wall, as if jealous of the chaos within. Thunder rang like a gong, shaking the platform. It felt as though the Earth was spinning off its axis.

"We've trusted each other this far," Opal shouted, scraping damp hair from her eyes. "Believe in me one last time. I know what I'm doing!"

"Okay!" Nico scrambled up after her. He shot a worried glance at Emma and Tyler. "Let's go, you two!"

Emma slid under the bars. Tyler shook his head once, hard, but at a hiss from the closest Taker he bounded onto the railing.

No time for dramatics. Barely time to breathe. Nico watched Opal release her hold and drop into the frothing purple water. Takers howled, reaching out to stop them. Nico saw Emma plunge shrieking into the cyclone, then he grabbed Tyler by the shoulder and launched them both over the side. They splashed down together and were immediately sucked into the vortex.

Nico felt a blast of cold, then a wave of scorching heat. He tried to scream but his mouth filled with water.

A new pull enveloped him. Similar to the Darkdeep, but vaster. Infinitely stronger.

There was no choice to be made. Nico was yanked into a mass of pulsing violet light. He plummeted toward a gleaming tear in reality and was wrenched through it. *Now* he could scream. And he did.

And then . . . he stopped. Because there was no sound, nothing to hear, though he could feel his vocal cords working.

He was . . . floating.

Not like on water, because the water was gone.

Like one floats in nothingness. Like thoughts float in the mind just before sleep comes.

A sense of awe filled him. This wasn't the void of the Darkdeep. Surrounding him was a prism of colors and shapes. Geometric forms blinked into existence like teardrops, then faded as quickly. He spotted Opal and Emma below him, sinking toward another shimmering rip in the fabric of the universe.

Nico looked up, saw the gash through which they'd entered. Tyler was hovering next to it.

A voice spoke inside Nico's head. It was Tyler's.

I can still see the oil rig, Tyler sent. He pressed a hand against the opening and it brightened, but didn't yield. *But this is sealed now! We can't go back!*

Guys, down here!

Opal.

Trying not to panic, Nico attempted to swim to the girls, but it was no good. He floundered in a circle.

Just think it, Opal sent. *It works like the Darkdeep, only slightly different.*

Nico stopped flailing and imagined himself descending. His body followed suit. He reached the girls as Tyler zoomed to a stop next to him, panting and sweating.

Isn't this cool? Emma sent, eyes bright.

Tyler threw up his hands. *We're stuck here! The Rift won't let us back into our world.*

Is this the other one? Emma looked around at the funhouse space they occupied. *Where's Thing? Where are all the Takers and Beasts, or whatever?*

This isn't it. Opal pointed to the second glimmering slash, the one below them. *This must be another in-between place. I bet Thing's world is through there.*

Nico examined the other portal. It gleamed white, like hot glaze on a donut. He could just see through the hazy patina—to a wild landscape of red and violet—but then two tiny green hands popped through the opening, and Nico whooshed backward in alarm.

A grinning head followed, then a blobbish body. Thing exited the rent with a slight popping sound, carrying something in its arms. *Perfect. You're all present. To reenter our own worlds we'll need to time our departures precisely.*

Nico stared in surprise. *What are you doing here?*

Helping you. Well, helping Opal, really. I was touched when she released me. Few beings in the universe possess such compassion. I thought I'd never see my realm again.

Thing smiled at Opal. She actually blushed.

So! I have a temporary solution for the Rift. Thing held out the item it carried. *Take this. It's something of your world that came to mine, long ago. It's what made me curious in the first place. Intrigued enough that I climbed through these tears without thinking. I just had to see what kind of beings could craft such an object.*

Nico stared at the object in Thing's hands. Outwardly, it was an ancient, rectangular box, made of stout wood and inlaid on both sides with alternating stone squares in a checkered pattern. Nico noticed a hinge along one side of the box—with a metal clasp attached to the other—and immediately guessed what it was. *A chessboard? That's it?*

Why would Thing bring this? Did it want to play? Nico started worrying he was having some sort of mental episode. He pinched his arm to make sure he was really there.

Some of Yvette's shipwreck on your world bled into mine. A large amount of debris was pulled through the Rift into this emptiness. Thing opened the chessboard and removed a game piece—a delicately shaped horse carved out of onyx—and stared at the knight fondly. *This little adventurer and its companions made it all the way to my realm. I took that as a sign, and decided to enter yours.* Thing sighed. *In my mind, I was a fearless adventurer. I wanted to see what sort of beings could create something so beautiful and clever. I paid dearly for my boldness.*

Nico's eyes popped. The Torchbearers' letter! He remembered the vague instructions Emma had read to the group at Tyler's kitchen table: Seek the platform. Tend the seal. Secure the Traveler and maintain the balance!

You're the Traveler, aren't you? Nico sent to Thing, regarding the little green creature with regret. *The one the Torchbearers wanted "secured." They really did keep you prisoner, didn't they?*

Thing nodded sadly. *They weren't cruel, but I was not allowed to leave.*

That's awful! Emma glared up at the tear back to their world. *The Torchbearers have a lot to answer for.*

Opal looked at Thing with sorrowful eyes. *I'd like to formally apologize to you on behalf of the Order. As the newest Torchbearers, we promise to never do anything that horrible ever again.*

Thing smiled. *Thank you, Opal. All of you. Though I might not make promises until you fully understand what you face. Your world is precious. Flawed or not, it needs Torchbearers to keep it safe. There are more realms than mine in this multiverse.*

But we can't get back, Tyler said glumly. *I tried. The Rift is blocked.*

We are currently in a gap between dimensions. Thing waved an arm at their kaleidoscope surroundings. *My returning here balances your presence in this space. If we leave at the same time, both Rifts will allow us to pass. And we shouldn't dawdle. Dozens of Takers fled back through here moments ago, but they'll return.*

No problem, Tyler said smugly. *We've got a Beast for that.*

Thing's beady eyes widened. *Interesting. Early Torchbearers reached a truce with the leviathan, using algae as a signal, but they were never partners. You seem to have accomplished something new.* Its expression grew calculating. *Years ago, the Order had a friend named Charles Dixon. I directed you to his false tomb so that Opal could retrieve the compass. His remains were removed with honor years before, to lie in a private graveyard, but the crypt proved useful as a place to store things. Dixon had little interest in rituals—and even less in monitoring the Deepness—but he was fascinated by the leviathan. No one truly bonded with the creature after he was lost. Perhaps you can take up his mantle, Tyler. The Order is currently without a Beastmaster.*

Tyler blinked rapidly. "A what-master?"

Beastmaster. An important position within the Order. The only one that can be held by someone not fully sworn as a Torchbearer.

Those torches in Dixon's tomb, Opal said suddenly, slapping a hand over her mouth in surprise. *The brands smelled funny when I lit them—like charred seaweed. But they weren't meant to be burned at all, were they?*

Thing shook its head. *Those were algae torches for signaling the Beast that had grown dry and stiff over time. You swung flaming algae at the leviathan, which no doubt confused it greatly. But it was an honest mistake.* Thing laughed in their heads. *Had those been real torches, I doubt the creature would've let you walk away unscathed.*

The flowing space around them pulsed. Thing frowned. *I'm afraid it's time to go.*

Emma took the chessboard from Thing's hands. *So we carry this back across, and the Rift will be sealed again?*

Thing gave her an inscrutable look. *For now.*

Nico felt his stomach do a backflip. *That's it? Carry the chessboard home and we're good?*

Colors rippled in the void. Thing made a sending of worry. *We've stayed here too long. It's upsetting the alignment. Go now. The Rift will close behind you as we restore the balance.*

But the Beast is still on our side, Nico said suddenly. *Maybe even a few Takers. How does that affect the trade-off?*

Thing's reply carried a twinge of impatience. *I don't have all the answers, Nico, but balance is not always one-for-one. I believe this will work for the present. That object leveled my existence in your realm, and I now sense nothing of my world in yours beyond the leviathan. So we must fix the loss of my presence alone.*

Opal slid forward and took Thing's hand. The gesture seemed to startle the little green being. *Thanks for giving us a second chance. Do you have a true name? I'm sorry we never asked.*

Thing stared at Opal for a long moment. *Dax*, it sent softly.

The space around them twisted. Nico felt himself stretched, then squished like a stress ball.

Go. Thing floated down to the rip in reality that accessed its world. *Quickly. We're out of time.*

Reality seemed to melt. Nico grabbed Tyler's hand, saw him take Emma's, who linked with Opal. As one they arrowed up toward the passage back into their world. Reaching the threshold, they turned and looked down.

Thing waved. They waved back. Then Thing faced the gateway to its realm and started through.

Here goes nothing, Opal said, taking the chessboard from Emma. Holding it in front of her, she stepped to the barrier and pushed. It parted easily and she stumbled forward, with only the hand holding Emma's still visible in the void.

Don't let go! Nico urged. Emma and Tyler went next in a rush. Nico came last. As he passed through the veil—into the frigid, murky Pacific Ocean—he felt something slide shut behind him. Releasing Tyler's hand, Nico swam to the surface and took a gasping breath.

They were inside the Rift's cylinder in the drilling chamber, but the water had stopped moving, its purple glow dulled to nearly nothing. There was no sign of any Takers, or the Beast. Nico still worried about both being on the loose—whatever Thing thought—but a groan from the catwalks above captured his full attention.

Rain poured down through the open roof. The platform was vibrating ominously, seemed ready to keel over. "Let's get out of here!" he shouted.

Tyler was helping Emma onto a ladder. Opal and Nico swam over to another set of metal rungs, Opal holding the chessboard overhead. The wall to Nico's left shifted precariously as they climbed. Up on the catwalk level, they fled through the door, scrambled down the outside steps, and raced away along the lonely spit of rocks.

Metal screeched behind them. Nico turned, watched the entire oil rig collapse with an echoing crash. "Oh man," Emma breathed. "Close one."

"Maybe we can call a cab?" Tyler said hopefully, pulling his hood up. The rain had begun to slacken, the weird glow fading like an exhaled breath. "Otherwise . . ."

Nico peered into the darkness. Clouds hid the moon. The world was pitch-black and would stay that way until morning. How long before people started searching for them? Would anyone think to look out here?

A spotlight cut across the waves. Nico heard the low purr of an engine. Moments later a cherry-red runabout pulled up to the breakwater. Logan waved from behind the wheel.

"Oh thank heavens," Tyler gasped. "Logan did the thing he was supposed to do!"

"So did we," Opal said, in an almost disbelieving tone. "We closed the Rift, you guys. Thing made it easy."

Nico nodded, yet felt unsettled. It *had* been easy. He remembered something Thing had said near the end: *For now.*

Logan tossed a line and they all scrambled aboard. "Sorry I'm late," he said. "But the town is in an uproar, you're all probably considered missing, and, now that I've added two counts of boat theft to my resume, I'm officially Timbers' highest-profile criminal."

"Are the figments still attacking?" Opal said worriedly, shoving the chessboard under her seat.

"Thing's army ran wild through downtown, but thankfully most everyone stayed inside. Then they all vanished at once. Whatever you did, it wasn't a second too soon. But we're never going to cover this up. Dozens of people saw real-deal monsters running down Main Street. Blaming it on Halloween isn't going to work."

"*We* didn't do anything about the figments," Tyler said in disbelief, but then he slapped the gunwale beside him. "It must've been when Thing went home! I bet its creations disappeared when the little blob crossed over. Thing helped us close the Rift, too."

Logan shook his head. "Tell me about it on the way back."

He reversed into deeper water, then spun the bow and headed for Timbers. Nico stared up at the night sky, which had returned to normal. *But will my life?* As they bounced across the waves, Nico couldn't shake a feeling that his world had changed forever.

32

OPAL

A rare November blue sky stretched across the horizon.

Opal and Emma waited on the front steps of the public library, surveying the damage littering downtown. A moment later, Nico and Tyler strode up together, followed by Logan appearing from the opposite direction.

"Are you good?" Opal asked as the boys approached.

"Incredibly, yes." Nico said. "I can't believe my dad bought it."

Tyler waggled his phone with a guilty grin. "No cell service—the greatest excuse ever."

Opal nodded, her expression growing contrite. "After I told my mom we had to hide in the gym to avoid freaks attacking the middle-school Halloween party, she actually hugged me. I think she was still pretty upset about someone smashing the bank's front window."

"Technically there *was* no service last night," Emma said.

"The tower's still out of commission today, and us hunkering down to avoid a rampaging mob makes sense." She shrugged. "My parents believed me, no questions asked." Then Emma frowned at her shoes. "But I have to write letters of apology to almost everyone in town for my role in the beach fiasco. People seem pretty mad about it. They think I helped plan a giant *Freakshow* prank for ratings. Some reward for saving their butts with a distraction."

They turned to Logan, who snorted a bitter laugh. "No one even noticed I was missing. I put the boat back, slipped home, and pretended to have been in my room the whole time."

"Thanks for taking the risk for us, Logan." Opal looked at Nico. "Did you notice the red tide has dissipated? I walked through Orca Park on my way here, and there's no trace of the bloom. That's almost as weird as the algae showing up in the first place."

Nico's shoulders rose and fell. "My dad left a stack of articles on my desk about the outbreaks, but this one didn't act normal. I think the Rift had everything to do with it. Maybe it was leaking iron into the ocean, and that spurred the algae growth?"

Tyler nodded slowly. "That might even be what riled up the Beast. Maybe the iron, and algae, and other weird stuff was messing with its habitat. The Beast seemed to know where Dixon's crypt was, and then it came to the island in Still Cove.

Our new buddy might've been trying to check in with the Torchbearers and found us instead. As crazy as *that* sounds."

"We need to go through those file cabinets in the Torchbearers' office," Nico said, scratching his cheek. "Though I have to find a way inside the Custom House that doesn't risk bumping into my dad every single time."

"As soon as we can," Opal agreed. "But we've got other business right now."

"My mom didn't love me heading out again so early," Tyler said. "You sure this is necessary?"

Opal nodded with a frown. "We have to find Colton Bridger. He knows almost everything, and might even have the beach attack on film. We can't let anything get onto the Internet."

"They're headed for the waterfront," Logan said. "I saw that ugly van roll by on my way over here. I bet they're taking the first ferry out."

"Shoot." Opal hurried down the steps, waving for the others to follow. "Let's go. That stupid film crew can still ruin everything."

Bridger practically snarled as Opal approached the *Freakshow* van.

"*You.*" He spat the word out the passenger window. "Get away from me. Miserable little heathen."

Nico and the others gathered behind Opal, on a sidewalk next to the loading area. They'd found Bridger sitting in his van, alone, parked in line and waiting for the ferry to start taking on vehicles.

Bridger's eyes glittered with malice. "I don't know what your role in this fiasco was—or how you did it—but you're responsible for those awful creatures, I'm sure of it. Soon *everyone* is going to know your secret."

"What secret?" Opal had lost all patience with Colton Bridger. He talked a big game, but he'd hidden when the figment army attacked, then cowered uselessly in front of the Beast like a terrified squirrel. Had *he* ever faced down creatures from another dimension, or closed a rift in space-time that threatened the entire world? No, he had *not*. He couldn't even keep it together when confronted by the very Beast he'd traveled there to find. Some adventure hunter.

Still, he and his crew had seen a lot. That was a problem.

Bridger yanked his ski hat down over his eyebrows. "We've got a *ton* of footage from last night, and I'm going to use every frame of it. The world will learn what's happening in this podunk backwater. You can bet your crappy little town on that."

"We saved you," Opal said, scowling at the petulant TV host. "I think the words you're looking for are 'thank you.' "

"*Thank you?*" Bridger yanked open the passenger door and stepped out of the van. "You clearly summoned the Beast, and it almost killed me! You even planted a spy in my production." He smiled coldly at Emma. "But you'll pay for it. I'm about to put this hick town on the map, and my ratings will skyrocket!"

Bridger turned and hopped back into the van, but Tyler grabbed the door before he could close it. "If you expose the Beast as real, bad people will come looking. People only interested in exploiting the creature for their own gain."

"That's what you wanted, wasn't it?" Bridger's voice was a knot of tension. His finger darted out at Logan. "Right, T-shirt boy? *Come visit Timbers, you might spot a sea monster!* Well, congratulations. I'm going to make that happen."

"You're deliberately causing a disaster!" Tyler shouted, eyes angry. "Some jerks will try to catch it. Or *shoot* it. And the Beast isn't messing around, either. People could die!"

Tyler was right. Opal felt sick.

"That's your problem." Bridger laughed in their faces. "You led me right to that terrible creature, twice. You tried to *murder* me. So now you'll taste what payback . . . *tastes* like."

"We didn't ask you to follow us around," Nico snapped. "And wasn't that your whole point in coming here anyway? To see the legendary Beast?"

The ferry whistle blew. Engines fired up along the line of vehicles. The rest of the *Freakshow* crew emerged from the waiting area and began piling into the van. Derek and Jacqueline nodded to Emma, who gave a little wave back.

Bridger shoved Tyler's hand out of the way and slammed the door.

Jake keyed the ignition. These strangers were leaving with Timbers' biggest secrets in their possession, and there was nothing Opal could do to stop them.

Bridger rolled down his window and sneered. "I'm going to be so freaking famous. And this place is going to be a war zone after my finale airs. Enjoy!"

A crowd of angry citizens was filtering down to where the van idled. Jake slapped Bridger on the chest and pointed. "Let's go," Bridger said, voice tense. He glared at Emma. "Half this town blames *us* for last night, thanks to your stupid speech. But I'll show the world what happened here. *I'LL SHOW THE WORLD!*"

The van pulled onto the ferry. Moments later, the heavy boat pushed off. As the vessel floated away, the film crew headed up to the ferry's passenger area, but Bridger never appeared. Opal thought he was probably too unnerved to set foot outside his vehicle.

"I do not like that guy." Emma shook her head. "He wanted sea monsters to be real but couldn't handle meeting one."

Nico's shoulders slumped. "He's going to *ruin* Timbers."

"People are the worst," Opal said, hugging her arms to her chest.

Tyler sighed. "The absolute worst."

Logan put a hand on Ty's shoulder. "Personally, I think

screaming nightmare creatures from another dimension are the worst."

"Let's call it a tie." Tyler scrubbed at his eyes. "Guys, we have to do *something*."

"There's nothing we can do." Emma's voice was somber. "And right now, I have to go home."

Logan peered down through the open skylight. "Is it working?"

"Yeah!" Emma said. "At least, I think so. I've got three bars."

Her tablet sat on the pedestal where Thing's jar used to be. Thanks to some complicated cell phone–streaming airplay-signal-bouncing—or whatever Tyler and Logan had finagled—things were set up so they could watch the final episode of *Freakshow* together on the houseboat.

The sun was shining outside, the air clear of sulfur stink for the first time in a week. Opal was playing chess with Tyler on the ancient board Thing had given them. She was losing— badly—but didn't really care. The intricate pieces reminded her of all that they'd accomplished.

"So I think I finally figured out what the Torchbearers' emergency letter was asking us to do," Tyler said, moving his queen diagonally into a position that made Opal nervous. "About the seal, and the Traveler, and all that."

Opal stared at the board, searching for a trap. "Okay?"

Tyler glanced at Nico, who was reading an article about volcanic ash. He was still investigating where the sulfur had come from, but so far had found no clear answer. Feeling Tyler's eyes, Nico sat back and motioned for his friend to continue.

"The seal was a chemical layer that the Torchbearers devised to cover the Rift and keep it more stable," Tyler said. "That was the first part: *Seek the platform. Tend the seal.* But the Rift itself was held closed by balancing what came through it. So when they asked us to 'secure the Traveler,' they really did want us to keep Thing on this side, locked inside its jar. That's what actually kept the Rift from breaking open."

"So we rebalanced the equation with this," Opal said, tapping the chessboard. "Which crossed back over in exchange for Thing. But that didn't do anything for the seal, right?"

Nico shook his head. "We didn't fix that, which means the Rift is closed but still vulnerable. And I'm not sure how we can ever create the right chemical mixture again, since the entire oil platform collapsed and the Rift's tank is now buried under all that rubble."

"Good riddance," Tyler said. "If we can't reach it, no one else can, either."

"I wish we could ask Thing," Emma said from over by the pedestal. "I kinda miss the little green gumball."

Tyler's head reared back. "Miss it? Did you forget how that monster tried to feed us to an army of figments?"

"Thing came through in the end," Opal countered. "It had been caged for decades by the Torchbearers. I don't blame it for not trusting us at first."

Logan walked into the room and joined the trio hovering over the gameboard. "You're done for," he told Opal calmly.

"It's not over yet," Opal shot back. Tyler just grinned, putting his hands behind his head.

"Did you talk with Sheriff Ritchie?" Nico asked Logan. Adding the disaster of Dark Halloween to the unsolved vandalism of Beast Night had local law enforcement wired tighter than a snare drum. Every person in Timbers was being interviewed about both nights. Mayor Hayt was terrified to schedule any future civic events, since the last two had resulted in town property being torn to shreds.

Logan rubbed the back of his neck. "My dad and I met with him yesterday. Both investigations are ongoing, but no one has asked to see my four-wheelers. I think I might be in the clear."

"Dump the tires into the cove," Tyler advised, moving his rook halfway up the chessboard. "You made enough money on Beast shirts to buy new ones, right?"

Logan shrugged. "I shut all that down. Didn't feel right anymore. Not since the Beast became our new pet or whatever."

"Not a pet," Tyler said sharply. "Our *ally*."

Opal scowled at Tyler over the game pieces. "You checkmated me, didn't you?"

"I sure did."

"I wonder where the Beast is now?" Emma said, gazing out the showroom window. "I keep watching for the big guy in Still Cove. I'm not sure whether I want to see it there or not."

"About that." Tyler rose and walked to his backpack, removing a thick book. "I finished this one last night, and look what I found." He flipped to the back and held a page open so everyone could see. A swirling torch was drawn there.

"The symbol from Dixon's crypt," Opal blurted. "And the plaque where we found his name."

Tyler nodded, setting the book down. "It's the mark of a special position within the Order." He cleared his throat. "The emblem of Beastmaster."

There was a silent moment, then Nico laughed. "So that's you now?"

Tyler glowered at his friend. "And why not? I know the most about it!"

Nico held up his hands. "I was joking. It's just so full circle. But the job is definitely yours."

"Uncontestedly yours," Logan quipped. "Congrats, Beastmaster."

Opal nodded quickly, as did Emma, both girls beaming at their skinny friend.

"I'll try to . . . to figure out how to work with it," Tyler promised, suddenly embarrassed. "And reward it somehow for saving our butts with those Takers."

"You might need to convince the Beast to leave," Nico said quietly. "If Bridger's stupid show makes this area unsafe. We might need a plan for sinking the houseboat, too."

The mood in the room deflated. Emma walked back over to her tablet. "Speak of the devil," she said. "The episode is downloading!"

Everyone in Timbers would be streaming it, even those who blamed Colton Bridger for Dark Halloween. People were angry and scared. Many believed the film crew had played everyone, and that the figment army was nothing more than special effects and hired goons in costumes shipped in secretly from out of town. Many *didn't* believe that, however, and paranoia festered in the streets.

Opal and her friends wanted to watch the finale alone. They couldn't bear witnessing the fallout of their secrets being exposed. The five newest Torchbearers weren't the only Beast truthers in Timbers anymore, which was going to have repercussions. If outsiders swarmed the area to search for a sea monster, Still Cove would top their list of places to look. Everything they had worked so hard to protect was at risk.

The group clustered around Emma by the pedestal. Tyler started chewing his lip. "Oh man," he mumbled, "this is gonna be so bad."

The *Freakshow* title sequence played in all its garish glory.

Then, for the first time, the opening shot was a close-up of Colton Bridger's face. "We set out to discover if Timber's Beast of legend was truly real," Bridger said, his expression grave. He was staring into the camera while standing on a windswept beach, but not one Opal recognized. It looked more like California, with bright blue water and white sand. "What we uncovered in Timbers shocked even me. Someone who has been everywhere. Someone who has seen it all."

"Basic much?" Logan muttered. "*I* could do this intro."

"I'm here to tell you," Bridger said, his voice growing fervent, "that this Pacific Northwest lumber town has been harboring a dark secret. One they will even *kill* to protect."

Tyler rolled his eyes. "Come *on*."

"The production values are not as high as I expected," Emma murmured. "He rushed to get this out so soon."

Bridger leaned close to the camera, a wild intensity in his eyes. Opal began to feel light-headed. "I agonized over the best way to present what you are about to see," he rumbled, his voice as rough as tree bark. "In the end, I decided to let the horror speak for itself."

"I don't know if I can watch," Tyler moaned. Opal reached over and squeezed his hand. She knew how he felt. Once this story broke, Timbers would never be the same.

A dark shot of Razor Point appeared. People were milling around the borders of the illuminated filming area, waiting for Bridger's reenactment to begin. Nico squirmed beside Opal, his foot tapping on the floor. Her own pulse sped to a million rpms.

"We were attacked by . . . *monsters*," Bridger intoned, as movement appeared at the black edges of the shot. "First, by a wave of creatures so horrible and inexplicable as to defy description." But nothing came into focus—the figments were just shadows on the fringes, with sounds and motions of regular people panicking in the foreground. No monsters were clearly visible on-screen.

"Seriously?" Emma said. "This doesn't show anything."

Opal wanted to laugh, but her heart remained in her throat. Bridger wasn't finished. In the next moment, a mass of figments filled the screen, rushing up the beach, sending townspeople running and screaming. Chaos reigned. Cameras and lights were knocked askew as people fled for their lives.

Opal dug her nails into her palm. She heard Nico whimper under his breath, a hand rising to rub his forehead. It was everything they'd tried to contain, laid bare for the world to see.

Only . . .

"What is . . ." Logan trailed off.

"Huh," Tyler grunted, shifting as he tilted his head.

Opal felt a nervous giggle rise in her throat.

"It looks really . . . *bad*," Emma said, leaning close to the screen. "Is this digital? I know the rest of the crew all quit when they got back to California, and Bridger did the final cut alone. He had a tantrum on Twitter about it, acting like he didn't need them. He said he didn't trust anyone else to work on his shocking breakthrough anyway."

The images were grainy. Choppy. *Campy.* Someone came right up to the camera and screamed into it like an extra in a Godzilla movie. A taloned figment ran past, but all you could see was something covered in weird feathers. Then Nico was suddenly on-screen, throwing rocks.

"Look, Nico!" Emma shouted. "You're an action hero!" Nico hid his eyes.

"That one," Logan blurted, pointing out a horned gorilla with scales. "That figment was scary as crap, but the way they filmed it—"

"It looks like somebody's dad in a rubber suit," Nico finished. "Is Bridger this bad at editing?"

"The main camera went down early," Tyler said, a note of hope creeping into his voice. "These shots must be from backup cameras on tripods. Some must've been rolling the whole time, but it was really dark out, and no one was framing shots or adjusting the lenses. They don't seem to have gotten anything up close or in good lighting."

"And then," Bridger said, his voice dropping to a whisper, "summoned by a group of children skilled in the dark arts, the *Beast* itself arrived . . . to feed."

"Mercy." Tyler's voice was a desperate supplication. "Please, no."

They all watched as the image changed to a crooked shot of dark ocean. A shiver ran through Opal. *That's where it happened.*

There was vague movement in the background, obscured by waves. Then a roar sounded.

The hair on Opal's arms stood.

The Beast's head bobbed into the frame, sinuous and deadly. But . . . there was something weird about it. The camera had switched to a low-light mode, though a haphazard spotlight beam was shining directly up at the Beast from the ground. The sea monster looked . . . startled. Like a buffalo caught in headlights. It snuffled once, like a sneeze, and then ducked out of the shot. Seconds later another roar sounded. The camera tipped over, and the screen went black.

"Behold," Bridger hissed, "the horror of . . . the Beast."

The show cut to a still of the sea monster's head, but it looked nothing like real life. It looked . . . silly. Like Bridger had filmed his fake puppet-beast.

"Um." Tyler's voice was flat. "What on earth."

Everyone was silent for several beats. Then they all started cracking up.

"It looks like a kid's bathtub toy!" Logan wheezed. He was literally down on the floor. "My little sister used to shoot videos like that with my dad's phone."

"As you can see," Bridger continued dramatically, "the legends are true. The Beast . . . is . . . *real*."

The Beast's head boinged past one last time. The episode ended with stark music. Nico turned purple with laughter.

Opal was helpless. She leaned her head on Nico's shoulder, trying to catch her breath.

"My stomach, you guys," Emma gasped. "I think I pulled a muscle."

Nico was already scrolling on his phone. He handed it to Logan. "Are you seeing this?"

"Oh man, the Internet is killing *Freakshow*," Logan crowed. "Look at these comments. Bridger is a laughingstock!"

Opal exhaled for what felt like the first time in days. She closed her eyes. They still had serious problems—plenty of people in Timbers knew something incredible had happened that night—but *Freakshow* shouldn't set off any serious shockwaves. The episode was being panned as a fake on every social media platform in existence. It was more likely to kill interest in the Beast than create any.

The Rift was closed. Thing was home. No one was going to believe that footage.

Opal opened her notebook, the one with the tiny asters drawn in the corner of each page. Next to one of the flowers she sketched a small gemstone. An opal. This book had likely belonged to a Torchbearer, but it was hers now. Someone had to tell the stories. And she could trust herself to do it.

Opal closed the notebook, tucked it into her backpack, and got to her feet. *One task left.*

"What's up?" Nico asked, as she moved toward the hidden door. The others were passing his phone back and forth, reading scathing comments about *Freakshow* to one another.

"Just checking the Darkdeep," Opal said. "I'm still spooked it tried to swallow the staircase, you know?"

Nico nodded, popping up. "I'll come with you."

They went downstairs. The Darkdeep was back to normal, contained in the well at the center of the room. They had no idea why it had risen so high, or why it had fallen back. Opal was just grateful it was still.

But then she stopped in her tracks.

"Nico," Opal said softly.

"I see it," he whispered back.

Something was floating in the black water.

A glass jar.

Opal and Nico shared a glance.

"Wanna pretend we never saw it?" Nico said hopefully.

"More than anything in the world. We can be back upstairs in three seconds."

They edged closer to the pool instead. Using her fingertips, Opal fished out the jar.

It wasn't empty.

"We could be home in thirty minutes," Opal suggested.

"I've got a ton of homework," Nico agreed.

Opal slowly unscrewed the lid. Inside was a scrap of paper, with something scrawled on it.

"We don't have to read that," Nico said. "Reading is very overrated."

Opal's eyes scanned the paper. "It's a message."

"In a bottle." Nico sighed. "How cliché can you be? Who do you think is pranking us, Logan or Tyler?"

Opal didn't laugh. A hollow space had opened in the pit of her stomach.

Wordlessly, she handed the note to Nico. The blood drained from his face as he read.

Torchbearers,

Thank you sincerely for sending me home.
But I fear the balance has not been restored.
There's something here that doesn't belong.

Or, I should say, someone.

Come and see what I have for you.
—D